Jesse H. Jones

Know the Truth

SALZWASSER
VERLAG

Jesse H. Jones

Know the Truth

Reprint of the original, first published in 1865.

1st Edition 2022 | ISBN: 978-3-75258-885-9

Verlag (Publisher): Salzwasser Verlag GmbH, Zeilweg 44, 60439 Frankfurt, Deutschland
Vertretungsberechtigt (Authorized to represent): E. Roepke, Zeilweg 44, 60439 Frankfurt, Deutschland
Druck (Print): Books on Demand GmbH, In de Tarpen 42, 22848 Norderstedt, Deutschland

KNOW THE TRUTH;

A CRITIQUE ON THE HAMILTONIAN THEORY OF LIMITATION,

INCLUDING

SOME STRICTURES UPON THE THEORIES OF REV. HENRY L. MANSEL AND MR. HERBERT SPENCER.

BY

JESSE H. JONES

"Give me to see, that I may know where to strike."

NEW YORK

1865.

PREFACE.

THIS book has been written simply in the interest of Truth. It was because the doctrines of the Hamiltonian School were believed to be dangerous errors, which this process of thought exposes, that it was undertaken.

Logically, and in the final analysis, there can be but two systems of philosophical theology in the world. The one will be Pantheism, or Atheism, — both of which contain the same essential principle, but viewed from different standpoints, — the other will be a pure Theism. In the schools of Brahma and Buddh, or in the schools of Christ, the truth is to be found. And this is so because every teacher is to be held responsible for all which can be logically deduced from his system; and every erroneous result which can be so deduced is decisive of the presence of an error in principle in the foundation; and all schemes of philosophy, by such a trial, are seen to be based on one of these two classes of schools. Just here a quotation from Dr. Laurens Hickok's "Rational Psychology" will be in point:

"Except as we determine the absolute to be personality wholly out of and beyond all the conditions and modes of space and time, we can by no possibility leave nature for the supernatural. The clear-sighted and honest intellect, resting in this conclusion that the conditions of space and time cannot be transcended, will be Atheistic; while the deluded intellect, which has put the false play of the discursive understanding in its abstract speculations for the decisions of an all-embracing reason, and deems itself so fortunate as to have found a deity within the modes of space and time, will be Pantheistic. The Pantheism will be ideal and transcendent, when it reaches its conclusions by a logical process in the abstract law of thought; and it will be material and empiric, when it concludes from the fixed connections of cause and effect in the generalized law of nature; but in neither case is the Pantheism any other than Atheism, for the Deity, circumscribed in the conditions of space and time with nature, is but nature still, and, whether in abstract thought or generalized reality, is no God."

The Hamiltonian system is logically Atheism. Perceiving that the Deity cannot be found in Nature, it denies that he can be known at all. What the mind cannot know at all, *it is irrational to believe.* If man cannot *know that* God is, and have a clear sight of his attributes as a rational ground of confidence in what he says, it is the height of blind credulity to believe in him. And more; if man cannot have such knowledge, he has *no standard* by which to measure teachings, and be *sure* he has the truth. Under such circumstances, faith is *impossible.* Faith can only be based on *Reason.* If there is no Reason, there can be no faith. Hence he who talks about faith, and denies Reason, does not know what faith is. The logician rightfully held that God could not be found in Nature; but he was just as wrong in asserting that man is wholly in Nature and cannot know God, as he was right in the former instance. The acceptance of his one truth, and one error, compels man to be an Atheist; because then he has no faculty by which to know aught of

God; and few thorough men will accept blind credulity as the basis of Religion.

The author's sense of obligation to President Hickok cannot be too strongly stated. But for his works, it is believed that this little treatise could never have been written. Indeed, the author looks for but scanty credit on the score of originality, since most of what he has written he has learned, directly or indirectly, from that profound thinker. He has deemed it his chief work, to apply the principles developed by others to the exposure of a great error. And if he shall be judged to have accomplished this, his ambition will have been satisfied.

After the substance of this treatise had been thought out, and while the author was committing it to paper, the essays on "Space and Time," and on "The Philosophy of the Unconditioned," in the numbers of the "North American Review" for July and October, 1864, happened to fall under his notice. Some persons will appreciate the delight and avidity with which he read them; and how grateful it was to an obscure student, almost wholly isolated in the world, to find the views which he had wrought out in his secluded chamber, so ably advocated in the leading review of his country. Not that he had gone as far, or examined the subjects in hand as thoroughly as has been there done. By no means. Rather what results he had attained accord with some of those therein laid down. Of those essays it is not too much to say, that, if they have not exhausted the topics of which they treat, they have settled forever the conclusions to be reached, and leave for other writers only illustration and comment. If the author shall seem to differ from them on a minor question, — that of quantitative infinity, — the difference will, it is believed, be found to be one of the form of expression only. And the difference is maintained from the conviction that no term in science should have more than one signification. It is better to adopt illimitable and indivisible, as the technical epithets of Space, in place of the commonly used terms infinite and absolute.

A metaphysical distinction has been incidentally touched upon in the following discussion, which deserves a more extensive consideration than the scope and plan of this work would permit to it here; and which, so far as the author's limited reading goes, has received very little attention from modern writers on metaphysics. He refers to the distinction between the animal nature and spiritual person, so repeatedly enounced by that profound metaphysical theologian, the apostle Paul, and by that pure spiritual pastor, the apostle John, in the terms "flesh" and "spirit." The thinkers of the world, even the best Christian philosophers, seem to have esteemed this a moral and religious distinction, and no more, when in fact it cleaves down through the whole human being, and forms the first great radical division in any proper analysis of man's soul, and classification of his constituent elements. *This is a purely natural division.* It is organic in man. It belonged as much to Adam in his purity, as it does to the most degraded wretch on the globe now. It is of such a character that, had it been properly understood and developed, the Hamiltonian system of philosophy could never have been constructed.

An adequate statement of the truth would be conducted as follows. First, the animal nature should be carefully analyzed, its province accurately defined, and both the laws and forms of its activity exactly stated. Second, a like examination of the spiritual person should follow; and third, the relations, interactions, and influences of the two parts upon each other should be, as extensively as possible, presented. But it is to be remarked, that, while the analysis, by the human intellect, of these two great departments of man's soul, may be exhaustive, it is doubtful if any but the All-seeing Eye can read all their relations and inter-communications. The development of the third point, by any one mind, must needs, therefore, be partial. Whether any portion of the above designated labor shall be hereafter entered upon, will depend upon circumstances beyond the control of the writer.

As will appear, it is believed, in the development of the subject, the great, the *vital* point upon which the whole controversy with the Hamiltonian school must turn, is a question of *fact*; viz., whether man has a Reason, as the faculty giving *a priori* principles, or not. If he has such a Reason, then by it the questions now at issue can be settled, and that finally. If he has no Reason, then he can have no knowledge, except of appearances and events, as perceived by the Sense and judged by the Understanding. Until, then, the question of fact is decided, it would be a gain if public attention was confined wholly to it. Establish first a well-ascertained and sure foundation before erecting a superstructure.

The method adopted in constructing this treatise does not admit the presentation of the matter in a symmetrical form. On the contrary, it involves some, perhaps many, repetitions. What has been said at one point respecting one author must be said again in reply to another. Yet the main object for which the work was undertaken could, it seemed, be thoroughly accomplished in no other way.

The author has in each case used American editions of the works named.

KNOW THE TRUTH.

PART I.

THE SEEKING AND THE FINDING.

In April, 1859, there was republished in Boston, from an English print, a volume entitled "The Limits of Religious Thought Examined," &c., "by Henry Longueville Mansel, B. D."

The high position occupied by the publishers, — a firm of Christian gentlemen, who, through a long career in the publication of books either devoutly religious, or, at least, having a high moral tone, and being marked by deep, earnest thought, have obtained the confidence of the religious community; the recommendations with which its advent was heralded, but most of all the intrinsic importance of the theme announced, and its consonance with many of the currents of mental activity in our midst, — gave the book an immediate and extensive circulation. Its subject lay at the foundation of all religious, and especially of all theological thinking. The author, basing his teaching on certain metaphysical tenets, claimed to have circumscribed the boundary to all positive, and so valid effort of the human intellect in its upward surging towards the Deity, and to have been able to say, "Thus far canst thou come, and no farther, and here must thy proud waves be stayed." And this effort was declaredly made in the interest of religion. It was asserted that from such a ground only, as was therein sought to be established, could infidelity be successfully assailed and destroyed. Moreover, the writer was a learned and able divine in the Anglican Church, orthodox in his views; and his volume was composed of lectures delivered upon what is known as "The Bampton Foundation;" — a bequest of a clergyman, the income of which, under certain rules, he directed should be employed forever, in furthering the cause of Christ, by Divinity Lecture Sermons in Oxford. Such a book, on such a theme, by such a man, and composed under such auspices, would necessarily receive the almost universal attention of religious thinkers, and would mark an era in human thought. Such was the fact in this country. New England, the birthplace and home of American Theology, gave it her most careful and studious examination. And the West alike with the East pored over its pages, and wrought upon its knotty questions. Clergymen especially, and theological students, perused it with the earnestness of those who search for hid treasures. And what was the result? We do not hesitate to say that it was unqualified rejection. The book now takes its place among religious productions, not as a contribution to our positive knowledge, not as a practicable new road, surveyed out through the Unknown Regions of Thought, but rather as possessing only a negative value, as a monument of warning, erected at that point on the roadside where the writer branched off in his explorations, and on which is inscribed, "In this direction the truth cannot be found."

The stir which this book produced, naturally brought prominently to public attention a writer heretofore not extensively read in this country, Sir William Hamilton, upon whose metaphysical teachings the lecturer avowedly based his whole scheme. The doctrines of the metaphysician were subjected to the same scrutinizing analysis, which dissolved the enunciations of the divine; and they, like these, were pronounced "wanting." This decision was not reached or expressed in any extensive and exhaustive criticism of these writers; in which the errors of their principles and the revolting nature of the results they attained, were presented; but it rather was a shoot from the spontaneous and deep-seated conviction, that the whole scheme, of both teacher and pupil, was utterly insufficient to satisfy the craving of man's highest nature. It was rejected because it *could* not be received.

Something more than a year ago, and while the American theological mind, resting in the above-stated conviction, was absorbed in the tremendous interests connected with the Great Rebellion, a new aspirant for honors appeared upon the stage. A book was published entitled "The Philosophy of Herbert Spencer: First Principles." This was announced as the foundation of a new system of Philosophy, which would command the confidence of the present, and extort the wonder of all succeeding ages. Avowing the same general principles with Mansel and Hamilton, this writer professed to have found a radical defect in their system, which being corrected, rendered that system complete and final; so that, from it as a base, he sets out to construct a new scheme of Universal Science. This man, too, has been read, not so extensively as his predecessors; because when one has seen a geometrical absurdity demonstrated, he does not care, unless from professional motives, to examine and disprove further attempts to bolster up the folly; but still so widely read, as to be generally associated with the other writers above mentioned, and, like them, rejected. Upon being examined, he is found to be a man of less scope and mental muscle than either of his teachers; yet going over the same ground and expressing the same ideas, scarcely in new language even; and it further appears that his discovery is made at the expense of his logic and consistency, and involves an unpardonable contradiction. Previous to the publication of the books just mentioned, an American writer had submitted to the world a system of thought upon the questions of which they treat, which certainly seems worthy of some notice from their authors. Yet it has received none. To introduce him we must retrace our steps for a little.

In 1848, Laurens P. Hickok, then a Professor in Auburn Theological Seminary, published a work entitled "Rational Psychology," in which he professed to establish, by *a priori* processes, positions which, if true, afford a ground for the answer, at once and forever, of all the difficulties raised by Sir William Hamiltou and his school. Being comparatively a new writer, his work attracted only a moiety of the attention it should have done. It was too much like Analytical Geometry and Calculus for the popular mind, or even for any but a few patient thinkers. For them it was marrow and fatness.

Since the followers of Sir William Hamilton, whom we will hereafter term Limitists, have neglected to take the great truths enunciated by the American metaphysician, and apply them to their own system, and so be convinced by their own study of the worthlessness of that system, it becomes their opponents, in the interest of truth, to perform this work in their stead; viz., upon the basis of immutable truth, to unravel each of their well-knit sophistries, to show to the world that it may "*know the truth;*" and thus to destroy a system which, if allowed undisputed sway, would sap the very foundations of Christian faith.

The philosophical system of the Limitists is built upon a single fundamental proposition, which carries all their deductions with it. He who would strike these effectually, must aim his blow, and give it with all his might, straight at that one object; sure that if he destroys that, the destruction of the whole fabric is involved therein. But, as the Limitists are determined not to confess the dissolution of their scheme, by the simple establishment of principles, which they cannot prove false, and which, if true, involve the absurdity of their own tenets, it is further necessary to go through their writings, and examine them passage by passage, and show the fallacy of each. In the former direction we can but re-utter some of the principles of the great American teacher. In the latter there is room for new effort; and this shall be our especial province.

The proposition upon which the whole scheme of the Limitists is founded, was originally enunciated by Sir William Hamilton, in the following terms. "The Unconditioned is incognizable and inconceivable; its notion being only negative of the conditioned, which last can alone be positively known or conceived." "In our opinion, the mind can conceive, and consequently can know, only the *limited and the conditionally limited.* The unconditionally unlimited, or the Infinite, the unconditionally limited, or the Absolute, cannot positively be construed to the mind; they can be conceived only by a thinking away from, or abstraction of, those very conditions under which thought itself is realized; consequently, the notion of the Unconditioned is only negative — negative of the conceivable itself. For example, on the one hand we can positively conceive, neither an absolute whole, that is, a whole so great, that we cannot also conceive it as a relative part of a still greater whole; nor an absolute part, that is, a part so small, that we cannot also conceive it as a relative whole, divisible into smaller parts. On the other hand, we cannot positively represent, or realize, or construe to the mind, (as here understanding and imagination coincide,) an infinite whole, for this could only be done by the infinite synthesis in thought of finite wholes, which would itself require an infinite time for its accomplishment; nor, for the same reason, can we follow out in thought an infinite divisibility of parts. . . . . . As the conditionally limited (which we may briefly call the conditioned) is thus the only possible object of knowledge, and of positive thought — thought necessarily supposes conditions. *To think* is *to condition;* and conditional limitation is the fundamental law of the possibility of thought." . . . . . "The conditioned is the mean between two extremes — two inconditionates, exclusive of each other, neither of which *can be conceived as possible*, but of which, on the principles of contradiction and excluded middle, one *must be admitted as necessary*."

This theory may be epitomized as follows: — "The Unconditioned denotes the genus of which the Infinite and Absolute are the species." This genus is inconceivable, is "negative of the conceivable itself." Hence both the species must be so also. Although they are thus incognizable, they may be defined; the one, the Infinite, as "that which is beyond all limits;" the other, the Absolute, as "a whole beyond all conditions:" or, concisely, the one is illimitable immensity, the other, unconditional totality. As defined, these are seen to be "mutually repugnant:" that is, if there is illimitable immensity, there cannot be absolute totality; and the reverse. Within these two all possible being is included; and, because either excludes the other, it can be in only one. Since both are inconceivable we can never know in which the conditioned or conceivable being is. Either would give us a being — God — capable of accounting for the Universe. This fact is assumed to be a sufficient ground for faith; and man may therefore rationally satisfy himself with the study of those matters which are cognizable — the conditioned.

It is not our purpose at this point to enter upon a criticism of the philosophical theory thus enounced. This will fall, in the natural course, upon a subsequent page. We have stated it here, for the purpose of placing in that strong light which it deserves, another topic, which has received altogether too little attention from the opponents of the Limitists. Underlying and involved in the above theory, there is a question of *fact*, of the utmost importance. Sir William Hamilton's metaphysic rests upon his psychology; and if his psychology is true, his system is impregnable. It is his diagnosis of the human mind, then, which demands our attention. He has presented this in the following passage: —

"While we regard as conclusive Kant's analysis of Time and Space into conditions of thought, we cannot help viewing his deduction of the 'Categories of Understanding' and the 'Ideas of Speculative Reason' as the work of a great but perverse ingenuity. The categories of understanding are merely subordinate forms of the conditioned. Why not, therefore, generalize the *Conditioned* — *Existence Conditioned*, as the supreme category, or categories, of thought? — and if it were necessary to analyze this form into its subaltern applications, why not develop these immediately out of the generic principle, instead of preposterously, and by a forced and partial analogy, deducing the laws of the understanding from a questionable division of logical proposition? Why distinguish Reason (Vernunft) from Understanding (Verstand), simply on the ground that the former is conversant about, or rather tends toward, the unconditioned; when it is sufficiently apparent, that the unconditioned is conceived as the negation of the conditioned, and also that the conception of contradictories is one? In the Kantian philosophy, both faculties perform the same function, both seek the one in the many; — the Idea (Idee) is only the Concept (Begriff) sublimated into the inconceivable; Reason only the Understanding which has 'overleaped itself.'"

Not stopping now to correct the entirely erroneous statement that "both faculties," *i. e.*, Understanding and Reason, "perform the same function," we are to notice the two leading points which are made, viz.: — 1. That there is no distinction between the Understanding and the Reason; or, in other words, there is no such faculty as the Reason is claimed to be, there is none but the Understanding; and, 2. A generalization is the highest form of human knowledge; both of which may be comprised in one affirmation; the Understanding is the highest faculty of knowledge belonging to the human soul. Upon this, a class of thinkers, following Plato and Kant, take issue with the logician, and assert that the distinction between the two faculties named above, has a substantial basis; that, in fact, they are different in *kind*, and that the mode of activity in the one is wholly unlike the mode of activity in the other. Thus, then, is the great issue between the Hamiltonian and Platonic schools made upon a question of *fact*. He who would attack the former school successfully, must aim his blow straight at their fundamental assumption; and he who shall establish the fact of the Pure Reason as an unquestionable faculty in the human soul, will, in such establishment, accomplish the destruction of the Hamiltonian system of philosophy. Believing this system to be thoroughly vicious in its tendencies; being such indeed, as would, if carried out, undermine the whole Christian religion; and what is of equal importance, being false to the facts in man's soul as God's creature, the writer will attempt to achieve the just named and so desirable result; and by the mode heretofore indicated.

It is required, then, to *prove* that there is a faculty belonging to the human soul, essentially diverse from the Sense or the Understanding; a faculty peculiar and unique, which possesses such qualities as have commonly been ascribed by its advocates to the Pure Reason; and thereby to establish such faculty as a fact, and under that name.

Previous to bringing forward any proofs, it is important to make an exact statement of what is to be proved. To this end, let the following points be noted: —

a. Its modes of activity are essentially diverse from those of the Sense or Understanding. The Sense is only capacity. According to the laws of its construction, it receives impressions from objects, either material, and so in a different place from that which it occupies, or imaginary, and so proceeding from the imaging faculty in itself. But it is only capacity to receive and transmit impressions. The Understanding, though more than this, even faculty, is faculty shut within the limits of the Sense. According to its laws, it takes up the presentations of the Sense, analyzes and classifies them, and deduces conclusions: but it can attain to nothing more than was already in the objects presented. It can construct a system; it cannot develop a science. It can observe a relation, it cannot intuit a law. What we seek is capacity, but of another and higher kind from that of the Sense. Sense can have no object except such, at least, as is constructed out of impressions received from without. What we seek does not observe outside phenomena; and can have no object except as inherent within itself. It is faculty moreover, but not faculty walled in by the Sense. It is faculty and capacity in one, which, possessing inherent within itself, as objects, the *a priori* conditional laws of the Universe, and the *a priori* conditional ideal forms which these laws, standing together according to their necessary relations, compose, transcends, in its activity and acquisitions, all limitations of a *Nature;* and attends to objects which belong to the Supernatural, and hence which absoluteness qualifies. We observe, therefore,

b. The objects of its activity are also essentially diverse in kind from those of the Sense and the Understanding. All the objects of the Sense must come primarily or secondarily, from a material Universe; and the discussions and conclusions of the Understanding must refer to such a Universe. The faculty which we seek must have for its objects, *laws,* or, if the term suit better, first principles, which are reasons why conduct must be one way, and not another; which, in their combinations, compose the forms conditional for all activity; and which, therefore, constitute within us an *a priori* standard by which to determine the validity of all judgments. To illustrate. Linnæus constructed a system of botanical classification, upon the basis of the number of stamens in a flower. This was satisfactory to the Sense and the Understanding. Later students have, however, discovered that certain *organic laws* extend as a framework through the whole vegetable kingdom; which, once seen, throw back the Linnæan system into company with the Ptolemaic Astronomy; and upon which laws a *science* of Botany becomes possible. That faculty which intuits these laws, is called the Pure Reason.

To recapitulate. What we seek is, in its modes and objects of activity, diverse from the Sense and Understanding. It is at once capacity and faculty, having as object first principles, possessing these as an *inherent heritage*, and able to compare with them as standard all objects of the Sense and judgments of the Understanding; and to decide thereby their validity. These principles, and combinations of principles, are known as *Ideas*, and, being innate, are denominated *innate Ideas*. It is their reality which Sir William Hamilton denies, declaring them to be only higher generalizations of the Understanding, and it is the faculty called the Pure Reason, in which they are supposed to inhere, whose actuality is now to be proved.

The effort to do this will be successful if it can be shown that the logician's statement of the facts is partial, and essentially defective; what are the phenomena which cannot be comprehended in his scheme; and, finally, that they can be accounted for on no other ground than that stated.

1. The statement of facts by the Limitists is partial and essentially defective. They start with the assumption that a generalization is the highest form of human knowledge. To appreciate this fully, let us examine the process they thus exalt. A generalization is a process of thought through which one advances from a discursus among facts, to a conclusion, embodying a seemingly general truth, common to all the facts of the class. For instance. The inhabitants of the north temperate zone have long observed it to be a fact, that north winds are cold; and so have arrived at the general conclusion that such winds will lower the temperature. A more extensive experience teaches them, however, that in the south temperate zone, north winds are warm, and their judgment has to be modified accordingly. A yet larger investigation shows that, at one period in geologic history, north winds, even in northern climes, were warm, and that tropical animals flourished in arctic regions; and the judgment is again modified. Now observe this most important

fact here brought out. *Every judgment may be modified by a larger experience.* Apply this to another class of facts. An apple is seen to fall when detached from the parent stem. An arrow, projected into the air, returns again. An invisible force keeps the moon in its orbit. Other like phenomena are observed; and, after patient investigation, it is found to be a fact, that there is a force in the system to which our planet belongs, which acts in a ratio inverse to the square of the distance, and which thus binds it together. But if a generalization is the highest form of knowledge, we can never be sure we are right, for a subsequent experience may teach us the reverse. We know we have not *all the facts.* We may again find that the north wind is elsewhere, or was once here, warm. Should a being come flying to us from another sphere so distant, that the largest telescope could catch no faintest ray, even, of its shining, and testify to us that there, the force we called gravitation, was inversely as the *cube* of the distance, we could only accept the testimony, and modify our judgment accordingly. Conclusions of to-day may be errors to-morrow; and we can never know we are right. The Limitists permit us only interminable examinations of interminable changes in phenomena; which afford no higher result than a new basis for new studies.

From this wearisome, Io-like wandering, the soul returns to itself, crying its wailing cry, "Is this true? Is this all?" when suddenly, as if frenzied by the presence of a god, it shouts exultingly "The truth! the truth! I see the eternal truth."

The assumption of the Limitists is not all the truth. Their diagnosis is both defective and false. It is defective, in that they have failed to perceive those qualities of *universality* and *necessity,* which most men instinctively accord to certain perceptions of the mind; and false, in that they deny the reality of those qualities, and of the certain perceptions as modified by them, and the actuality of that mental faculty which gives the perceptions, and thus qualified. They state a part of the truth, and deny a part. The whole truth is, the mind both generalizes and intuits.

It is the *essential* tenet of their whole scheme, that the human mind nowhere, and under no circumstance, makes an affirmation which it unreservedly qualifies as necessary and universal. Their doctrine is, that these affirmations *seem* to be such, but that a searching examination shows this seeming to be only a bank of fog. For instance. The mind seems to affirm that two and two *must* make four. "Not so," says the Limitist. "As a fact, we see that two and two do make four, but it may make five, or any other sum. For don't you see? if two and two must make four, then the Infinite must see it so; and if he must see it so, he is thereby conditioned; and what is worse, we know just as much about it as he does." In reply to all such quibbles, it is to be said, — there is no seeming about it! If the mind is not utterly mendacious, it affirms, positively and unreservedly, "Two and two are four, *must* be four; and to see it so, *is conditional for* ALL *intellect*." Take another illustration. The mind instinctively, often unconsciously, always compulsorily, affirms that the sentiment, In society the rights of the individual can never trench upon the rights of the body politic, — is a necessary, and universally applicable principle; which, however much it may be violated, can never be changed. The whole fabric of society is based upon this. Could a mind think this away, it could not construct a practical system of society upon what would be left, — its negation. But the Limitists step in here, and say, "All this seems so, perhaps, but then the mind is so weak, that it can never be sure. You must modify (correct?) this seeming, by the consideration that, if it is so, then the Infinite must know it so, and the finite and Infinite must know it alike, and the Infinite will be limited and conditioned thereby, which would be impious." Again, the intellect unreservedly asserts, "There is no seeming in the matter. The utterance is true, absolutely and universally true, and every intellect *must* see it so."

Illustrations like the above might be drawn from every science of which the human mind is cognizant. But more are not needed. Enough has been adduced to establish the *fact* of those qualities, universality and necessity, as inherent in certain mental affirmations. Having thus pointed out the essential defect of the logician's scheme, it is required to state:

2. What the phenomena are which cannot be comprehended therein.

In general, it may be said that all those perceptions and assertions of the mind, which are instinctive, and which it involuntarily qualifies as universal and necessary, are not, and cannot be comprehended in Sir William Hamilton's scheme. To give an exhaustive presentation of all the *a priori* laws of the mind, would be beyond the scope of the present undertaking, and would be unnecessary to its success. This will be secured by presenting a classification of them, and sufficient examples under each class. Moreover, to avoid a labor which would not be in place here, we shall attempt no new classification; but shall accept without question, as ample for our purpose, that set forth by one of our purest and every way best thinkers, — Rev. Mark Hopkins, D. D., President of Williams College, Mass.

"The ideas and beliefs which come to us thus, may be divided into, first, mathematical ideas and axioms. These are at the foundation of the abstract sciences, having for their subject, quantity. In the second division are those which pertain to mere being and its relations. Upon these rest all sciences pertaining to actual being and its relations. The third division comprises those which pertain to beauty. These are at the foundation of æsthetical science. In the fourth division are those which pertain to morals and religion. Of these the pervading element is the sense of obligation or duty. Of this the idea necessarily arises in connection with the choice by a rational being of a supreme end, and with the performance of actions supposed to bear upon that." — *Moral Science*, p. 161.

First. — Mathematical ideas and axioms.

Take, for instance, the multiplication table. Can any one, except a Limitist, be induced to believe that it was originally *constructed;* that a will put it together, and might take it apart? Seven times seven now, make forty-nine. Will any one say that it might have been made to make forty-seven; or that at some future time such may be the case? Or again, take the axiom "Things which are equal to the same thing are equal to one another." Will some one say, that the intellectual beings in the universe might, with equal propriety, have been so constructed as to affirm that, in some instances, things which are equal to the same thing are *unequal* to one another? Or consider the properties of a triangle. Will our limitist teachers instruct us that these properties are a matter of indifference; that for aught we know, the triangle might have been made to have three right angles? Yet again. Examine the syllogism. Was its law constructed?

All M is X;
All Z is M;
All Z is X.

Will any one say that *perhaps,* we don't know but it might have been so made, as to appear to us that the conclusion was Some Z is not X? Or will the Limitists run into that miserable petty subterfuge of an assertion, "All this *seems* to us as it is, and we cannot see how it could be different; but then, our minds are so feeble, they are confined in such narrow limits, that it would be the height of presumption to assert positively with regard to stronger minds, and those of wider scope? Perhaps they see things differently." *Perhaps* they do; but if they do, their minds or ours falsify! The question is one of *veracity,* nothing more. Throughout all the range of mathematics, the positive and *unqualified* affirmation of the mind is that its intuitions are absolute and universal; that they are *a priori* laws conditional of *all* intellect; that of the Deity just as much as that of man. Feebleness and want of scope have nothing to do with mind in its affirmation, "Seven times seven *must* make forty-nine; *and cannot by any possibility of effort make any other product;*" and every intellect, *if it sees at all, must see it so.* And so on through the catalogue. From this, it follows in this instance, that human knowledge is *exhaustive*, and so is exactly similar, and equal to the Deity's knowledge.

Second. Those ideas and beliefs which pertain to mere being and its relations.

Take, for instance, the axiom, A material body cannot exist in the Universe without standing in some relation to all the other material bodies in that Universe. Either this is absolutely true, or it is not. If it is so true, then every intellectual being to whom it presents itself as object at all, must see it as every other does. One may see more relations than another; but the axiom in its intrinsic nature must be seen alike by all. If it is not absolutely true, then the converse, or any partially contradictory proposition, may be true. For example. A material body may exist in the Universe, and stand in no relation to some of the other material bodies in that Universe. But, few men will hesitate to say, that this is not only utterly unthinkable, but that it could only become thinkable by a denial and destruction of the laws of thought; or, in other words, by the stultification of the mind.

Take another instance, arising from the fact of parentage and offspring, in the sentient beings of the world. A pair, no matter to what class they belong, by the fact of becoming parents, establish a new relation for themselves; and, "after their kind," they are under bonds to their young. And, to a greater or less extent, their young have a claim upon them. As we ascend in the scale of being, the duty imposed is greater, and the claim of the offspring stronger. Whether it be the fierce eagle, or the timid dove, or the chirping sparrow; whether it be the prowling lion, or the distrustful deer, or the cowering hare; or whether it be the races of man who are examined, the relations established by parentage are everywhere recognized. Now, will one say that all this might be changed for aught we know; that, what we call law, is only a judgment of mankind; and so that this relation did not exist at first, but was the product of growth? And will one further say that there is no necessity or universality in this relation; but that the races might, for aught we know, have just as well been established with a parentage which involved no relation at all; that the fabled indifference of the ostrich, intensified a hundredfold, might have been the law of sentient being? Yet such results logically flow from the principles of the Limitists. Precisely the same line of argument might be pursued respecting the laws of human society. But it is not needed here. It is evident now, that what gives validity to judgments *is the fact that they accord with an a priori principle in the mind.*

Third. The ideas and beliefs which pertain to beauty. A science of beauty has not yet been sufficiently developed to permit of so extensive an illustration of this class as the others. Yet enough is established for our purpose. Let us consider beauty as in proportioned form. It is said that certain Greek mathematicians, subsequently to the Christian era, studied out a mathematical formula for the human body, and constructed a statue according to it; and that both were pronounced at the time *perfect*. Both statue and formula are now lost. Be the story true, or a legend, there is valid ground for the assertion, that the mind instinctively assumes, in all its criticisms, the axiom, There is a perfect ideal by which as standard, all art must be judged. The very fact that the mind, though acknowledging the imperfection of its own ideal, unconsciously asserts, that somewhere, in some mind, there is an ideal, in which a perfect hand joins a perfect arm, and a perfect foot a perfect leg, and these a perfect trunk; and a perfect neck supports a perfect head, adorned by perfect features, and thus there is a perfect ideal, is *decisive* that such an ideal exists. And this conclusion is true, because God who made us, and constructed the ground from whence this instinctive affirmation springs, is true.

Take another instance. Few men, who have studied Gothic spires, have failed to observe that the height of some, in proportion to their base, is too great, and that of others, too small. The mind irresistibly affirms, that between these opposite imperfections, there is a golden mean, at which the proportion shall be *perfect.* When the formula of this proportion shall be studied out, any workman, who is skilled with tools, can construct a perfect spire. The law once discovered and promulgated, becomes common knowledge. Mechanical skill will be all that can differentiate one workman from another. The fact that the law has not been discovered yet, throws no discredit upon the positive affirmation of the mind, that there must be such a law; any more than the fact of Newton's ignorance of the law of gravitation, when he saw the apple fall, discredited his instinctive affirmation, upon seeing that phenomenon, there is a law in accordance with which it fell.

Now how comes the mind instinctively and positively to make these assertions. If they were judgments, the mind would only speak of probabilities; but here, it qualifies the assertion with necessity. Men, however positive in their temperament, do not say, "I know it will rain to-morrow," but only, "In all probability it will." Not so here. Here the mind refuses to express itself doubtfully. Its utterance is the extreme of positiveness. It says *must.* And if its affirmation is not true, then there is no *reason* why those works of art which are held in highest esteem, should be adjudged better than the efforts of the tyro, except the whim of the individual, or the arbitrary determination of their admirers.

Fourth. The ideas and beliefs which pertain to morals and religion.

We now enter a sphere of which no understanding could by any possibility ever guess, much less investigate. Here no sense could ever penetrate; there is no object for it to perceive. Here all judgments are impertinent; for in this sphere are only laws, and duties, and obligations. An understanding cannot "conceive" of a moral law, because such a law is inconceivable; and it cannot perceive one, because it has no eye. If it were competent to explain every phenomenon in the other classes, it would be utterly impotent to explain a single phenomenon in this. What is moral obligation? Whence does it arise, or how is it imposed? and who will enforce it, and how will it be enforced? All these, and numerous such other questions, cannot be raised even by the Understanding, much less answered by it. The moral law of the Universe is one which can be learned from no judgment, or combination of judgments. It can be learned only by being *seen*. The moral law is no conclusion, which may be modified by a subsequent experience. It is an affirmation which is *imperative*. To illustrate. It is an axiom, that the fact of free moral agency involves the fact of obligation. Man is a free moral agent; and so, under the obligation imposed. At the first, it was optional with the Deity whether he would create man or not. But will any one assert that, having determined to create man such as he is, it was optional with him, whether man should be under the obligation, or not? Can man be a free moral agent, and be free from the duties inherent therein? Does not the mind instinctively and necessarily affirm, that the fact of free moral agency assures the fact of such a relation to God's moral government, that obligation *must* follow? One cannot hesitate to say, that the formula, A free agent may be released from his obligation to moral law, is absolutely unthinkable.

Again, no judgment can attain to the moral law of the Universe; and yet man knows it. Jesus Christ, when he proclaimed that law in the words "Thou shalt love the Lord thy God with all thy mind and strength, and thy neighbor as thyself," only uttered what no man can, in thought, deny. A man can no more think selfishness as the moral law of the Universe, than he can think two and two to be five. Man not only sees the law, but he feels and acknowledges the obligation, even in his rebellion. In fact there would be no rebellion, no sense of sin, if there were no obligation. Whence comes the authority of the law? No power can give it authority, or enforce obedience. Power can crush a Universe, it cannot change a heart. The law has, and can have authority; it imposes, and can impose obligation; only because *it is an a priori law of the Universe*, alike binding upon *all* moral beings, upon God as well as man; and is so seen immediately, and necessarily, by a direct intuition. Man finds this law fundamental to his self; and as well, a necessarily fundamental law of *all* moral beings. *Therefore* he acknowledges it. And the very efforts he makes to set up a throne for Passion, over against the throne of Benevolence, is an involuntary acknowledgment of the authority of that law he seeks to rival.

It was said above, that neither Sense nor Understanding can take any cognizance of the objects of investigation which fall in this class. This is because the Sense can gather no material over which the Understanding can run. Is the moral law matter? No. How then can the Sense observe it? One answer may possibly be made, viz.: It is deduced from the conduct of men; and sense observes that. To this it is replied

a. The allegation is not true. Most men violate the moral law of the Universe. Their conduct accords with the law of selfishness. Such conclusions as that of Hobbes, that war is the natural condition of Society, are those which would follow from a consideration of man, as he appears to the Sense.

b. If it were true, the question obtrudes itself,—How came it there? *How came this fundamental law to be?* and to this the Sense and Understanding return no shadow of answer.

But from the stand-point of a Pure Reason, all is clear. All the ideas and beliefs, every process of thought which belongs to this sphere, are absolute and universal. They *must* be what they are; and so are conditional of all moral beings. Here what the human mind sees, is just what the Deity sees; and it sees just as the Divine mind sees, so that the truth, as far as so seen, is *common* to both.

Although the facts which have been adduced above, are inexplicable by the Limitists, and are decisive of the actuality of the Reason, as it has been heretofore described, yet another line of argument of great weight must not be omitted. There are in language certain *positive* terms, which the Limitists, and the advocates of the Reason agree in asserting cannot convey any meaning to, or be explained by the Sense and Understanding. Such are the words infinite and absolute. The mere presence of such words in language, as positive terms, is a decisive evidence of the fact, that there is also a faculty which entertains positive ideas corresponding to them. Sir William Hamilton's position in this matter, is not only erroneous, but astonishing. He asserts that these words express only "negative notions." "They," the infinite and absolute, "can be conceived only by a thinking away from, or abstraction of, those very conditions under which thought itself is realized; consequently, the notion of the Unconditioned is only negative — negative of the conceivable itself." But, if this is true, how came these words in the language at all? Negative ideas produce negative expressions. Indeed, the Limitists are confidently challenged to designate another case in language, in which a positive term can be alleged to have a *purely* negative signification. Take an illustration to which we shall recur further on. The question has been raised, whether a sixth sense can be. Can the Limitists find in language, or can they construct, a positive term which will represent the negation of a sixth sense? We find in language the positive terms, ear and hearing; but can such positive terms be found, which will correspond to the phrase, no sixth sense? In this instance, in physics, the absurdity is seen at once. Why is not as readily seen the equal absurdity of affirming that, in metaphysics, positive terms have grown up in the language which are simple negations? Here, for the present, the presentation of facts may rest. Let us recapitulate those which have been adduced. The axioms in mathematics, the principles of the relations of being, the laws of æsthetics, and most of all the whole system of principles pertaining to morals and religion, standing, as they do, a series of mental affirmations, which all mankind, except the Limitists, qualify as necessary and universal, compel assent to the proposition, that there must be a faculty different in kind from the Sense and Understanding, — for these have already been found impotent — which can be ground to account for all these facts satisfactorily. And the presence in language of such positive terms as absolute and infinite, is a most valuable auxiliary argument. The faculty which is required, — the faculty which qualifies all the products of its activity with the characteristics above named, is the Pure Reason. And its actuality may therefore be deemed established.

The Pure Reason having thus been proved to be, it is next required to show the mode of its activity. This can best be done, by first noticing the *kind* of results which it produces. The Reason gives us, not thoughts, but ideas. These are simple, pure, primary, necessary. It is evident that any such object of mental examination can be known only in, and by, itself. It cannot be analyzed, for it is simple. It cannot be compared, for it is pure; and so possesses no element which can be ground for a comparison. It cannot be deduced, for it is primary and necessary. *It can only be seen.* Such an object must be known under the following circumstances. It must be inherent in the seeing faculty, and must be *immediately and directly seen* by that faculty; all this in such a manner, that the abstraction of the object seen, would annihilate the faculty itself. Now, how is it with the Reason? Above we found it to be both capacity and faculty: capacity in that it possessed as integral elements, *a priori* first principles, as objects of sight; faculty in that it saw, brought forward, and made available, those principles. The mode of activity of the Pure Reason is then a *seeing*, direct, immediate, *sure;* which holds pure truth *fast*, right in the very centre of the field of vision. This act of the Reason in thus seeing pure truth is best denominated an intuition of the Reason. And here it may be said,—If perception and perceive could be strictly confined to the Sense; concept and conceive to the Understanding; and intuition and intuit to the Reason, a great gain would be made in accuracy of expression regarding these departments of the mind.

Having thus, as it is believed, established the fact of the existence of a Pure Reason, and shown the mode of its activity, it devolves to declare the function of that faculty.

The function of the Pure Reason is, first:—to intuit, by an immediate perception, the *a priori* elemental principles which condition all being; second,—to intuit, by a like immediate perception, those principles, combined in *a priori* systematic processes, which are the conditional ideal forms for all being; and third,—again to intuit, by another immediate perception, precisely similar in kind to the others, the fact, at least, of the perfectly harmonious combination of all *a priori* elemental principles, in all possible systematic processes, into a perfect unity,—an absolute, infinite Person,—God.

To illustrate.

1. The Reason asserts that "Malice is criminal;" and that it is *necessarily* criminal; or, in other words, that no act, of any will, can make it otherwise than it is. The assertion, then, that "Malice is criminal," is an axiom, and conditions all being, God as well as man.

2. The Reason asserts that every mathematical form must be seen in Space and Time, and it affirms the same necessity in this as in the former case.

3. The full illustration of this point would be Anselm's *a priori* argument for the existence of God. His statement of it should, however, be so modified as to appear, not as an *a priori* argument for the existence of God, but as an ampli-

fied declaration of the fact, that the existence of God is a first principle of Reason; and as such, can no more be denied than the multiplication table. Objection. — This doctrine degrades God to the level of the finite; both being alike conditioned. Answer. — By no means; as will be seen from the two following points.

1. It is universally acknowledged that God must be self-existent, which means, if it means anything, that the existence of God is *beyond his own control;* or, in other words, that self-existence is an *a priori* elemental principle, which conditions God's existing at all.

2. In the two instances under consideration, the word condition has entirely different significations. God is conditioned only by *Himself.* Not only is this conditioning not a limitation, properly speaking, but the very absence of limitation. The fact that He is absolute and infinite, is a condition of His existence. Man's conditions are the very opposite of these. He is relative, instead of absolute; finite, instead of infinite; dependent, instead of self-existent. Hence he differs in *kind* from God as do his conditions.

Such being the function of the Pure Reason, it is fully competent to solve the difficulties raised by Sir William Hamilton and his followers; and the statement of such solution is the work immediately in hand.

Much of the difficulty and obscurity which have, thus far, attended every discussion of this subject, will be removed by examining the definitions given to certain terms; — either by statement, or by implication in the use made of them; — by exposing the errors involved; and by clearly expressing the true signification of each term.

By way of criticism the general statement may be made, — that the Limitists — as was natural from their rejection of the faculty of the Pure Reason — use only such terms, and in such senses, as are pertinent to those subjects which come under the purvey of the Understanding and the Sense; but which are entirely impertinent, in reference to the sphere of spiritual subjects. The two following phases of this error are sufficient to illustrate the criticism.

1. The terms Infinite and Absolute are used to express abstractions. For instance, "*the infinite*, from a human point of view, is merely a name for the absence of those conditions under which thought is possible." "It is thus manifest that a consciousness of the Absolute is equally self-contradictory with that of the Infinite." — *Limits of Religious Thought*, pp. 94 and 96. If asked "Absolute" what? "Infinite" what? Will you allow person, or other definite term to be supplied? Mansel would reply — No! no possible answer can be given by man.

Now, without passing at all upon the question whether these terms can represent concrete objects of thought or not, it is to be said, that the use of them to express abstract notions, is utterly unsound. The mere fact of abstraction is an undoubted limitation. There may be an Infinite and Absolute Person. By no possibility can there be an abstract Infinite.

2. But a more glaring and unpardonable error is made by the Limitists in their use of the words infinite and absolute, as expressing quantity. Take a few examples from many.

"For example, we can positively conceive, neither an absolute whole, that is, a whole so great that we cannot also conceive it as a relative part of a still greater whole; nor an absolute part, that is, a part so small, that we cannot also conceive it as a relative whole, divisible into smaller parts. On the other hand, we cannot positively represent, or realize, or construe to the mind (as here understanding and imagination coincide), an infinite whole, for this could only be done by the infinite synthesis in thought of finite wholes which would itself require an infinite time for its accomplishment; nor, for the same reason, can we follow out in thought an infinite divisibility of parts." — *Hamilton's Essays*, p. 20.

"The metaphysical representation of the Deity as absolute and infinite, must necessarily, as the profoundest metaphysicians have acknowledged, amount to nothing less than the sum of all reality." — *Limits of Religious Thought*, p. 76.

"Is the First Cause finite or infinite? . . . . . To think of the First Cause as finite, is to think of it as limited. To think of it as limited, necessarily implies a conception of something beyond its limits; it is absolutely impossible to conceive a thing as bounded, without conceiving a region surrounding its boundaries." — *Spencer's First Principles*, p. 37.

The last extract tempts one to ask Mr. Spencer if he ever stood on the north side of the affections. Besides the extracts selected, any person reading the authors above named, will find numerous phrases like these: "infinite whole," "infinite sum," "infinite number," "infinite series," by which they express sometimes a mathematical, and sometimes a material amount.

Upon this whole topic it is to be said, that the terms infinite and absolute have, and can have, no relevancy to any object of the Sense or of the Understanding, judging according to the Sense, or to any number. There is no whole, no sum, no number, no amount, but is definite and limited; and to use those words with the word infinite, is as absurd as to say an infinite finite. And to use words thus, is to "multiply words without knowledge."

Again, the lines of thought which these writers pursue, do not tend in any degree to clear up the fogs in which they have lost themselves, but only make the muddle thicker. Take, for instance, the following extract: —

"Thus we are landed in an inextricable dilemma. The Absolute cannot be conceived as conscious, neither can it be conceived as unconscious; it cannot be conceived as complex, neither can it be conceived as simple; it cannot be conceived by difference, neither can it be conceived by the absence of difference; it cannot be identified with the Universe, neither can it be distinguished from it. The One and the Many, regarded as the beginning of existence, are thus alike incomprehensible." — *Limits of Religious Thought*," p. 79.

The soul, while oaring her way with weary wing, over the watery waste of such a philosophy, can find no rest for the sole of her foot, except on that floating carcase of a doctrine, Chaos is God. The simple fact that such confusion logically results from the premises of the Limitists, is a sufficient warrant for rejecting their whole system of thought, — principle and process; and for striking for a new base of operations. But where shall such a base be sought for? On what immutable Ararat can the soul find her ark, and a sure resting-place? Man seeks a Rock upon which he can climb and cry, I KNOW that this is truth. Where is the Everlasting Rock? In our search for the answer to these queries, we may be aided by setting forth the goal to be reached, — the object to be obtained.

By observation and reflection man comes to know that he is living in, and forms part of, a system of things, which he comprehensively terms the Universe. The problem is, — *To find an Ultimate Ground, a Final Cause, which shall be adequate to account for the existence and sustentation of this Universe.* There are but two possible directions from which the solution of this problem can come. It must be found either within the Universe, or without the Universe.

Can it be found within the Universe? If it can, one of two positions must be true. Either a part of the Universe is cause for the existence of the whole of the Universe; or the Universe is self-existent. Upon the first position nothing need be said. Its absurdity is manifested in the very statement of it. A full discussion, or, in fact, anything more than a notice of the doctrine of Pantheism, set forth in the second point, would be beyond the intention of the author. The qnestions at issue lie not between theists and pantheists, but between those who alike reject Pantheism as erroneous. The writer confesses himself astonished that a class of rational men could ever have been found, who should have attempted to find the Ultimate Ground of the Universe *in itself.* All that man can know of the facts of the Universe, he learns by observation; and the sum of the knowledge he thus gains is, that a vast system of physical objects exists. From the facts observed, he draws conclusions: but the stream cannot rise higher than its fountain. With reference to any lesser object, as a watch, the same process goes on. A watch is. It has parts; and these parts move in definite relations to each other; and to secure a given object. If now, any person, upon being asked to account for the existence of the watch, should confine himself wholly to an examination of the nature of the springs, the wheels, the hands, face, &c., endeavoring to find the reason of its being within itself, the world would laugh at him. How much more justly may the world laugh, yea, shout its ridicule, at the mole-eyed man who rummages among the springs and wheels of the vast machine of the Universe, to find the reason of *its* being. In the former instance, the bystander would exclaim, — "The watch is an evidence of intelligence. Man is the only intelligent being on the earth; and is superior to the watch. Man made the watch." And his assertion would be true. *A fortiori* would a bystander of the Universe exclaim, "The Universe is an evidence of intelligence. An intelligent Being, superior to the Universe, made the Universe." And his assertion is true. We are driven then to our last position; but it is the Gibraltar of Philosophy.

THE ULTIMATE GROUND OF THE UNIVERSE MUST BE SOUGHT FOR, AND CAN ONLY BE FOUND, WITHOUT THE UNIVERSE.

From this starting-point alone can we proceed, with any hope of reaching the goal. Setting out on our new course, we will gain a step by noticing a fact involved in the illustration just given. The bystander exclaims, "The watch is an evidence of intelligence." In this very utterance is necessarily expressed the fact of two diverse spheres of existence: the one the sphere of matter, the other the sphere of mind. One cannot think of matter except as inferior, nor of mind except as superior. These two, matter and mind, comprise all possible existence. The Reason not only cannot see *how* any other existence can be, but affirms *that* no other can be. Mind, then, is the Ultimate Ground of the Universe. What mind?

By examination, man perceives what appears to be an order in the Universe, concludes that there is such an order, assumes the conclusion to be valid, and names the order Nature. Turning his eye upon himself, he finds himself not only associated with, but, through a portion of his faculties, forming a part of that Nature. But a longer, sharper scrutiny, a profounder examination, reveals to him his soul's most secret depth; and the fact of his spiritual personality glows refulgent in the calm light of consciousness. He sees himself, indeed, in Nature; but he thrills with joy at the quickly acquired knowledge that Nature is only a nest, in which he, a purely supernatural being, must flutter for a time, until he shall be grown, and ready to plume his flight for the Spirit Land. If then, man, though bound in Nature, finds his central self utterly diverse from, and superior to Nature, so that he instinctively cries, "My soul is worth more than a Universe of gold and diamonds;" *a fortiori* must that Being, who is the Ultimate Ground, not only of Nature, but of those supernatural intelligences who live in Nature, be supernatural, spiritual, and supreme?

Just above, it was seen that matter and mind comprise all possible existence. It has now been found that mind, in its highest form, even in man, is pure spirit; and as such, wholly supernatural. It has further been determined, that the object of our search must be the Supreme Spirit.

Just at this point it is suitable to notice, what is, perhaps, the most egregious and unpardonable blunder the Limitists have made. In order to do this satisfactorily, the following analysis of the human mind is presented. The soul is a spiritual person, and an animal nature. To this animal nature belong the Sense and the Understanding. It is universally acknowledged, — at least the Limitists will not deny, — that the Sense and the Understanding are wholly within, and conditioned by Nature. Observe then their folly. They deny that a part can account for a whole; they reject Pantheism; *and yet they employ only those faculties which they confess are wholly within and conditioned by Nature* — for they deny the existence of the Pure Reason, the perceptive faculty of the spiritual person — *to search, only in Nature, for the cause of Nature.* A fly would buzz among the wheels of a clock to as little purpose.

The result arrived at just above, now claims our careful attention.

The Ultimate Ground of the Universe is THE SUPREME SPIRIT.

To appreciate this result, we must return to our analysis of man. In his spiritual personality we have found him wholly supernatural. We have further found that, only as a spiritual person is he capable of pursuing this investigation to a final and valid termination. If, then, we would complete our undertaking, we must ascend into a sphere whose light no eagle's eye can ever bear; and whose atmosphere his daring wing can never beat. There no sense can ever enter; no judgments are needed. Through Reason — the soul's far-darting eye, — and through Reason alone, can we gaze on the Immutable.

Turning this searching eye upon ourselves, we find that man, as spiritual person, is a Pure Reason, — the faculty which gives him *a priori* first principles, as the standard for conduct and the forms for activity, — a Spiritual Sensibility, which answers with emotive music to the call of the Reason; and lastly, a Will, in which the Person dwells central, solitary, and supreme, the final arbiter of its own destiny. Every such being is therefore a miniature final cause.

The goal of our search must be near at hand. In man appears the very likeness of the Being we seek. His highest powers unmistakably shadow forth the form of that Being, who is The Final. Man originates; but he is dependent for his power, and the sphere of that power is confined to his own soul. We seek a being who can originate, who is utterly independent; and the sphere of whose activity extends wherever, without himself, he chooses. Man, after a process of culture, comes to intuit some first principles, in some combinations. We seek a being who necessarily sees, at once and forever, all possible first principles, in all possible relations, as the ideal forms for all possible effort. Man stumbles along on the road of life, frequently ignorant of the way, but more frequently perversely violating the eternal law which he finds written on his heart. We seek a being who never stumbles, but who is perfectly wise; and whose conduct is in immutable accord with the *a priori* standards of his Reason. Man is a spiritual person, dependent for existence, and limited to himself in his exertions. He whom we seek will be found to be also a spiritual person who is self-existent, and who sets his own bounds to his activity.

That the line of thought we are now pursuing is the true one, and that the result which we approach, and are about to utter, is well founded, receives decisive confirmation from the following facts. Man perceives that malice must be criminal. Just so the Eternal Eye must see it. A similar remark is true of mathematical, and all other *a priori* laws. Sometimes, at least, there awakens in man's bosom the unutterable thrill of benevolence; and thus he tastes of the crystal river which flows, calmly and forever, through the bosom of the "Everlasting Father." For his own conduct, man is the final cause. In this is he, must he be, the likeness of the Ultimate. Spiritual personality is the highest possible form of being. It is then a form common to God and man. Here, therefore, Philosophy and Revelation are at one. With startling, and yet grateful unanimity, they affirm the solemn truth, "GOD MADE MAN IN HIS OWN IMAGE."

We reach the goal at last. The Final Truth stands full in the field of our vision. "I am Alpha and Omega, the beginning and the ending, saith Jehovah, who is, and who was, and who is to come, the Almighty." THAT SPIRITUAL PERSON WHO IS SELF-EXISTENT, ABSOLUTE, AND INFINITE, IS THE ULTIMATE GROUND, THE FINAL CAUSE OF THE UNIVERSE.

The problem of the Universe is solved. We stand within the portico of the sublime temple of truth. Mortal has lifted, at last, the veil of Isis, and looked upon the eternal mysteries.

It is manifest now, how irrelevant and irreverent those expressions must be, in which the terms infinite and absolute are employed as signifying abstractions or amounts. They can have no meaning with reference to the Universe. But what their true significance is, stands out with unmistakable clearness and precision.

1. *Absoluteness is that distinctive spiritual* QUALITY *of the necessary Being which establishes Him as unqualified except by Himself, and as complete.*

2. Absoluteness and Unconditionedness are, — the one the positive, and the other the negative term expressive of the same idea.

3. *Infinity is that distinctive spiritual* QUALITY *of the necessary Being which gives to Him universality.*

Absoluteness and Infinity are, then, spiritual qualities of the self-existent Person, which, distinguishing Him from all other persons, constitute Him unique and supreme.

It is a law of Logic, which even the child must acknowledge, that whenever, by a process of thought, a result has been attained and set forth, he who propounds the result is directly responsible for all that is logically involved in it. The authority of that law is here both acknowledged and invoked. The most rigid and exhaustive logical development of the premises heretofore obtained, which the human mind is capable of, is challenged, in the confidence that there can be found therein no jot of discrepancy, no tittle of contradiction. As germain, and important to the matter in hand, some steps in this development will be noted.

In solving the problem placed before us, viz: To account for the being and continuance of the Universe, we have found that the Universe and its Cause are two distinct and yet intimately and necessarily connected beings, the one dependent upon the other, and that other utterly independent; and so that the one is limited and finite, and the other absolute and infinite; that the one is partly thing and partly person, and that to both thing and person limitation and finiteness belong; while the other is wholly person, and consequently the pure, absolute, and infinite Person. We have further found that absoluteness and infinity are spiritual qualities of that one Person, which are incommunicable, and differentiate Him from all other possible beings; and which establish Him as the uncaused, self-active ground for all possible beings besides. It is then a Person with all the limitations and conditions of personality, — a Person at once limited and unlimited, conditioned and unconditioned, related and unrelated, whose limitations, conditions, and relations are entirely consistent with his absoluteness and infinity, who is the final Cause, the Ultimate Ground of the Universe.

The finite person is self-conscious, and in a measure self-comprehending; but he only partially perceives the workings of his own being. *A fortiori*, must the infinite Person be self-conscious, and exhaustively self-comprehending. The finite person is an intellect, sensibility, and will; but these are circumscribed by innumerable limitations. So must the infinite Person be intellect, sensibility, and will; but His intellect must be Universal Genius; His sensibility Pure Delight, and His will, as choice, Universal Benevolence, and as act, Omnipotence.

1. As intellect, the infinite Person is Universal Genius.

Then, he "must possess the primary copies or patterns of what it is possible may be, in his own subjective apprehension;" or, in other words, "The pure ideals of all possible entities, lie as pure reason conceptions in the light of the divine intelligence, and in these must be found the rules after which the creative agency must go forth." These *a priori* "pure ideals" are *conditional* of his knowledge. They are the sum and limit of all possible knowledge. He must know them as they are. He cannot intuit, or think otherwise than in accordance with them. However many there may be of these ideals, the number is fixed and definite, and must be so; and so the infinite Person must see it. In fine, in the fact of exhaustive self-comprehension is involved the fact, that the number of his qualities, attributes, faculties, forms of activity, and acts, are, and must be limited, definite, and so known to him; and yet he is infinite and absolute, and thoroughly knows himself to be so.

2. As sensibility, the infinite Person is Pure Delight.

Then he exists in a state of unalloyed and complete bliss, produced by the ceaseless consciousness of his perfect worth and worthiness, and his entire complacency therein. Yet he is pleased with the good conduct, and displeased with the evil conduct, of the moral beings he has made. And if two are good, and one better than another, he loves the one more than the other. Yet all this in no way modifies, or limits, or lessens his own absolute self-satisfaction and happiness.

3. As will, the infinite Person is, in choice, Universal Benevolence; in act, Omnipotence.

a. In choice, the whole personality, — both the spontaneous and self activity, are entirely and concordantly active in the one direction. Some of the objects towards which this state manifests itself may be very small. The fact that each receives the attention appropriate to his place in the system of beings in no way modifies the Great Heart, which spontaneously prompts to all good acts. But

b. In act, the infinite Person, though omnipotent, is, always must be, limited. His ability to act is limited and determined by the "pure ideals," in which "must be found the rules after which the creative agency must go forth." In act he is also limited by his choice. The fact that he is Universal Benevolence estops him from performing any act which is not in exact accordance therewith. He cannot construct a rational being, to whom two and two will appear five; and if he should attempt to, he would cease to be perfect Goodness. Again, the infinite Person performs an act — of Creation. The act is, must be, limited and definite; and so must the product — the Universe be. He cannot create an unlimited Universe, nor perform an infinite act. The very words unlimited Universe, and as well the notions they express, are contradictory, and annihilate each other. Further, an infinite act, even if possible, would not, could not create, or have any relation to the construction of a Universe. An infinite act must be the realization of an infinite ideal. The infinite Person has a thorough comprehension of himself; and consequently a complete idea of himself. That idea, being the idea of the infinite Person, is infinite; and it is the only possible infinite idea. He finds this idea realized in himself. But, should it be in his power to realize it *again,* that exertion of power would be an infinite act, and its product another infinite Person. No other infinite act, and no other result, are rationally supposable.

The Universe, then, however large it be, is, must be, limited and definite. Its magnitude may be inconceivable to us; but in the mind of its Creator every atom is numbered. No spirit may ever have skirted its boundary; but that boundary is as clear and distinct to his eye as the outline of the Alps against a clear sky is to the traveller's. The questions Where? How far? How long? How much? and the like, are pertinent only *in* the Universe; and their answers are always limited and definite.

The line of thought we have been pursuing is deemed by a large class of thinkers not only paradoxical, but utterly contradictory and self-destructive. We speak of a Person, a term which necessarily involves limitation and condition, as infinite and absolute. We speak of this infinity and absoluteness as spiritual qualities, which are conditional and limiting to him. We speak of him as conditioned by an inability to be finite. In fine, to those good people, the Limitists, our sense seems utter nonsense. It is required, therefore, for the completion of this portion of our task, to present a rational ground upon which these apparent contradictions shall become manifestly consistent.

In those sentences where the infinite Person is spoken of as limited and unlimited, &c., it is evident that there is a play upon words, and that they apply to different qualities in the personality. It is not said, of course, that the number of his faculties is limited and unlimited; or that his self-complacency is boundless and constrained; or that his act is conditioned and unconditioned. Nor are these seeming paradoxes stated to puzzle and disturb. They are written to express a great, fundamental, and all-important truth, which seems never once to have shadowed the minds of the Limitists, — a truth which, when once seen, dispels forever all the ghostly battalions of difficulties which they have raised. The truth is this.

That Being whose limitations, conditions, and relations are wholly subjective, *i. e.* find their whole base and spring in his self; and who is therefore entirely free from all possible limitations, conditions, and relations, from without himself; and who possesses, therefore, all possible fulness of all possible excellences, and finds the perennial acme of happiness in self-contemplation, and the consciousness of his perfect worth; and being such is ground for all other possible being; is, in the true philosophical sense, unrelated, unconditioned, unlimited. Or, in other words, the conditions imposed by Universal Genius upon the absolute and infinite Person are *different in kind* from the conditions imposed upon finite persons and physical things. The former in no way diminish aught from the fulness of their possessor's endowments; the latter not only do so diminish, but render it impossible for their possessor to supply the deficiency.

The following dictum will, then, concisely and exactly express the truth we have attained.

Those only are conditions, in the philosophical sense, which diminish the fulness of the possessor's endowments.

An admirable illustration of this truth can be drawn from some reflections of Laurens P. Hickok, D. D., which we quote. "What we need is not merely a rule by which to direct *the process* in the attainment of any artistic end, but we must find the legislator who may determine the end itself. . . . . . Whence is the ultimate behest that is to determine the archetype, and control the pure spontaneity in its action.

. . . .

"Must the artist work merely because there is an inner want to gratify, with no higher end than the gratification of the highest constitutional craving? Can we find nothing beyond a want, which shall from its own behest demand that this, and not its opposite, shall be? Grant that the round worlds and all their furniture are *good* — but why good? Certainly as means to an end. Grant that this end, the happiness of sentient beings, is *good* — but why good? Because it supplies the want of the Supreme Architect. And is this the *supreme good?* Surely if it is, we are altogether within nature's conditions, call our ultimate attainment by what name we may. We have no origin for our legislation, only as the highest architect finds such wants within himself, and the archetypal rule for gratifying his wants in the most effectual manner; and precisely as the ox goes to his fodder in the shortest way, so he goes to his work in making and peopling worlds in the most direct manner. Here is no will; no personality; no pure autonomy. The artist finds himself so constituted that he must work in this manner, or the craving of his own nature becomes intolerable to himself, and the gratifying of this craving is *the highest good.*"

We attain hereby a mark by which to distinguish the diminishing from the undiminishing condition. A sense of want, *a craving,* is the necessary result of a diminishing condition. Hence the presence of any craving is the distinguishing mark of the finite; and that plenitude of endowments which excludes all possible craving or lack, is the distinguishing mark of the infinite and absolute Person. In this plenitude his infinity and absoluteness consist; and it is, therefore, conditional of them. Upon this plenitude, as conditional of this Person's perfection, Dr. Hickok speaks further, as follows: —

"We must find that which shall itself be the reason and law for benevolence, and for the sake of which the artist shall be put to his beneficent agency above all considerations that he finds his nature craving it. It must be that for whose sake, happiness, even that which, as kind and benevolent, craves on all sides the boon to bless others, itself should be. Not sensient nor artistic autonomy, but a pure ethic autonomy, which knows that within itself there is an excellency which obliges for the sake of itself. This is never to be found, nor anything very analogous to it, in sensient nature and a dictate from some generalized experience. It lies within the rational spirit, and is law in the heart, as an inward imperative in its own right, and must there be found. . . . . . This inward witnessing capacitates for self-legislating and self-rewarding. It is inward consciousness of a worth imperative above want; an end in itself, and not means to another end; a user of things, but not itself to be used by anything; and, on account of its intrinsic excellency, an authoritative determiner for its own behoof of the entire artistic agency with all its products, and thus a conscience excusing or accusing.

"This inward witnessing of the absolute to his own worthiness, gives the ultimate estimate to nature, which needs and can attain to nothing higher, than that it should satisfy this worthiness as end; and thereby in all his works, he fixes, in his own light, upon the subjective archetype, and attains to the objective result of that which is befitting his own dignity. It is, therefore, in no craving want which must be gratified, but from the interest of an inner behest, which should be executed for his own worthiness' sake, that 'God has created all things, and for his pleasure they are and were created.'"

In the light of the foregoing discussion and illustrations, the division of conditions into two classes — the one class, conditions proper, comprising those which diminish the endowments of the being upon whom they lie, and are ground for a craving or lack; and the other class, comprising those conditions which do not diminish the endowments of the being upon whom they lie, and which are, therefore, ground for perfect plenitude of endowments, and of self-satisfaction on account thereof — is seen to be thoroughly philosophical. And let it be here noted, that the very construction, or, if the term suit better, perception of this distinction, is a decisive evidence of the fact, and a direct product of the operation of the Pure Reason. If our intellect comprised only what the Limitists acknowledge it to be, a Sense and an Understanding, not only could no other but diminishing conditions be thought of, but by no possibility could a hint that there were any others flit through the mind. Such a mind, being wholly in nature, and conditioned by nature, *cannot* climb up out of nature, and perceive aught there. But those conditions which lie upon the infinite Person are supernatural and spiritual; and could not be even vaguely guessed at, much more examined critically and classified, but by a being possessed of a faculty the same in kind with the intellect in which such spiritual conditions inhere.

The actual processes which go on in the mind are as follows. The Sense, possessing a purely mechanical structure, a structure not differing in *kind* from that of the vegetable, — both being alike entirely conditioned by the law of cause and effect, — perceives phenomena. The relation of the object to the sensorium, or of the image to the sensory, and the forms under which the Sense shall receive the impression, are fixed. Because the Sense acts compulsorily, in fixed mechanical forms, it is, by this very construction, incapable, not only of receiving impressions and examining phenomena outside of those forms, but it can never be startled with the guess that there *is* anything else than what is received therein. For instance: A man born blind, though he can have no possible notion of what light is, knows that light is, from the testimony of those who can see. But if a race of men born blind should be found, who had never had any communication with men who could see, it is notorious that they could have no possible notion even that light was. A suspicion of its existence could never cross their minds. This position is strengthened and established beyond controversy, by the failure of the mind in its efforts to construct an entirely new sense. Every attempt only intensifies our appreciation of the futility of the effort. From fragments of the five senses we might, perhaps, construct a patchwork sixth; but the mind makes no presentation to itself of a new sense. The reason is, that, to do so, the Sense, as mental faculty, must transcend the very conditions of its existence. It is precisely with the Understanding as with the lower faculty. It cannot transcend its limits. It can add no item to the sum of human knowledge, except as it deduces it from a presentation by the Sense. Hence its conditions correspond to those in its associate faculty.

It is manifest, then, that a being with only these faculties may construct a *system*, but can never develop a *science.* It can arrange, classify, by such standards as its fancy may select, the phenomena in nature; but this must be in accordance with some sensuous form. *No law can be seen,* by which it ought to be so, and not otherwise. Such classification must always be determined by the number of stamens in the flower, for instance; and that standard, though arbitrary, will be as good as any other, *unless there comes a higher faculty* which, overlooking all nature, perceives the *a priori* law working in nature, which gives the ultimate ground for an exhaustive development of a science which in its *idea* cannot be improved. It is manifest, further, that those conditions, to which we have applied the epithet proper, lie upon the two faculties we have been considering. In this we agree with the Limitists.

It now behooves to present the fact that the faculty whose existence was proved in the earlier part of our work, is competent to overlook, and so comprehend nature, and all the conditions of nature, and thereby assign to said conditions their true and inferior place, while it soars out of nature, and intuits those *a priori* laws which, though the conditions of, are wholly unconditioned *by nature;* but which are both the conditions of and conditioned by the supernatural; and this in an entirely different sense from the other. This is the province of the Pure Reason. Standing on some lofty peak, above all clouds of sense, under the full blaze of eternal truth, the soul sees all nature spread like a vast map before her searching eye, sharply observes, and appreciates all the conditions of nature; and then, while holding it full in the field of her vision, with equal fulness perceives that other land, the spiritual plains of the supernatural, sees them too in all their conditionings; and sees, with a clearness of vision never approximated by the earthly eye, the fact that these supernatural conditions are no deprivation which awaken a want, but that they inhere and cohere, as final ground for absolute plenitude of endowments and fulness of bliss, in the Self-existent Person.

It will be objected to the position now attained, that it involves the doctrine that the Pure Reason in the finite spiritual person is on a par with the Universal Genius in the infinite spiritual Person. The objection is fallacious, because based upon the assumption that likeness in mode of action involves entire similarity. The mode of action in the finite Pure Reason is precisely similar to that of the Universal Genius; the objects perceived by both are the same, they are seen in the same light, and so are in accord; but the *range* of the finite is one, and the *range* of the infinite is another; and so diverse also are the circumstances attending the act of seeing. The range of the finite Reason is, *always must be, partial:* the range of the infinite Reason is, *always must be, exhaustive* (not infinite). In circumstances, the finite

Reason is created dependent for existence, must begin in a *germ* in which it is inactive, and *must* be developed by association with nature, and under forms of nature; and can never, by any possibility of growth, attain to that perfectness in which it shall be satisfied, or to a point in development from which it can continue its advance as *pure spirit.* It always must be spirit in a body; even though that be a spiritual body. The infinite Reason is self-existent, and therefore independent; and is, and always must be, in the absolute possessiou of all possible knowledge, and so cannot grow. Hence, while the infinite and finite reasons see the same object in the same light, and therefore *alike,* the difference in range, and the difference in circumstance, must forever constitute them dissimilar. The exact likeness of sight just noticed is the *necessary a priori* ground upon which a moral government is *possible.*

In thus declaring the basis upon which the above distinction between the two classes of conditions rests, we have been led to distinguish more clearly between the faculties of the mind, and especially to observe how the Pure Reason enables us thereby to solve the problems she has raised. In this radical distinction lies the rational ground for the explication of all the problems which the Limitists raise. It also appears that the terms must, possible, and the like, being used to express no idea of restraint, as coming from without upon the infinite Person, or of lack or craving, as subsisting within him, are properly employed in expressing the fact that his *Self, as a priori ground for his activity,* is, though the only, yet a real, positive, and irremovable limit, condition, and law of his action. Of two possible ends he may freely choose either. Of all possible modes of action he may choose one; but the constituting laws of his Self he *cannot,* and the moral laws of his Self he *will not,* violate.

That point has now been reached at which this branch of the discussion in hand may be closed. The final base from which to conduct an examination of the questions respecting absoluteness and infinity has been attained. In the progress to this consummation it was found that a radical psychological error lay at the root of the philosophy taught by the Limitists. Their theory was seen to be partial, and essentially defective. Qualities which they do not recognize were found to belong to certain mental affirmations. Four classes of these affirmations or ideas were named and illustrated; and by them the fact of the Reason was established. Then its mode of activity and its functions were stated; and finally the great truth which solves the problem of the ages was, by this faculty, attained and stated. It became evident that the final cause of the Universe must be found without the Universe; and it was then seen that

That spiritual Person who is self-existent, absolute, and infinite, is the Ultimate Ground, the Final Cause, of the Universe.

Definitions of the terms absolute and infinite suitable to such a position were then given, with a few concluding reflections. From the result thus secured the way is prepared for an examination of the general principles and their special applications which the Limitists maintain, and this will occupy our future pages.

PART II.

AN EXAMINATION OF THE FUNDAMENTAL PROPOSITION OF THE LIMITISTS, AND OF CERTAIN GENERAL COROLLARIES UNDER IT.

It has been attempted in the former pages to find a valid and final basis of truth, one which would satisfy the cravings of the human soul, and afford it a sure rest. In the fact that God made man in his own image, and that thus there is, *to a certain extent*, a community of faculties, a community of knowledge, a community of obligations, and a community of interests, have we found such a basis. We have hereby learned that a part of man's knowledge is necessary and final; in other words, that he can know the truth, and be sure that his knowledge is correct. If the proofs which have been offered of the fact of the Pure Reason, and the statements which have been made of the mode of its activity and of its functions, and, further, of the problem of the Universe, and the true method for solving it, shall have been satisfactory to the reader, he will now be ready to consider the analysis of Sir William Hamilton's fundamental proposition, which was promised on an early page. We there gave, it was thought, sufficiently full extracts for a fair presentation of his theory, and followed them with a candid epitome. In recurring to the subject now, and for the purpose named, we are constrained at the outset to make an acknowledgment.

It would be simple folly, a childish egotism, to pass by in silence the masterly article on this subject in the "North American Review" for October, 1864, and after it to pretend to offer anything new. Whatever the author might have wrought out in his own mental workshop, — and his work was far less able than what is there given, — that article has left nothing to be said. He has therefore been tempted to one of two courses: either to transfer it to these pages, or pass by the subject entirely. Either course may, perhaps, be better than the one finally chosen; which is, while pursuing the order of his own thought, to add a few short extracts therefrom. One possibility encourages him in this, which is, that some persons may see this volume, who have no access to the Review, and to whom, therefore, these pages will be valuable. To save needless repetition, this discussion will presuppose that the reader has turned back and perused the extracts and epitome above alluded to.

Upon the very threshold of Sir William Hamilton's statement, one is met by a logical *faux pas* which is truly amazing. Immediately after the assertion that "the mind can know only the *limited and the conditionally limited,*" and in the very sentence in which he denies the possibility of a knowledge of the Infinite and Absolute, *he proceeds to define those words in definite and known terms!* The Infinite he defines as "the unconditionally unlimited," and the Absolute as "the unconditionally limited." Or, to save him, will one say that the defining terms are unknown? So much the worse, then! "The Infinite," an unknown term, may be represented by x; and the unconditionally unlimited, a compound unknown term, by ab. Now, who has the right to say, either in mathematics or metaphysics, in any philosophy, that $x = ab$? Yet such dicta are the basis of "The Philosophy of the Unconditioned." But, one of two suppositions is possible. Either the terms infinite and absolute are known terms and definable, or they are unknown terms and undefinable. Yet, Hamilton says, they are unknown and definable. Which does he mean? If he is held to the former, they are unknown; then all else that he has written about them are batches of meaningless words. If he is held to the latter, they are definable; then are they known, and his system is denied in the assertion of it. Since his words are so contradictory, he must be judged by his deeds; and in these he always assumes that we have a positive knowledge of the infinite and absolute, else he would not have argued the matter; for there can be no argument about nothing. Our analysis of his theory, then, must be conducted upon this hypothesis.

Turn back for a moment to the page upon which his theory is quoted, and read the last sentence. Is his utterance a "principle," or is it a judgment? Is it an axiom, or is it a guess. The logician asserts that we know only the conditioned, and yet bases his assertion upon "the principles," &c. What is a principle, and how is it known? If it is an axiom, then he has denied his own philosophy in the very sentence in which he uttered it. And this, we have no hesitation in saying, is just what he did. He blindly assumed certain "fundamental laws of thought," — to quote another of his phrases, — to establish the impotence of the mind to know those laws *as fundamental.* Again, if his philosophy is valid, the words "must," "necessary," and the like, are entirely out of place; for they are unconditional. In the conditioned there is, can be, no must, no necessity.

From these excursions about the principle let us now return to the principle itself. It may be stated concisely thus: There are two extremes, — "the Absolute" and the "Infinite." These include all being. They are contradictories, that is, one must be, to the exclusion of the other. But the mind can "conceive" of neither. What, then, is the logical conclusion? *That the mind cannot conceive of anything.* What is his conclusion? That the mind can conceive of something between the infinite and the absolute, which is neither the one nor the other, but a *tertium quid* — the conditioned. Where did this *tertium quid* come from, when he had already comprehended everything in the two extremes? If there is a mean, the conditioned, and the two extremes, then "excluded middle" has nothing to do with the matter at all.

To avoid the inevitable conclusion of his logic as just stated, Hamilton erected the subterfuge of *mental imbecility.* To deny any knowledge to man, was to expose himself to ridicule. He, therefore, and his followers after him, drew a line in the domain of knowledge, and assigned to the hither side of it all knowledge that can come through generalizations in the Understanding; and then asserted that the contradictions which appeared in the mind, when one examined those questions which lie on the further side of that line, resulted from the impotency of the mind to comprehend the questions themselves. This was, is, their psychology. How satisfactory it may be to Man, a hundred years, perhaps, will show. But strike out the last assertion, and write, Both are cognizable; and then let us proceed with our reasoning. The essayist in the North American presents the theory under four heads, as follows: —

"1. The Infinite and Absolute as defined, are contradictory and exclusive of each other; yet, one must be true.

"2. Neither of them can be conceived as possible.

"3. Each is inconceivable; and the inconceivability of each is referable to the same cause, namely, mental imbecility.

"4. As opposite extremes, they include everything conceivable between them."

The first and fourth points require our especial attention.

1. Let us particularly mark, then, that it is *as defined,* that the terms are "contradictory." The question, therefore, turns upon the definitions. Undoubtedly the definitions are erroneous; but in order to see wherein, the following general reflections may be made: —

The terms infinite and absolute, as used by philosophers, have two distinct applications: one to Space and Time, and one to God. Such definitions as are suitable to the latter application, and self-consistent, have already been given. Though reluctant to admit into a philosophical treatise a term bearing two distinct meanings, we shall waive for a little our scruples, — though choosing, for ourselves, to use the equivalent rather than the term.

Such definitions are needed, then, as that absolute Space and Time shall not be contradictory to infinite Space and Time. Let us first observe Hamilton's theory. According to it, Space, for instance, is either unconditional illimitation, or it is unconditional limitation; in other words, it is illimitable, or it is a limited whole. The first part of the assertion is true. That Space is illimitable, is unquestionably a self-evident truth. Any one who candidly considers the subject will see not only that the mind cannot assign limits to Space, but that the attempt is an absurdity just alike in kind with the attempt to think two and two five. The last part is a psychological blunder, has no pertinence to the question, and is not what Hamilton was groping for. He was searching for the truth, that *there is no absolute unit in Space.* A limited whole has nothing to do with the matter in hand — absoluteness — at all. The illimitability of Space, which has just been established as an axiom, precludes this. What, then, is the opposite pole of thought? We have just declared it. There is no absolute unit of Space; or, in other words, all division is *in* Space, but Space is indivisible. This, also, is an axiom, is self-evident. We attain, then, two poles of thought, and definitions of the two terms given, which are exhaustive and consistent.

"Space is illimitable.
Space is indivisible."

The one is the infinity of Space, the other is the absoluteness of Space. The fact, then, is, all limitation is *in* Space, and all division is *in* Space; but Space is neither limited or divided. One of the logician's extremes is seen, then, to have no foundation in fact; and that which is found to be true is also found to be consistent with, nay, essential to, what should have been the other.

Having hitherto expressed a decided protest against any attempt to find out God through the forms of Space and

Time, a repetition will not be needed here. God is only to be sought for, found, and studied, by such methods as are suitable to the supreme spiritual Person. Hence all the attempts of the Limitists to reason from spatial and temporal difficulties over to those questions which belong to God, are simply absurd. The questions respecting Space and Time are to be discussed by themselves. And the questions respecting God are to be discussed by themselves. He who tries to reason from the one to the other is not less absurd than he who should try to reason from a farm to the multiplication table.

In Sir William Hamilton's behalf it should be stated, that there is just a modicum of truth underlying his theory,— just enough to give it a degree of plausibility. The Sense, as faculty for the perception of physical objects, or their images, and the Understanding as discursive faculty for passing over and forming judgments upon the materials gathered by the Sense, lie under the shadow of a law very like the one he stated. The Sense was made *incapable* of perceiving an ultimate atom or of comprehending the universe. From the fact that the Sense never has perceived these objects, the Understanding concludes that it never will. Only by the insight and oversight of that higher faculty, the Pure Reason, do we come to know that it never *can*. It was because those lower faculties are thus walled in by the conditions of Space and Time, and are unable to perceive or conceive anything out of those conditions, and because, in considering them, he failed to see the other mental powers, that Sir William Hamilton constructed his Philosophy of the Unconditioned.

2. Neither of them can be conceived as possible.

Literally, this is true. The word "conceive" applies strictly to the work of the Understanding; and that faculty can never have any notion of the Infinite or Absolute. But, assuming that "conceive" is a general term for cognize, the conclusion developed just above is inevitable. If all being is in one or the other, and neither can be known, nothing can be known.

3. They cannot be known, because of mental imbecility. If man can know nothing because of mental imbecility, why suppose that he has a mental faculty at all? Why not enounce, as the fundamental principle of one's theory, the assertion, All men are idiots? This would be logically consistent. The truth is, the logician was in a dilemma. He must confess that men know something. By a false psychology he had ruled the Reason out of the mind, and so had left himself no faculty by which to form any notion of absoluteness and infinity; and yet they would thrust themselves before him, and demand an explanation. Hence, he constructed a subterfuge. He would have been more consistent if he had said, There is no absolute and infinite. The conditioned is the whole of existence; and this the mind knows.

"4. As opposite extremes, they include everything conceivable between them."

What the essayist in the North American says upon this point is so apt, and so accords with our own previous reflections, that we will not forbear making an extract. "The last of the four theses will best be re-stated in Hamilton's own words; the italics are his. 'The conditioned is the mean between two extremes — two inconditionates, exclusive of each other, neither of which *can be conceived as possible*, but of which, on the principles of contradiction and excluded middle, one *must be admitted as necessary*.' This sentence excites unmixed wonder. To mention in the same breath the law of excluded middle, and two contradictions with a mean between them, requires a hardihood unparalleled in the history of philosophy, except by Hegel. If the two contradictory extremes are themselves incogitable, yet include a cogitable mean, why insist upon the necessity of accepting either extreme? This neccssity of accepting one of two contradictories is wholly based upon the supposed impossibility of a mean; if the mean exists, that may be true, and both the contradictories false. But if a mean between the two contradictories be both impossible and absurd, (and we have hitherto so interpreted the law of excluded middle,) Hamilton's conditioned entirely vanishes."

Upon a system which, in whatever aspect one looks at it, is found to be but a bundle of contradictions and absurdities, further criticism would appear to be unnecessary.

Having, impliedly at least, accepted as true Sir William Hamilton's psychological error, — the rejection of the Reason as the intellectual faculty of the spiritual person, — and having, with him, used the terms limit, condition, and the like, in such significations as are pertinent to the Sense and Understanding only, the Limitists proceed to present in a paradoxical light many questions which arise concerning "the Infinite." They take the ground that, to our view, he can be neither person, nor intellect, nor consciousness; for each of these implies limitation; and yet that it is impossible for us to know aught of him, except as such. Then having, as they think, completely confused the mind, they draw hence new support for their conclusion, that we can attain to no satisfactory knowledge on the subject. The following extracts selected from many will show this.

"Now, in the first place, the very conception of Consciousness, in whatever mode it may be manifested, necessarily implies distinction between one object and another. To be conscious, we must be conscious of something; and that something can only be known as that which it is, by being distinguished from that which it is not. But distinction is necessarily a limitation; for, if one object is to be distinguished from another, it must possess some form of existence which the other has not, or it must not possess some form which the other has. But it is obvious that the Infinite cannot be distinguished, as such, from the Finite, by the absence of any quality which the Finite possesses; for such absence would be a limitation. Nor yet can it be distinguished by the presence of an attribute which the Finite has not; for as no finite part can be a constituent of an infinite whole, this differential characteristic must itself be infinite; and must at the same time have nothing in common with the finite. . . . . .

"That a man can be conscious of the Infinite, is thus a supposition which, in the very terms in which it is expressed, annihilates itself. Consciousness is essentially a limitation; for it is the determination of the mind to one actual out of many possible modifications. But the Infinite, if it is conceived at all, must be conceived as potentially everything, and actually nothing; for if there is anything in general which it cannot become, it is thereby limited; and if there is anything in particular which it actually is, it is thereby excluded from being any other thing. But again, it must also be conceived as actually everything, and potentially nothing; for an unrealized potentiality is likewise a limitation. If the infinite can be that which it is not, it is by that very possibility marked out as incomplete, and capable of a higher perfection. If it is actually everything, it possesses no characteristic feature by which it can be distinguished from anything else, and discerned as an object of consciousness. . .

"Rationalism is thus only consistent with itself when it refuses to attribute consciousness to God. Consciousness, in the only form in which we can conceive it, implies limitation and change, — the perception of one object out of many, and a comparison of that object with others. To be always conscious of the same object, is, humanly speaking, not to be conscious at all; and, beyond its human manifestation, we can have no conception of what consciousness is." — *Limits of Religious Thought*, pp. 93–95.

"As the conditionally limited (which we may briefly call the conditioned) is thus the only possible object of knowledge and of positive thought — thought necessarily supposes conditions. To *think* is to *condition*; and conditional limitation is the fundamental law of the possibility of thought. . . .

"Thought cannot transcend consciousness; consciousness is only possible under the antithesis of a subject and object of thought; known only in correlation, and mutually limiting each other; while, independently of this, all that we know either of subject or object, either of mind or matter, is only a knowledge in each of the particular, of the plural, of the different, of the modified, of the phenomenal. We admit that the consequence of this doctrine is — that philosophy, if viewed as more than a science of the conditioned, is impossible. Departing from the particular, we admit that we can never, in our highest generalizations, rise above the finite; that our knowledge, whether of mind or matter, can be nothing more than a knowledge of the relative manifestations of an existence, which in itself it is our highest wisdom to recognize as beyond the reach of philosophy."

"In all this, so far as human intelligence is concerned, we cordially agree; for a more complete admission could not be imagined, not only that a knowledge, and even a notion, of the absolute is impossible for man, but that we are unable to conceive the possibility of such a knowledge even in the Deity himself, without contradicting our human conceptions of the possibility of intelligence itself." — *Sir William Hamilton's Essays*, pp. 21, 22, 38.

"The various mental attributes which we ascribe to God — Benevolence, Holiness, Justice, Wisdom, for example — can be conceived by us only as existing in a benevolent and holy and just and wise Being, who is not identical with any one of his attributes, but the common subject of them all; in one word, a *Person*. But Personality, as we conceive it, is essentially a limitation and relation. Our own personality is presented to us as relative and limited; and it is from that presentation that all our representative notions of personality are derived. Personality is presented to us as a relation between the conscious self and the various modes of his consciousness. There is no personality in abstract thought without a thinker: there is no thinker unless he exercises some mode of thought. Personality is also a limitation; for the thought and the thinker are distinguished from and limit each other; and the various modes of thought are distinguished each from each by limitation likewise. . . . . ." — *Limits of Religious Thought*, p. 102.

"Personality, with all its limitations, though far from exhibiting the absolute nature of God as He is, is yet truer, grander, more elevating, more religious, than those barren, vague, meaningless abstractions in which men babble about nothing under the name of the Infinite and Personal conscious existence, limited though it be, is yet the noblest of all existence of which man can dream. . . . . . It is by consciousness alone that we know that God exists, or that we are able to offer Him any service. It is only by conceiving Him as a Conscious Being, that we can stand in any religious relation to Him at all; that we can form such a representation of Him as is demanded by our spiritual wants, insufficient though it be to satisfy our intellectual curiosity." — *Limits of Religious Thought*, p. 104.

The conclusions of these writers upon this whole topic are as follows: —

"The mind is not represented as conceiving two propositions subversive of each other as equally possible; *but only as unable to understand* as possible two extremes; one of which, however, on the ground of their mutual repugnance, it is compelled to recognize as true. . . . . . And by a wonderful revelation we are thus, in the very consciousness of our inability to conceive aught above the relative and finite, inspired with a belief in the existence of something unconditioned beyond the sphere of all comprehensible reality." — *Sir William Hamilton's Essays*, p. 22.

"To sum up briefly this portion of my argument. The conception of the Absolute and Infinite, from whatever side we view it, appears encompassed with contradictions. There is a contradiction in supposing such an object to exist, whether alone or in conjunction with others; and there is a contradiction in supposing it not to exist. There is a contradiction in conceiving it as one; and there is a contradiction in conceiving it as many. There is a contradiction in conceiving it as personal; and there is a contradiction in conceiving it as impersonal. It cannot, without contradiction, be represented as active; nor, without equal contradiction, be represented as inactive. It cannot be conceived as the sum of all existence; nor yet can it be conceived as a part only of that sum." — *Limits of Religious Thought*, pp. 84, 85.

We have quoted thus largely, preferring that the Limitists should speak for themselves. Their doctrine, as taught, not simply in these passages, but throughout their writings, may be briefly summed up as follows.

The human mind, whenever it attempts to investigate the profoundest subjects which come before it, and which it is goaded to examine, finds itself in an inextricable maze of contradictions; and, after vainly struggling for a while to get out, becomes nonplussed, confused, confounded, dazed; and, falling down helpless and effortless in the maze, and with devout humility acknowledging its impotence, it finds that the "highest reason" is to pass beyond the sphere and out of the light of reason, into the sphere of a superrational and therefore dark, and therefore *blind* faith.

But it is to be stated, and here we strike to the centre of the errors of the Limitists, that a perception and confession of mental impotence is *not* the logical deduction from their premises. Lustrous as may be their names in logic, — and Sir William Hamilton is esteemed a sun in the logical firmament, — no one of them ever saw, or else dared to acknowledge, the logical sequence from their principles. They have climbed upon the dizzy heights of thought, and out on their verge; and there they stand, hesitating and shivering, like naked men on Alpine precipices, with no eagle wings to spread and soar away towards the Eternal Truth; and not daring to take the awful plunge before them. Behold the gulf from which they shrink. Mr. Mansel says: —

"It is our duty, then, to think of God as personal; and it is our duty to believe that He is infinite. It is true that we cannot reconcile these two representations with each other, as our conception of personality involves attributes apparently contradictory to the notion of infinity. But it does not follow that this contradiction exists anywhere but in our own minds: it does not follow that it implies any impossibility in the absolute nature of God. The apparent contradiction, in this case, as in those previously noticed, is the necessary consequence of an attempt on the part of the human thinker to transcend the boundaries of his own consciousness. It proves that there are limits to man's power of thought; and it proves no more." — *Limits of Religious Thought*, p. 106.

Or, to put it in sharp and accurate, plain and unmistakable English. "It is our duty to think of God as personal," when to think of Him as personal is to think a lie; "to believe that He is infinite," when so to believe is to believe the lie already thought; and when to believe a lie is to incur the penalty decreed by the Bible — God's book — upon all who believe lies. And this is the religious teaching of a professed Christian minister in one of the first Universities in the world. Not that Mr. Mansel meant to teach this. By no means. But it logically follows from his premises. In his philosophy the mind instinctively, necessarily, and with equal authority in each case, asserts

That there must be an infinite Being;
That that Being must be Self-conscious,
Must be unlimited; and that
Consciousness is a limitation.

These assertions are contradictory and self-destructive. What follows then? That the mind is impotent? No! It follows that the mind is a deceiver! We learn again the lesson we have learned before. It is not weakness, it is falsehood: it is not want of capacity, it is want of integrity that is proved by this contradiction. Man is worse than a hopeless, mental imbecile, he is a hopeless, mental cheat.

But is the result true? How can it be, when with all its

might the mind revolts from it, as nature does from a vacuum? True that the human mind is an incorrigible falsifier? With the indignation of outraged honesty, man's soul rejects the insulting aspersion, and reasserts its own integrity and authority. Ages of controversy have failed to obliterate or cry down the spontaneous utterance of the soul, "I have within myself the ultimate standard of truth."

It now devolves to account for the aberrations of the Limitists. The ground of all their difficulties is simple and plain. While denying to the human mind the faculty of the Pure Reason, they have, *by the (to them) undistinguished use of that faculty*, raised questions which the Understanding by no possibility could raise, which the Reason alone is capable of presenting, and which that Reason alone can solve; and have attempted to solve them solely by the assistance, and in the forms of, the Sense and the Understanding. Their problems belong to a spiritual person; and they attempt to solve them by the inferior modes of an animal nature. Better, by far, could they see with their ears. All their processes are developed on the vicious assumption, that the highest form of knowledge possible to the human mind is a generalization in the Understanding, upon facts given in the Sense: a form of knowledge which is always one, whether the substance be distinguished in the form, be a peach, as diverse from an apple; or a star, as one among a million. The meagreness and utter insufficiency of this doctrine, to account for all the phenomena of the human mind, we have heretofore shown; and shall therefore need only now to distinguish certain special phases of their fundamental error.

As heretofore, there will be continual occasion to note how the doctrine of the Limitists, that the Understanding is man's highest faculty of knowledge, and the logical sequences therefrom respecting the laws of thought and consciousness vitiate their whole system. One of their most important errors is thus expressed: — "To be conscious, we must be conscious of something; and that something can only be known as that which it is, by being distinguished from that which it is not." "Thought cannot transcend consciousness; consciousness is only possible under the antithesis of subject and object of thought known only in correlation, and mutually limiting each other; while, independently of this, all that we know either of subject or object, either of mind or matter, is only a knowledge in each of the particular, of the plural, of the different, of the modified, of the phenomenal." In other words, our highest possible form of knowledge is that by which we examine the peach, distinguish its qualities among themselves, and discriminate between them and the qualities of the apple. And Sir William Hamilton fairly and truly acknowledges that, as a consequence, science, except as a system of objects of sense, is impossible.

The fact is, as has been made already sufficiently apparent, that the diagnosis by the Limitists of the constitution of the mind is erroneous. Their dictum, that all knowledge must be attained through "relation, plurality, and difference," is not true. There is a kind of knowledge which we obtain by a direct and immediate *sight*; and that, too, under such conditions as are no limitation upon the object thought. For instance, the mind, by a direct intuition, affirms, "Malice is criminal." It also affirms that this is an eternal, immutable, universal law, conditional for all possibility of moral beings. This direct and immediate sight, and the consciousness attending it, are *full* of that one object, and so are occupied only with it; and it does NOT come under any forms of relation, plurality, and difference. So is it with all *a priori* laws. The mode of the pure reason is thus seen to be the direct opposite of that of the Understanding and the Sense.

Intimately connected with the foregoing is a question whose importance cannot be overstated. It is one which involves the very possibility of God's existence as a self-conscious person. To present it, we recur again to the extracts made just above from Sir William Hamilton. "Consciousness is only possible under the antithesis of a subject and object of thought, known only in correlation, and mutually limiting each other." Subsequently, he makes the acknowledgment as logically following from this: "that we are unable to conceive the possibility of such knowledge," *i. e.* of the absolute, "even in the Deity himself." That is, God can be believed to be self-conscious only on the ground that the human intellect is a cheat. The theory which underlies this assertion of the logician — a theory not peculiar to the Limitists, but which has, perhaps, been hitherto universally maintained by philosophers — may be concisely stated thus. In every correlation of subject and object,— in every instance where they are to be contrasted, — the subject must be one, and the object must be *another and different.* Hamilton, in another place, utters it thus: "Look back for a moment into yourselves, and you will find, that what constitutes intelligence in our feeble consciousness, is, that there are there several terms, of which the one perceives the other, of which the other is perceived by the first; in this consists self-knowledge," &c. Mark the "several terms," and that the one can only see the other, never itself.

This position is both a logical and psychological error. It is a logical error because it *assumes*, without argument, that there is involved in the terms subject and object such a logical contradiction and contradistinction that the subject cannot be object to itself. This assumption is groundless. As a matter of fact, it is *generally* true that, so far as man is concerned, the subject is one, and the object another and different. But this by no means proves that it is *always* so; it only raises the presumption that such may be the case. And when one comes to examine the question in itself, there is absolutely no logical ground for the assumption. It is found to be a question upon which no decision from logical considerations can have any validity, because *it is purely psycho-*

logical, and can only be decided by evidence upon a matter of fact. Furthermore, it is a psychological error, because a careful examination shows that, in some instances, the opposite is the fact; that, in certain experiences, the subject and object are identical.

This fact that the subject and object are often identical in the searching eye of human reason, and *always so* under the eye of Universal Genius, is of too vast scope and too vital importance to be passed with a mere allusion. It seems amazing that a truth which, the instant it is stated, solves a thousand difficulties which philosophy has raised, should never yet have been affirmed by any of the great spiritual-eyed thinkers, and that it should have found utterance, only to be denied, by the pen of the Limitists. A word of personal reminiscence may be allowed here. The writer came to see this truth during a process of thought, having for its object the solution of the problem, How can the infinite Person be self-comprehending, and still infinite? While considering this, and without ever having received a hint from any source that the possibility of such a problem had dawned on a human mind before, there blazed upon him suddenly, like a heaven full of light, this, which appeared the incomparably profounder question: How can any soul, not God only, but any soul, be a self-examiner? Why don't the Limitists entertain and explain this? It was only years after that he met the negative statement in Herbert Spencer's book. The difficulty is, that the Limitists have represented to their minds the mode of the seeing of the Reason, by a sensuous image, as the eye; and because the eye cannot see itself, have concluded that the Reason cannot see itself. It is always dangerous to argue from an illustration; and, in this instance, it has been fatal. If man was only an animal nature, and so only a *receiver* of impressions, with a capacity to generalize from the impressions received, the doctrine of the Limitists would be true. But once establish that man is also a spiritual *person*, with a reason, which sees truth by immediate intuition, and their whole teaching becomes worthless. The Reason is not receptivity merely, or mainly; it is originator. In its own light it gives to itself *a priori* truth, and itself as seeing that truth; and so the subject and object are identical. This is one of the differentiating qualities of the spiritual person.

Our position may be more accurately stated and more amply illustrated and sustained as follows:

Sometimes, in the created spiritual person, and always in the self-existent, the absolute and infinite spiritual Person, the subject and object are IDENTICAL.

1. Sometimes in the created spiritual person, the subject and object are identical. The question is a question of fact. In illustrating the fact, it will be proved. When a man looks at his hands, he sees they are instruments for *his* use. When he considers his physical sense, he still perceives it to be instrument for *his* use. In all his conclusions, judgments, he still finds, not himself, but *his* instrument. Even in the Pure Reason he finds only *his* faculty; though it be the highest possible to intellect. Yet still he searches, searches for the *I am*; which claims, and holds, and uses, the faculties and capacities. There is a phrase universally familiar to American Christians, a fruit of New England Theology, which leads us directly to the goal we seek. It is the phrase, "self-examination." In all thorough, religious self-examination the subject and object are identical. In the ordinary labors and experiences of life, man says, "I can do this or that;" and he therein considers only his aptitudes and capabilities. But in this last, this profoundest act, the assertion is not, "I can do this or that." It is, "I am this or that." The person stands unveiled before itself, in the awful sanctuary of God's presence. The decision to be made is not upon the use of one faculty or another. It is upon the *end* for which all labor shall be performed. The character of the person is under consideration, and is to be determined. The selfhood, with all its wondrous mysteries, is at once

subject and object. The I am in man, alike in kind to that most impenetrable mystery, the eternal I AM of "the everlasting Father," is now stirred to consider its most solemn duty. How shall the finite I am accord *itself* to the pure purpose of the infinite I AM? It may be, possibly is, that some persons have never been conscious of this experience. To some, from a natural inaptitude, and to others, from a perverse disinclination, it may never come. Some have so little gift of introspection, that their inner experiences are never observed and analyzed. Their conduct may be beautiful, but they never know it. Their impressions ever come from without. Another class of persons shun such an experience as Balshazzar would have shunned, if he could, the handwriting on the wall. Their whole souls are absorbed in the pursuit of earthly things. They are intoxicated with sensuous gratification. The fore-thrown shadow of the coming thought of self-examination awakens within them a vague instinctive dread; and they shudder, turn away, and by every effort avoid it. Sometimes they succeed; and through the gates of death rush headlong into the spirit-land, only to be tortured forever there with the experience they so successfully eluded here. For the many thousands, who know by experience what a calm, candid, searching, self-examination is, now that their attention has been drawn to its full psychological import, no further word is necessary. They know that in that supreme insight there was seen and known, at one and the same instant, in a spontaneous and simultaneous action of the soul, the seer and the seen as one, as identical. And this experience is so wide-spread, that the wonder is that it has not heretofore been assigned its suitable place in philosophy.

2. Always in the self-existent, the absolute and infinite, spiritual Person, the subject and object are identical. This question, though one of fact, cannot be determined *by us*, by our experience; it must be shown to follow logically from certain *a priori* first principles. This may be done as fol-

lows. Eternity, independence, universality, are qualities of God. Being eternal, he is ever the same. Being independent, he excludes the possibility of another Being to whom he is necessarily related. Being universal, he possessés all possible endowment, and is ground for all possible existence; so that no being can exist but by his will. As Universal Genius, all possible objects of knowledge or intellectual effort are immanent before the eye of his Reason; and this is a *permanent state.* He is an object of knowledge, comprehending all others; and therefore he *exhaustively* knows himself. He distinguishes his Self as object, from no what else, because there is no else to distinguish his Self from; but having an exhaustive self-comprehension, he distinguishes within that Self all possible forms of being each from each.

He is absolute, and never learns or changes. There is nothing to learn and nothing to change to, except to a wicked state; and for this there *can be to him no temptation.* He is ever the same, and hence there can be no instant in time when he does not *exhaustively* know himself. Thus always in him are the subject and object identical.

These two great principles, viz: That the Pure Reason sees *a priori* truth *immediately*, and out of all relation, plurality and difference, and that in the Pure Reason, in self-examination, the subject and object are identical, by their simple statement explode, as a Pythagorean system, the mental astronomy of the Limitists. Reason is the sun, and the Sense and the Understanding, with their satellite faculties, the circumvolving planets.

The use of terms by the Limitists has been as vicious as their processes of thought, and has naturally sprung from their fundamental error. We will note one in the following sentence. "Consciousness, in the only form in which we can conceive it, implies limitation and change, — the perception of one object out of many, and a comparison of that object with others." Conceive is the vicious word. Strictly, it is usable only with regard to things in Nature, and can have no relevancy to such subjects as are now under consideration. It is a word which expresses *only* such operations as lie in the Sense and Understanding. The following definition explains this: "The concept refers to all the things whose common or similar attributes or traits it conceives (con-cepis), or *grasps together* into one class and one act of mind." — *Bowen's Logic*, p. 7. This is not the mode of the Reason's action at all. It does not run over a variety of objects and select out from them the points of similarity, and grasp these together into one act of mind. It sees one object in its unity as pure law, or first truth; and examines that in its own light. Hence, the proper word is, *intuits*. Seen from this standpoint, consciousness does *not* imply limitation and change. A first truth we always see as *absolute*, — we are conscious of this sight; and yet we know that neither consciousness nor sight is any limitation upon the truth. We would paraphrase the sentence thus: Consciousness, in the highest form in which we know it, implies and possesses *permanence*; and is the light in which pure truth is seen as pure object by itself, and forever the same.

It is curious to observe how the Understanding and the Pure Reason run along side by side in the same sentence; the inferior faculty encumbering and defeating the efforts of the other. Take the following for example.

"If the infinite can be that which it is not, it is by that very possibility marked out as incomplete, and capable of a higher perfection. If it is actually everything, it possesses no characteristic feature by which it can be distinguished from anything else, and discerned as an object of consciousness." The presence in language of the word infinite and its cognates is decisive evidence of the presence of a faculty capable of entertaining it as a subject for investigation. This faculty, the Reason having presented the subject for consideration, the Understanding seizes upon it and drags it down into her den, and says, "can be that which it is not." This she says, because she cannot act, except to conceive, and cannot conceive, except to distinguish this from something else; and so cannot perceive that the very utterance of the word "infinite" excludes the word "else." The Understanding conceives the finite as one and independent, and the infinite as one and independent. Then the Reason steps in, and says the infinite is all-comprehending. This conflicts with the Understanding's *conception*, and so the puzzle comes. In laboring for a solution, the Reason's affirmation is expressed hypothetically: "If it (the infinite) is actually everything;" and thereupon the Understanding puts in its blind, impertinent assertion, "it possesses no characteristic feature by which it can be distinguished from anything else. *There is nothing else from which to distinguish it.* The perception of the Reason is as follows. The infinite Person comprehends intellectually, and is ground for potentially and actually, all that is possible and real; and so there can be no else with which to compare him. Because, possessing all fulness, he is actually everything, by this characteristic feature of completeness he distinguishes himself from nothing, which is all there is, (if no-thing — void — can be said to *be,*) beside him; and from any part, which there is within him. Thus is he object to himself in his own consciousness.

This vicious working of the Understanding against the Reason, in the same sentences, can be more fully illustrated from the following extracts. "God, as necessarily determined to pass from absolute essence to relative manifestation, is determined to pass either *from the better to the worse, or from the worse to the better.* A third possibility that both states are equal, as contradictory in itself, and as contradicted by our author, it is not necessary to consider." —*Sir William Hamilton's Essays*, p. 42. "Again, how can the Relative be conceived as coming into being? If it is a distinct reality from the absolute, it must be conceived as passing from non-existence into existence. But to conceive an object as non-existent is again a self-contradiction; for that which is conceived exists, as an object of thought, in and by that conception. We may abstain from thinking of an object at all; but if we think of it, we cannot but think of it as existing. It is possible at one time not to think of an object at all, and at another to think of it as already in being; but to think of it in the act of becoming, in the progress from not being into being, is to think that which, in the very thought, annihilates itself. Here again the Pantheistic hypothesis seems forced upon us. We can think of creation only as a change in the condition of that which already exists; and thus the creature is conceivable only as a phenomenal mode of the being of the Creator."—*Limits of Religious Thought*, p. 81.

"God," a word which has *no significance* except to the Reason: "as necessarily determined,"—a phrase which belongs only to the Understanding. The opposite is the truth: "to pass from absolute essence." This can have no meaning except to the Pure Reason: "to relative manifestation." This belongs to the Understanding. It contradicts the other; and the process is absurd. The mind balks in the attempt to think it. In creation there is no such process as "passing from absolute essence to relative manifestation." The words imply that God, in passing from the state of absolute essence, ceased to be absolute essence, and became "relative manifestation." All this is absurd; and is in the Understanding and Sense. God never *became*. The Creator is still absolute essence, as before creation; and the logician's this or that are both false; and his third possibility is not a contradiction, but the truth. The fact of creation may be thus stated. The infinite Person, freely according his will to the behest of his worth, and yet equally free to not so accord his will, put forth from himself the creative energy; and this under such modes, that he neither lost nor gained by the act; but that, though the latter state was diverse from the first, still neither was better than the other, but both were equally good. Before creation, he possessed absolute plenitude of endowments. All possible ideals were present before his eye. All possible joy continued a changeless state in his sensibility. His will, as choice, was absolute benevolence; and, as act, was competent to all possible effort. To push the ideal out, and make it real, added nothing to, and subtracted nothing from, his fulness.

The fact must be learned that muscular action and the working of pure spirit are so diverse, that the inferior mode cannot be an illustration of the superior. A change in a pure spirit, which neither adds nor subtracts, leaves the good unchanged. Hence, when the infinite Person created, he passed neither from better to worse, nor from worse to better; but the two states, though diverse, were equally good.

We proceed now to the other extract. "Again, how can the relative," etc. "If the Relative is a distinct reality from the absolute," then each is *self-existent*, and independent. The sentence annihilates itself. "It must be conceived as passing from non-existence into existence." The image here is from the Sense, as usual, and vicious accordingly. It is, that the soul is to look into void, and see, out of that void, existence come, without there being any cause for that existence coming. This would be the phenomenon to the Sense. And the Sense is utterly unable to account for the phenomenon. The object in the Sense must appear as *form*; but in the Reason it is idea. Mr. Mansel's presentation may well be illustrated by a trick of jugglery. The performer stands before his audience, dressed in tights, and presents the palms of his hands to the spectators, apparently empty. He then closes his right hand, and then opening it again, appears holding a bouquet of delicious flowers, which he hands about to the astonished gazers. The bouquet seems to come from nothing, *i. e.* to have no cause. It appears "to pass from non-existence to existence." But common sense corrects the cheating seeming, and asserts, "There is an adequate cause for the coming of the bunch of flowers, though we cannot see it." Precisely similar is creation. Could there have been a Sense present at that instant, creation would have seemed to it a juggler's trick. Out of nothing something would have seemed to come. But under the correcting guide of the Pure Reason, an adequate cause is found. Before creation, the infinite Person did not manifest himself; and so was actually alone. At creation his power, which before was immanent, he now made emanent; and put it forth in the forms chosen from his Reason, and according to the requirement of his own worth. Nothing was added to God. That which was ideal he now made actual. The form as Idea was one, the power as Potentiality was another, and each was in him by itself. He put forth the power into the form, the Potentiality into the Idea, and the Universe was. Thus it was that "the Relative came into being." In the same manner it might be shown how, all along through the writings of the Limitists, the Understanding runs along by the Reason, and vitiates her efforts to solve her problems. We shall have occasion to do something of this farther on.

The topic now under discussion could not be esteemed finished without an examination of the celebrated dictum, "To think is to condition." Those who have held this to be universally true, have also received its logical sequence, that to the finite intellect God cannot appear self-comprehending. In our present light, the dictum is known to be, not a universal, but only a partial, truth. It is incumbent, therefore, to circumscribe its true sphere, and fix it there. We shall best enter upon this labor by answering the question, What is thinking?

First. In general, and loosely, any mental operation is called thinking. Second. Specifically, all acts of reflection are thinkings. Under this head we notice two points. *a.* That act of the Understanding in which an object presented by the Sense is analyzed, and its special and generic elements noted, and is thus classified, and its relations determined, is properly a thinking. Thus, in the object cat I distinguish specifically that it is domestic, and generically that it is carnivorous. *b.* That act of the finite spiritual person by which he compares the judgments of the Understanding with the *a priori* laws of the Pure Reason, and by this final standard decides their truth or error. Thus, the judgment of the young Indian warrior is, that he ought to hunt down and slay the man who killed his father in battle. The standard of Reason is, that Malice is criminal. This judgment is found to involve malice, and so is found to be wrong. Third, the intuitions of the reason. These, in the finite person, come *after* a process of reflection, and are partly consequent upon it; yet they take place in another faculty, which is developed by this process; but they are such, that by no process of reflection *alone* could they be. Thinking, in the Universal Genius, is the *sight*, at once and forever, of all possible object of mental effort. It is necessary and *spontaneous*, and so is an endowment, not an attainment; and is possessed without effort. We are prepared now to entertain the following statements: —

A. So far as it represents thinking as the active, *i. e.* causative ground, or agent of the condition, the dictum is not true. The fact of the thinking is not, cannot be, the ground of the condition. The condition of the object thought, whatever the form of thinking may be, must lie as far back at least as the ground of the thinker. Thus, God's self, as ground for his Genius, must also be ground for *all* conditions. Yet men think of an object *in its conditions.* This is because the same Being who constructed the objects in their conditions, constructed also man as thinker, *correlated to those conditions*, so that he should think upon things *as they are.* In this view, to think is not to condition, but is mental activity in the conditions already imposed. Thus it is with the Understanding; and the process of thinking, as above designated, goes on in accordance with the law stated in *a*, of the second general definition. It follows, therefore,

B. That so far as the dictum expresses the fact, that within the sphere of conditions proper, — observing the distinction of conditions into two classes heretofore made, — the finite intellect must act under them, and see those objects upon which they lie, accordingly, — as, for instance, a geometrical figure must be seen in Time and Space, — so far it is true, and no farther. For instance: To see an eagle flying, is to see it under all the conditions imposed upon the bird as flying, and the observer as seeing. But when men intuit the *a priori* truth, Malice is criminal, they perceive that it lies under no conditions proper, but is absolute and universal. We perceive, then,

C. That for all mental operations which have as object pure laws and ideal forms, and that Being in whom all these inhere, this dictum is not true. The thinker may be conditioned in the proper sense of that term; yet he entertains objects of thought which are unconditioned; and they are not affected by it. Thus, it does not affect the universality of the principle in morals above noted that I perceive it to be such, and that necessarily.

Assuming, then, that by the dictum, To think is to condition, is meant, not that the thinker, by the act of thinking, constructs the conditions, but that he recognizes in himself, as thinking subject, and in the object thought, the several conditions (proper) thereof, — the following statements will define the province of this dictum.

1. The Universe as physical object, the observing Sense, and the discursive Understanding, lie wholly within it.

2. Created spiritual persons, *as constituted beings*, also lie wholly within it. *But it extends no farther.* On the other hand,

3. Created spiritual persons, in their capacities to intuit pure laws, and pure ideal forms; and those laws and forms themselves lie wholly without it.

4. So also does God the absolute Being in whom those laws and forms inhere. Or, in general terms,

When conditions (proper) already lie upon the object thought, since the thinker must needs see the object under its conditions, it is true that, To think is to condition. But so far as it is meant that thinking is such a kind of operation that it cannot proceed except the object be conditioned, it is not true; for there are processes of thought whose objects are unconditioned.

The question, "What are Space and Time?" with which Mr. Spencer opens his chapter on "Ultimate Scientific Ideas," introduces a subject common to all the Limitists, and which, therefore, should be considered in this part of our work. A remark made a few pages back, respecting an essay in the "North American Review" for October 1864, applies with equal force here in reference to another essay by the same writer, in the preceding July number of that periodical. At most, his view can only be unfolded. He has left nothing to be added. In discussing a subject so abstruse and difficult as this, it would seem, in the present stage of human thought at least, most satisfactory to set out from the Reason rather than the Sense, from the idea rather than the phenomenon; and so will we do.

In general, then, it may be said that Space and Time are *a priori* conditions of created being. The following extracts are in point. "Pure Space, therefore, as given in the primitive intuition, is pure form for any possible phenomenon. As unconjoined in the unity of any form, it is given in the primitive intuition, and is a cognition necessary and universal. Though now obtained from experience, and in chronological order subsequent to experience, yet is it no deduction from experience, nor at all given by experience; but it is wholly independent of all experience, prior to it, and without which it were impossible that any experience of outer object should be." "Pure Time, as given in the intuition, is immediately beheld to be conditional for all possible period, prior to any period being actually limited, and necessarily continuing, though all bounded period be taken away." — *Rational Psychology*, pp. 125, 128.

Again, a clearly defined distinction may be made between them as conditions. Space is the *a priori* condition of *material* being. Should a spiritual person, as the soul of a man, be stripped of all its material appurtenances, and left to exist as pure spirit, it could hold no communication with any other being but God; and no other being but he could hold any communication with it. It would exist out of all relation to Space. Not so, however, with Time. Time is the *a priori* condition of all created being, of the spiritual as well as material. In the case just alluded to, the isolated spiritual person would have a consciousness of succession and duration, although he would have no standard by which to measure that duration; he could think in processes, and only in processes, and thus would be necessarily related to Time. Dr. Hickok has expressed this thus: "Space in reference to time has no significancy. Time is the pure form for phenomena as given in the internal sense only, and in these there can be only succession. The inner phenomenon may endure in time, but can have neither length, breadth, nor thickness in space. A thought, or other mental phenomenon, may fill a period, but cannot have superficial or solid content; it may be before or after another, but not above or below it, nor with any outer or inner side." — *Rational Psychology*, p. 135.

Space and Time may also be distinguished thus: "Space has three dimensions," or, rather, there can be three dimensions in space, — length, breadth, and thickness. In other words, it is solid room. "Time has but one dimension," or, rather, but one dimension can enter into Time, — length. In Time there can only be procession. Space and Time may then be called, the one "statical," the other "dynamical," illimitation. Following the essayist already referred to, they may be defined as follows:

"Space is the infinite and indivisible Receptacle of Matter.

"Time is the infinite and indivisible Receptacle of Existence."

Both, then, are marked by receptivity, indivisibility, and illimitability. The one is receptivity, that material object may come into it; the other, that event may occur in it. There is for neither a final unit nor any limit. All objects are divisible in Space, and all periods in Time; and thus also are all limits comprehended, but they are without limit. Turning now from these more general aspects of the subject, a detailed examination may be conducted as follows.

The fundamental law given by the Reason is, as was seen above, that Space and Time are *a priori* conditions of created being. We can best consider this law in its application to the facts, by observing two general divisions, with two subdivisions under each. Space and Time have, then, two general phases, one within, and one without, the mind. Each of these has two special phases. The former, one in the Sense, and one in the Understanding. The latter, one within, and one without, the Universe.

First general phase, within the mind. First special phase, in the Sense. "As pure form in the primitive intuition, they are wholly limitless, and void of any conjunction in unity, having themselves no figure nor period, and having within themselves no figure nor period, but only pure diversity, in which any possible conjunction of definite figures and periods may, in some way, be effected." In other words, they are pure, *a priori*, formal laws, which are conditional to the being of any sense as the perceiver of a phenomenon; and yet this sense could present no figure or period, till some figure or period was produced into it by an external agency. As such necessary formal laws, Space and Time "have a necessity of being independently of all phenomena." Or, in other words, the fact that all phenomena *must* appear in them, lies beyond the province of power. This, however, is no more a limit to the Deity than it is a limit to him that he cannot hate his creatures and be good. In our experience the Sense gives two kinds of phenomena: the one the actual phenomena of actual objects, the other, ideal phenomena with ideal objects. The one is awakened by the presentation, in the physical sense, of a material object, as a house; the other, by the activity of the imaging faculty, engaged in constructing some form in the inner or mental sense, from forms actually observed. Upon both alike the formal law of Space and Time must lie.

Second special phase, in the Understanding. Although there is pure form, if there was no more than this, no notion of a system of things could be. Each object would have its own space, and each event its own time. But one object and event could not be seen in any relation to another object and event. In order that this shall be, there must be some ground by which all the spaces and times of phenomena shall be joined into a unity of Space and Time; so that all objects shall be seen in one Space, and all events in one Time. "A notional connective for the phenomena may determine these phenomena in their places and periods in the whole of all space and of all time, and so may give both the phenomena and their space and time in an objective experience." The operation of the Understanding is, then, the connection, by a notional, of all particular spaces and times; *i. e.* the space and time of each phenomenon in the Sense, into a comprehensive unity of Space and Time, in which all phenomena can be seen to occur; and thus a system can be. In a word, not only must each phenomenon be seen in its own space and time, but all phenomena must be seen in *one* Space and Time. This connection of the manifold into unity is the peculiar work of the Understanding. An examination of the facts as above set forth enables us to construct a general formula for the application to all minds of the fundamental law given by the Reason. That law, that all objects must be seen in Space, and all events in Time, involves the subordinate law:

That no mind can observe material objects or any events except under the conditions of Space and Time; or, to change the phraseology, *Space and Time are* a priori *conditional to the being of any mind or faculty in a mind capable of observing a material object or any event.* This will, perhaps, be deemed to be, in substance, Kant's theory. However that may be, this is true, but is only *a part of the truth.*

The rest will appear just below. The reader will notice that no exception is made to the law here laid down, and will start at the thought that this law lies upon the Deity equally as upon created beings. No exception is made, because none can be truthfully made. The intellect is just as unqualified in its assertion on this point as in those noticed on an earlier page of this work. Equally with the laws of numbers does the law of Space and Time condition all intellect. The Deity can no more see a house out of all relation to Space and Time than he can see how to make two and two five.

Second general phase, without the mind. First special phase, within the Universe. All that we are now to examine is objective to us; and all the questions which can arise are questions of fact. Let us search for the fact carefully and hold it fearlessly. To recur to the general law. It was found at the outset that Reason gave the idea of Space and Time as pure conditions for matter and event. We are now to observe the pure become the actual condition; or, in other words, we are to see the condition *realized*. Since, then, we are to observe material objects and events in a material system, it is fitting to use the Sense and the Understanding; and our statements and conclusions will conform to those faculties.

We have a concept of the Universe as a vast system in the form of a sphere in which all things are included. This spherical system is complete, definite, limited, and so has boundaries. A portion of "immeasurable void" — Space — has been occupied. Where there was nothing, something has become. Now it is evident that the possibility of our having a concept of the Universe, or of a space and a time in the Universe, is based upon the presence of an actual, underlying, all-pervading substance, which fills and forms the boundaries of the Universe, and thus enables spaces and times to be. We have no concept except as in limits, and those limits are conceived to be substance. In other words, space is distance, and time is duration, in our concept. Take away the boundaries which mark the distance, and the procession of events which forms the duration, and in the concept pure negation is left. To illustrate. Suppose there be in our presence a cubic yard of vacuum. Is this vacuum an entity? Not at all. It can neither be perceived by the Sense nor conceived by the Understanding. Yet it is a space. Speaking carelessly, we should say that this cube was object to us. Why? Because it is enclosed by substantial boundaries. All, then, that is object, all that is entity, is substance. In our concept, therefore, a space is solid distance within the substance, and the totality of all distances in the Universe is conceived to be Space. Again; suppose there pass before our mind a procession of events. One event has a fixed recurrence. In our concept the procession of events is a time, and the recurring event marks a period in time. The events proceeding are all that there is in the concept; and apart from the procession a conception of time is impossible. The procession of all the events of the Universe, that is *duration*, is our concept of Time. Thus, within the Universe, space is solid distance and time is duration; and neither has any actuality except as the Universe is. Let us assume for a moment that our concept is the final truth, and observe the result. In that concept space is limited by matter, and matter is conceived of as unlimited. This result is natural and necessary, because matter, substance, "a space-filling force," is the underlying notional upon which as ground any concept is possible. If matter is truly illimitable, then materialistic pantheism, which is really atheism, logically follows. Again; in our concept time is duration, and duration is conceived of as unlimited. If so, the during event is unlimited. From this hypothesis idealistic pantheism logically follows. But bring our concept into the clear light, and under the searching eye of Reason, and all ground for those systems vanishes instantly. Instead of finding matter illimitable and the limit for a space, Space is seen to be illimitable and pure condition, that matter may establish a limit within it. And Time, instead of being duration, and so limited by the during event, is found to be illimitable and pure condition, that event may have duration in it. This brings us to the

Second special phase, without or independent of the Universe. We have been considering facts in an objective experience, and have used therefor the Sense and Understanding, as was proper. What we are now to consider is a subject of which all experience is impossible. It can therefore be examined only by that faculty which presents it, the Pure Reason. Remove now from our presence all material object in Space, and all during event in Time; in a word, remove the Universe, and what will be left? As the Universe had a beginning, and both it and all things in it are conditioned by Space and Time, so also let it have an end. Will its conditions cease in its ceasing? Could another Universe arise, upon which would be imposed no conditions of Space and Time? These questions are answered in the statement of them. Those conditions must remain. When we have abstracted from our *concept* all substance and duration, there is left only *void.* Hence, in our concept it would be proper to say that without the Universe is void, and before the Universe there was void. Also, that in void there is no thing, no where, and no when; or, void is the negation of actual substance, space, and time. But pure Space and Time, as *a priori* conditions that material object and during event may be, have not ceased. There is still *room,* that an object may become. There is still *opportunity,* that an event may occur. By the Reason it is seen that these conditions have the same necessary being for material object and occurring event, as the conditions of mental activity have for mind; and they have their peculiar characteristics exactly according with what they do condition, just as the laws of thought have their peculiar characteristics, which exactly suit them to what they condition. If there be a spiritual person, the moral law must be given in the intuition as necessarily binding upon him; and this is an *a priori* condition of the being of such person. Precisely similar is the relation between Space and Time as *a priori* conditions, and object and event upon which they lie. The moral law has its characteristics, which fit it to condition spiritual person. Space and Time have their characteristics, which fit them to condition object and event. Space, then, as room, and Time as opportunity, and both as *a priori* conditions of a Universe, must have the same necessity of being that God has. They *must* be, as he *must* be. But observe, they are pure conditions, and no more. They are neither things nor persons. The idea of them in the Reason is simple and unanalyzable. They can be assigned their logical position, but further than this the mind cannot go.

The devout religious soul will start, perhaps, at some of the positions stated above. We have not wrought to pain such soul, but only for truth, and the clue of escape from all dilemmas. The only question to be raised is, are they true? If a more patient investigation than we have given to this subject shall show our positions false, then we shall only have failed as others before us have; but we shall love the truth which shall be found none the less. But if they shall be found true, then is it certain that God always knew them so and was always pleased with them, and no derogation to his dignity can come from the proclamation of them, however much they may contravene hitherto cherished opinions. Most blessed next after the Saviour's tender words of forgiveness are those pure words of the apostle John, "No lie is of the truth."

The conclusions to which we have arrived enable us to state how it is that primarily God was out of all relation to Space and Time. He was out of all relation to Space, because he is not material object, thereby having limits, form, and position in Space. He was out of all relation to Time, because he holds immediately, and at once, all possible objects of knowledge before the Eye of his mind. Hence he can learn nothing, and can experience no process of thought. Within his mind no event occurs, no substance endures. Yet, while this is true, it is equally true that, as the Creator, he is conditioned by Space and Time, just as he is conditioned by himself; and it may be found by future examination that they are essential to that Self. But, whatever conclusion may be arrived at respecting so difficult and abstract a subject, this much is certain: God, as the infinite and absolute spiritual Person, self-existent and supreme, is the great Fact; and Space and Time, whatever they are, will, *can* in no wise interfere with and compromise his perfectness and supremacy. It is a pleasure to be able to close this discussion with reflections profound and wise as those contained in the following extract from the essay heretofore alluded to.

"The reciprocal relations of Space, Time, and God, are veiled in impenetrable darkness. Many minds hesitate to attribute real infinity to Space and Time, lest it should conflict with the infinity of God. Such timidity has but a slender title to respect. If the Laws of Thought necessitate any conclusion whatever, they necessitate the conclusion that Space and Time are each infinite; and if we cannot reconcile this result with the infinity of God, there is no alternative but to accept of scepticism with as good a grace as possible. No man is worthy to join in the search for truth, who trembles at the sight of it when found. But a profound faith in the unity of all truth destroys scepticism by anticipation, and prophesies the solutions of reason. Space is infinite, Time is infinite, God is infinite; three infinites coexist. Limitation is possible only between existences of the same kind. There could not be two infinite Spaces, two infinite Times, or two infinite Gods; but while infinites of the same kind cannot coexist, infinites of unlike kinds may. When an hour limits a rod, infinite Time will limit infinite Space; when a year and an acre limit wisdom, holiness, and love, infinite Space and Time will limit the infinite God. *But not before.* Time exists ubiquitously, Space exists eternally, God exists ubiquitously and eternally. The nature of the relations between the three infinites, so long as Space and Time are ontologically incognizable, is utterly and absolutely incomprehensible; but to assume contradiction, exclusion, or mutual limitation to be among these relations, is as gratuitous as it is irreverent."

PART III.

AN EXAMINATION IN DETAIL OF CERTAIN IMPORTANT PASSAGES IN THE WRITINGS OF THE LIMITISTS.

ADDITIONAL REFLECTIONS UPON THE WRITINGS OF SIR WILLIAM HAMILTON.

It never formed any part of the plan of this work to give an extended examination of the logician's system of metaphysics, or even to notice it particularly. From the first, it was only proposed to attempt the refutation of that peculiar theory which he enounced in his celebrated essay, "The Philosophy of the Unconditioned," a monograph that has generally been received as a fair and sufficient presentation thereof; and which he supplemented, but never superseded. If the arguments adduced, and illustrations presented, in the first part, in behalf of the fact of the Pure Reason, are satisfactory, and the analysis and attempted refutation of the celebrated dictum based upon two extremes, an excluded middle and a mean, in the second part, are accepted as sufficient, as also the criticisms upon certain general corollaries, and the explanation of certain general questions, then, so far at least as Sir William Hamilton is concerned, but little, if any, further remark will be expected. A few subordinate passages in the essay above referred to may, however, it is believed, be touched with profit by the hand of criticism and explanation. To these, therefore, the reader's attention is now called.

In remarking upon Cousin's philosophy, Hamilton says: "Now, it is manifest that the whole doctrine of M. Cousin is involved in the proposition, *that the Unconditioned, the*

Absolute, the Infinite, is immediately known in consciousness, and this by difference, plurality, and relation." It is hardly necessary to repeat here the criticism, that the terms infinite, absolute, &c. are entirely out of place when used to express abstractions. As before, we ask, infinite — what? The fact of abstraction is one of the greatest of limitations, and vitiates every such utterance of the Limitists. The truth may be thus stated: — The infinite Person, or the necessary principle as inhering in that Person, is *immediately* known in consciousness, and this, *not* by difference, plurality, and relation, but by a direct intuition of the Pure Reason. In this act the object seen — the idea — is held right in the Reason's eye; and so is seen by itself and in itself. Hence it is not known by difference, because there is no other object but the one before that eye, with which to compare it. Neither is it known by plurality, because it is seen by itself, and there is no other object contemplated, with which to join it. Nor is it known by relation, because it is seen to be what it is *in itself*, and as out of all relation. A little below, in the same paragraph, Hamilton again remarks upon Cousin, thus: — "The recognition of the absolute as a constitutive principle of intelligence, our author regards as at once the condition and the end of philosophy." The true idea, accurately stated, is as follows. The fact that, by a constituting law of intelligence, the Pure Reason immediately intuits absoluteness as the distinctive quality of *a priori* first principles, and of the infinite Person in whom they inhere, is the condition, and the application of that fact is the end of philosophy.

These two erroneous positions the logician follows with his celebrated "statement of the opinions which may be entertained regarding the Unconditioned, as an immediate object of knowledge and of thought." The four "opinions," to which he reduces all those held by philosophers, are too well known to need quotation here. They are noticed now, only to afford an opportunity for the presentation of a fifth, and, as it is believed, the true opinion, which is as follows.

The infinite Person is "inconceivable," but is cognizable as a fact, is known to be, and is, to a certain extent, known to be such and such; all this, by an immediate intuition of the Pure Reason, of which the spiritual person is definitely conscious; and that Person is so seen to be primarily unconditioned, *i. e.* out of all relation, difference, and plurality.

"Inconceivable." As we have repeatedly said, this word has no force except with regard to things in nature.

Is cognizable as a fact, &c. Nothing can be more certain than that an *exhaustive* knowledge of the Deity is impossible to any creature. But equally certain is it, that, except as we have some true, positive, *reliable* knowledge of him *as he is*, we cannot be moral beings under his moral government. Take, for instance, the moral law as the expression of God's nature. 1. Either "God is love," or he is not love — hate; or he is indifferent, *i. e.* love has no relation to him. If the last alternative is true, then the other two have no relevancy to the subject in hand. Upon such a supposition, it is unquestionably true that he is utterly inscrutable. Then are we in just the condition which the Limitists assert. But observe the results respecting ourselves. Our whole moral nature is the most bitter, tantalizing falsehood which it is possible for us to entertain as an object of knowledge. We feel that we ought to love the perfect Being. At times we go starving for love to him and beg that bread. He has no love to give. He never felt a pulsation of affection. He sits alone on his icy throne, in a realm of eternal snow; and, covered with the canopy, and shut in by the panoply, of inscrutable mystery, he mocks our cry. We beg for bread. He gives us a stone. Does such a picture instantly shock, yea, horrify, all our finer sensibilities? Does the soul cry out in agony, her rejection of such a conclusion? In that cry we hear the truth in God's voice; for he made the soul. Still less can the thought be entertained that he is hate. It is impossible, then, to think of God except as *love*. We know what love is. We know what God is. There is a somewhat common to the Deity and his spiritual creatures. This enables us to attain a final law, as follows.

In so far as God's creatures have faculties and capacities in common with him, in so far do they know him positively; but in all matters to which their peculiarities as creatures pertain, they only know him negatively; i. e. *they know that he is the opposite of themselves.*

That passage which was quoted in a former page, simply to prove that Sir William Hamilton denied the reality of the Reason as distinct from the Understanding, requires and will now receive a particular examination. He says: "In the Kantian philosophy, both faculties perform the same function; both seek the one in the many; — the Idea (Idee) is only the Concept (Begriff) sublimated into the inconceivable; Reason only the Understanding which has 'overleaped itself.'" In this sentence, and the remarks which follow it, the logician shows that he neither comprehends the assigned function and province of the Reason, nor possesses any accurate knowledge of the mental phenomena upon which he passes judgment. A diagnosis could not well be more thoroughly erroneous than his. For "both faculties" do *not* "perform the same function." Only the Understanding seeks "the one in the many." The Reason seeks *the many in the one.* The functions and modes of activity of the two faculties are exactly opposite. The Understanding runs about through the universe, and gathers up what facts it may, and concludes truth therefrom. The Reason sees the truth *first,* as necessary *a priori* law, and holding it up as standard, measures facts by it, or uses the Sense to find the facts in which it inheres. Besides, the author, in this assertion, is guilty of a most glaring *petitio principii.* For, the very question at issue is, whether "both faculties" do "perform the same function"; whether "both" do "seek the one in the many." In order not to leave the hither side of the question built upon a bare assertion, it will be proper to revert to a few of those proofs adduced heretofore. The

Reason sees the truth first. Take now the assertion, Malice is criminal. Is this primarily learned by experience; or is it an intuitive conviction, which conditions experience. Or, in more general terms, does a child need to be taught what guilt is, before it can feel guilty, as it is taught its letters before it can read; or does the feeling of guilt arise within it spontaneously, upon a breach of known law. If the latter be the true experience, then it can only be accounted for upon the ground that an idea of right and wrong, as an *a priori* law, is organic in man; and, by our definition, the presentation of this law to the attention in consciousness is the act of the Reason. Upon such a theory the one principle was not sought, and is not found, in the many acts, but the many acts are compared with, and judged by, that one standard, which was seen *first*, and as necessarily true. Take another illustration. All religions, in accounting for the universe, have one common point of agreement, which is, that some being or beings, superior to it and men, produced it. And, except perhaps among the most degraded, the more subtle notion of a final cause, though often developed in a crude form, is associated with the other. These notions must be accounted for. How shall it be done? Are they the result of experience? Then, the first human beings had no such notions. But another and more palpable objection arises. Are they the result of individual experience? Then there would be as many religions as individuals. But, very ignorant people have the experience,—persons who never learned anything but the rudest forms of work, from the accumulated experience of others; nor by their own experience, to make the smallest improvement in a simple agricultural instrument. How, then, could they learn by experience one of the profoundest speculative ideas? As a last resort, it may be said they were taught it by philosophers. But this is negatived by the fact, that philosophers do not, to any considerable extent, teach the people, either immediately or mediately; but that generally those who have the least philosophy have the largest influence. And what is most in point, none of these hypotheses will account for the fact, that the gist of the idea, however crude its form, is everywhere the same. Be it a Fetish, or Brahm, or God, in the kernel final cause will be found. It would seem that any candid mind must acknowledge that no combined effort of men, were this possible, could secure such universal exactitude. But turn now and examine any individual in the same direction, as we did just above, respecting the question of right and wrong, and a plain answer will come directly. The notion of first cause, however crude and rudimentary its form, is organic. It arises, then, spontaneously, and the individual takes it — "the one," — and in it finds a reason for the phenomena of nature — "the many," — and is satisfied. And this is an experience not peculiar to the philosopher; but is shared equally by the illiterate, — those entirely unacquainted with scientific abstractions. These illustrations might be carried to an almost indefinite length, showing that commonly, in the every-day experiences of life, men are accustomed not only to observe phenomena and form conclusions, as "It is cloudy to-day, and may rain to-morrow," but also to measure phenomena by an original and fixed standard, as, "This man is malicious, and therefore wicked." Between the two modes of procedure, the following distinction may always be observed. Conclusions are always doubtful, only probable. Decisions are always certain. Conclusions give us what may be, decisions what must be. The former result from concepts and experience, the latter from intuitions and logical processes. Thus is made plain the fact that, to give it the most favorable aspect, Sir William Hamilton, in his eagerness to maintain his theory, has entirely mistaken one class of human experiences, and so was led to deny the actuality of the most profound and important faculty of the human mind. In view of the foregoing results, one need not hesitate to say that, whether he ever attempted it or not, Kant never "has clearly shown that the idea of the unconditioned can have no objective reality," for it is impossible to do this, the opposite being the truth. Its objective reality is God; it therefore "conveys" to us the most important "knowledge," and "involves" no "contradictions." Moreover, unconditionedness is a "simple," "positive," "notion," and not "a fasciculus of negations"; but is an attribute of God, who comprehends all positives. A little after, Hamilton says: "And while he [Kant] appropriated Reason as a specific faculty to take cognizance of these negations, hypostatized as positive, under the Platonic name of *Ideas*," &c. Here, again, the psychological question arises, Is the Reason such a faculty? Are its supposed objects negations? Are they hypostatized as positive? Evidently, if we establish an affirmative answer to the first question, a negative to the others follows directly, and the logician's system is a failure. Again, the discrimination of "thought into *positive* and *negative* is simply absurd. All thought is *positive*. The phrase, negative thought, is only a convenient expression for the refusal of the mind to think. But "Ideas" are not thoughts at all, in the strict sense of that term. It refers to the operations of the mind upon objects which have been presented. Ideas are a part of such objects. All objects in the mind are positive. The phrase, negative object, is a contradiction. But, without any deduction, we see immediately that ideas are positives. The common consciousness of the human race affirms this.

The following remark upon Cousin requires some notice. "For those who, with M. Cousin, regard the notion of the unconditioned as a positive and real knowledge of existence in its all-comprehensive unity, and who consequently employ the terms *Absolute, Infinite, Unconditioned*, as only various expressions for the same identity, are imperatively bound to prove that their idea of *the One corresponds, either with that Unconditioned we have distinguished as the Absolute, or with that Unconditioned we have distinguished as the Infinite, or that it includes both, or that it excludes both.* This they have not done, and, we suspect, have never attempted to do." The italics are Hamilton's. The above statement is invalid, for the following reasons. The Absolute, therein named, has been shown to be irrelevant to the matter in hand, and an absurdity. It is self-evident that the term "limited whole," as applied to Space and Time, is a violation of the laws of thought. Since we seek the truth, that Absolute must be rejected. Again, the definitions of the terms absolute and infinite, which have been found consistent, and pertinent to Space and Time, have been further found irrelevant and meaningless, when applied to the Being, the One, who is the Creator. That Being, existing primarily out of all relation to Space and Time, must, if known at all, be studied, and known as he is. The terms infinite and absolute will, of necessity, then, when applied to him, have entirely different significations from what they will when applied to Space and Time. So, then, no decision of questions arising in this latter sphere will have other than a negative value in the former. The questions in that sphere must be decided on their own merits, as must those in this. What is really required, then, is, that the One, the Person, be shown to be both absolute and infinite, and that these, as qualities, consistently inhere in that *unity*. As this has already been done in the first Part of this treatise, nothing need be added here.

Some pages afterwards, in again remarking upon M. Cousin, Hamilton quotes from him as follows: "The condition of intelligence *is difference*; and an act of knowledge is only possible where there exists a plurality of terms." In a subsequent paragraph the essayist argues from this, thus: "But, on the other hand, it is asserted, that the condition of intelligence, as knowing, is plurality and difference; consequently, the condition of the absolute as existing, and under which it must be known, and the condition of intelligence, as capable of knowing, are incompatible. For, if we suppose the absolute cognizable, it must be identified either, first, with the subject knowing; or, second, with the object known; or, third, with the indifference of both." Rejecting the first two, Hamilton says: "The *third* hypothesis, on the other hand, is *contradictory of the plurality of intelligence;* for, if the subject of consciousness be known as one, a plurality of terms is not the necessary condition of intelligence. The alternative is therefore necessary: Either the absolute cannot be known or conceived at all, or our author is wrong in subjecting thought to the conditions of plurality and difference."

In these extracts may be detected an error which, so far as the author is informed, has been hitherto overlooked by philosophers. The logician presents an alternative which is unquestionably valid. Yet with almost, if not entire unanimity, writers have been accustomed to assign plurality, relation, difference, and — to adopt a valuable suggestion of Mr. Spencer — likeness, as conditions of all knowledge; and among them those who have claimed for man a positive knowledge of the absolute. The error by which they have been drawn into this contradiction is purely psychological; and arises, like the other errors which we have pointed out, from an attempt to carry over the laws of the animal nature, the Sense and Understanding, by which man learns of, and concludes about, things in nature, to the Pure Reason, by which he sees and knows, with an *absolutely certain* knowledge, principles and laws; and to subject this faculty to those conditions. Now, there can be no doubt but that if the logician's premiss is true, the conclusion is unavoidable. If "an act of knowledge is only possible where there exists a plurality of terms," then is it impossible that we should know God, *or that he should know himself.* The logic is impregnable. But the conclusion is revolting. What must be done, then? Erect some makeshift subterfuge of mental impotence? It will not meet the exigency of the case. It will not satisfy the demand of the soul. Nay, more, she casts it out utterly, as a most gross insult. Unquestionably, but one course is left; and that is so plain, that one cannot see how even a Limitist could have overlooked it. Correct the premiss. Study out the true psychology, and that will give us perfect consistency. Hold with a death-grip to the principle that *every truth is in complete harmony with every other truth;* and hold with no less tenacity to the principle that the human intellect is true. And what is the true premiss which through an irrefutable logic will give us a satisfactory, a true, an undoubted conclusion. This. A plurality of terms is *not* the necessary condition of intelligence; but objects which are pure, simple, unanalyzable, may be directly known by an intellect. Or, to be more explicit. Plurality, relation, difference, and likeness, are necessary conditions of intelligence through the Sense and Understanding; but they do not in the least degree lie upon the Reason, which sees its objects as pure, simple ideas which are *self-evident*, and, consequently, are not subject to those conditions. Whatever knowledge we may have of "mammals," we undoubtedly gain under the conditions of plurality, relation, difference, and likeness; for "mammals" are things in nature. But absoluteness is a pure, simple, unanalyzable idea in the Reason, and as such is seen and known by a direct insight as out of all plurality, relation, difference, and likeness: for this is a *quality* of the self-existent Person, and so belongs wholly to the sphere of the supernatural, and can be examined only by a spiritual person who is also supernatural.

Let us illustrate these two kinds of knowledge. 1. The knowledge given by the Sense and Understanding. This is of material objects. Take, for example, an apple. The Sense observes it as one of many apples, and that many characteristics belong to it as one apple. Among these, color, skin, pulp, juices, flavor, &c. may be mentioned. It observes, also, that it bears a relation to the stem and tree on which it grows, and, as well, that its several qualities have relations among themselves. One color belongs to the skin, another to the pulp. The skin, as cover, relates to the pulp as covered, and the like. The apple, moreover, is distinguished from other fruits by marks of difference and marks of likeness. It has a different skin, a different pulp, and a different flavor. Yet, it is like other fruits, in that it grows on a tree, and possesses those marks just named, which, though differing among themselves, according to the fruit in which they inhere, have a commonality of kind, as compared with other objects. This distinguishing, analyzing, and classifying of characteristics, and connecting them into a unity, as an apple, is the work of the Sense and Understanding.

2. The knowledge given by the Pure Reason. This is of *a priori* laws, of these laws combined in pure archetypal forms, and of God as the Supreme Being who comprehends all laws and forms. A fundamental difference in the two modes of activity immediately strikes one's attention. In the former case, the mode was by distinguishment and *analysis*. In the latter it is by comprehension and *synthesis*. Take the idea of moral obligation to illustrate this topic. No one but a Limitist will, it is believed, contend against the position of Dr. Hopkins, "that this idea of obligation or *oughtness* is a simple idea." This being once acceded, carries with it the whole theory which the author seeks to maintain. How may "a simple idea" be known? It cannot be distinguished or analyzed. Being simple, it is *sui generis*. Hence, it cannot be known by plurality or relation, difference or likeness. If known at all, it must be known *as it is in itself*, by a spontaneous insight. Such, in fact, is the mode of the activity of the Pure Reason, and such are the objects of that activity. In maintaining, then, the doctrine of "intellectual intuition," M. Cousin was right, but wrong in subjecting all knowledge "to the conditions of plurality and difference."

Near the close of the essay under examination Sir Wm. Hamilton states certain problems, which he is "confident" Cousin cannot solve. There is nothing very difficult about them; and it is a wonder that he should have so presented them. Following the passage — which is here quoted — will be found what appear simple and easy solutions.

"But (to say nothing of remoter difficulties) — (1) how liberty can be conceived, supposing always a plurality of modes of activity, without a knowledge of that plurality; — (2) how a faculty can resolve to act by preference in a particular manner, and not determine itself by final causes; — (3) how intelligence can influence a blind power, without operating as an efficient cause; — (4) or how, in fine, morality can be founded on a liberty which at best only escapes necessity by taking refuge with chance; — these are problems which M. Cousin, in none of his works, has stated, and which we are confident he is unable to solve."

1. Liberty cannot be *conceived.* It must be intuited. There is "a plurality of modes," and there is "a knowledge of that plurality." 2. "A faculty" cannot resolve to act; cannot have a preference; and cannot determine itself *at all.* Only a *spiritual person* can *resolve,* can have a preference, can determine. 3. Intelligence cannot influence. Blind power cannot be influenced. Only a spiritual person can be influenced, and he by object through the intelligence as medium, and only he can be an efficient cause. 4. Morality cannot "be founded on a liberty, which only escapes necessity by taking refuge with chance;" and, what is more, such a liberty is impossible, and to speak of it as possible is absurd. What vitiates the processes of thought of the Limitists so largely, crops out very plainly here: viz., the employment both in thinking and expressions of faculties, capacities, and qualities, as if they possessed all the powers of persons. This habit is thoroughly erroneous, and destructive of truth. The truth desired to answer this whole passage, may be stated in exact terms thus: The infinite and absolute spiritual Person, the ultimate and indestructible, and indivisible and composite unit, possesses as a necessary quality of personality pure liberty; which is freedom from compulsion or restraint in the choice of one of two possible ends. This Person intuits a multitude of modes of activity. He possesses also perfect wisdom, which enables him, having

chosen the right end, to determine with unerring accuracy which one of all the modes of activity is the best to secure the end. Involved in the choice of the end, is the determination to put in force the best means for securing that end. Hence this Person decides that the best mode shall *be*. He also possesses all-power. This is *his* endowment, not that of his intelligence. The intelligence is not person, but *faculty* in the person. So is it with the *power*. So then this Person, intuiting through his intelligence what is befitting his dignity, puts forth, in accordance therewith, his power; and is efficient cause. Such a being is neither under necessity nor chance. He is not under necessity, because there is no constraint which compels him to choose the right end, rather than the wrong one. He is not under chance, because he is *certain* which is the best mode of action to gain the end chosen. In this distinction between ends and modes of activity, which has been so clearly set forth by Rev. Mark Hopkins, D. D., and in the motions of spiritual persons in each sphere, lie the ground for answering *all* difficulties raised by the advocates of necessity or chance. With these remarks we close the discussion of Hamilton's philosophical system, and proceed to take up the teachings of his followers.

REVIEW OF "LIMITS OF RELIGIOUS THOUGHT."

THIS volume is one which will always awaken in the mind of the candid and reflective reader a feeling of profound respect. The writer is manifestly a deeply religious man. The book bears the marks of piety, and an earnest search after the truth respecting that august Being whom its author reverentially worships. However far wrong we may believe him to have gone in his speculative theory, his devout spirit must ever inspire esteem. Though it is ours to criticize and condemn the intellectual principles upon which his work is based, we cannot but desire to be like him, in rendering solemn homage to the Being he deems inscrutable.

In proceeding with our examination, all the defects which were formerly noticed as belonging to the system of the Limitists will here be found plainly observable. Following his teacher, Mr. Mansel holds the Understanding to be the highest faculty of the human intellect, and the consequent corollary that a judgment is its highest form of knowledge. The word "conceive" he therefore uses as expressive of the act of the mind in grasping together various marks into a concept, when that word and act of mind are utterly irrelevant to the object to which he applies them; and hence they can have no meaning as used. We shall see him speak of "starting from the divine, and reasoning down to the human"; or of "starting from the human, and reasoning up to the divine"; where, upon the hypothesis that the two are entirely diverse, no reasoning process, based upon either one, can reach the other. On the other hand, if any knowledge of God is possible to the created mind, it is only on the ground that there is a similarity, an exact likeness in certain respects, between the two; in other words, that the Creator plainly declared a simple fact, in literal language, when he said, "God made man in his own image." If man's mind is wholly unlike God's mind, he cannot know truth as God knows it. And if the human intellect is thus faulty, man cannot be the subject of a moral government, for every subject of a moral government is amenable to law. In order to be so amenable, he must know the law *as it is.* No phantasmagoria of law, no silhouette will do. It must be immediately seen, and known to be binding. Truth is *one.* He, then, who sees it as it is, and knows it to be binding, sees it as God sees it, and feels the same obligation that God feels. And such an one must man be if he is a moral agent. Whether he is such an agent or not, we will not argue here; since all governments and laws of society are founded upon the hypothesis that he is, it may well be assumed as granted.

Of the "three terms, familiar as household words," which Mr. Mansel, in his second lecture, proceeds to examine, it is to be said, that "First Cause," if properly mentioned at all, should have been put last; and that "Infinite" and "Absolute" are not pertinent to Cause, but to Person. So then when we consider "the Deity as He is," we consider him, not as Cause, for this is *incidental,* but as the infinite and absolute Person, for these three marks are *essential.* Further, these last-mentioned terms express ideas in the Reason; while the term Cause expresses "an *a priori* Element of connection, and thus a primitive understanding-conception." Hardly more satisfactory than his use of the term Cause is his definition of the terms absolute and infinite. He defines "the Absolute" to be "that which exists in and by itself, having no necessary relation to any other Being," when it is rather the exclusion of the possibility of any other Being. Again, he defines "the Infinite" to be "that which is free from all possible limitation; that than which a greater is inconceivable; and which, consequently, can receive no additional attribute or mode of existence which it had not from all eternity." "That which" means the thing which, for which is neuter. Mr. Mansel's infinite is, then, the *Thing*. This *Thing* "is free from all possible limitation." How can that be when the Being he thus defines is, must be, necessarily existent, and so is bound by one of the greatest of limitations, the inability to cease to be. But some light may be thrown upon his use of the term "limitation" by the subsequent portions of his definition. The Thing "which is free from all possible limitation" is "that than which a greater is inconceivable." Moreover, this greatest of all possible things possesses all possible "attributes," and is in every possible "mode of existence" "from all eternity." Respecting the phrase "than which a greater is inconceivable," two suppositions may be made. Either there may be a thing "greater" than, and diverse from, all other things; or there may be a thing greater than, and including all, other things. Probably the latter is Mr. Mansel's thought; but it is Materialistic Pantheism. This Being must be in every "mode of existence" "from all eternity." Personality is a "mode of existence"; therefore this Being must forever have been in that mode. But impersonality is also a mode of existence, therefore this Being must forever have been in that mode. Yet again these two modes are contradictory and mutually exclusive; then this Being must have been from all eternity in two contradictory and mutually exclusive modes of existence! Is further remark necessary to show that Mr. Mansel's definition is thoroughly vitiated by the understanding-conception that infinity is amount, and is, therefore, utterly worthless? Can there be a thing so great as to be without limits? Has greatness anything to do with infinity? Manifestly not. It becomes necessary, then, to recur to and amplify those definitions which we have already given to the terms he uses.

Absoluteness and infinity are qualities of the necessary Being.

Absoluteness is that quality of the necessary Being by which he is endowed with self-existence, self-dependence, and totality. Or in other words, having this quality, he is wholly independent of any other being; and also the possibility of the existence of any other independent Being is excluded; and so he is the Complete, the Final, upon whom all possible beings must depend.

Infinity is that quality of the necessary Being which gives him universality in the totality. It expresses the fact, that he possesses all possible endowments in perfection.

Possessing these qualities, that Being is free from any external restraint or limitation; but those restraints and limitations, which his very constituting elements themselves impose, are not removed by these qualities. For instance, the possession of Love, Mercy, Justice, Wisdom, Power, and the like, are essential to God's entirety; and the possession of them in *perfect harmony* is essential to his perfectness in the entirety. This fact of perfect harmony, exact balance, bars him from the *undue* exercise of any one of his attributes; or, concisely, his perfection restrains him from being imperfect. We revert, then, to the fundamental distinction, attained heretofore, between improper limitations, or those which are involved in perfection; and proper limitations, or those which are involved in deficiency and dependence; and applying it here, we see that those limitations, which we speak of as belonging to God, are not indicative of a lack, but rather are necessarily incidental to that possession of all possible perfection which constitutes him the Ultimate.

In this view infinity can have no relevancy to "number." It is not that God has one, or one million endowments. It asks no question about the number; and cares not for it. It is satisfied in the assertion that he possesses *all that are possible*, and in perfect harmony. It is, further, an idea, not a concept. It must be intuited, for it cannot be "conceived." No analogy of "line" or "surface" has any pertinence; because these are concepts, belonging wholly in the Understanding and Sense, where no idea can come. Yet it may be, *is*, the quality of an intelligence endowed with a limited number of attributes; — for there can be no number without limitation, since the phrase unlimited number is a contradiction of terms; — but this limitation involves no lack, because there are no "others," which can be "thereby related to it, as cognate or opposite modes of consciousness." Without doubt it is, in a certain sense, true, that "the metaphysical representation of the Deity, as absolute and infinite, must necessarily, as the profoundest metaphysicians have acknowledged, amount to nothing less than the sum of all reality." This sense is that all reality is by him, and for him, and from him; and is utterly dependent upon him. But Hegel's conclusion by no means follows, in which he says: "What kind of an Absolute Being is that which does not contain in itself all that is actual, even evil included." This is founded upon the suppressed premiss, that such a Being *must* do what he does, and his creatures *must* do what they do; and so evil must come. Thus much only can be admitted, and this may be admitted, without derogating aught from God's perfectness: viz., that he sees in the ideals of his Reason *how* his laws may be violated, and so, how sin may and will be in this moral system; but it is a perversion of words to say that this knowledge on the part of God is evil.

The knowing how a moral agent may break the perfect law, is involved in the knowing how such agent may keep that law. But the fact of the knowledge does not involve any whit of consent to the act of violation. On the other hand, it may, does, become the ground for the putting forth of every wise effort to prevent that act. Again; evil is produced by those persons whom God has made, who violate his moral laws. He being perfectly wise and perfectly good, for perfectly wise and good reasons sustains them in the ability to sin. There can be, in the nature of things, no persons at all, without this ability to sin. But God does not direct them to sin; neither when they do sin does any stain fall upon him for sustaining their existence during their sinning. That definition of the term absolute, upon which Hegel bases his assertion, is one fit only for the Sense and Understanding; as if God was the physical sum of all existence. It is Materialistic Pantheism. But by observing the definitions and distinctions, which have been heretofore laid down, it may be readily seen how an actual mode of existence, as that of finite person, may be denied to God, and no lack be indicated thereby. Hegel's blasphemy may, then, be answered as follows: God is the infinite and absolute spiritual Person. Personality is the form of his being. The form cannot be empty. Organized essence fills the form. Infinity and absoluteness are *qualities* of the Person as thus organized. The quality of absoluteness, for instance, as transfusing the essence, is the endowment of pure independence, and involves the exclusion of the possibility of any other independent Being, and the possession of the ability to create every possible dependent being. In so far, then, as Hegel's assertion means that no being can exist, and do evil, except he is created and sustained by the Deity, it is true. But in so far as it means — and this is undoubtedly what Hegel did mean — that God must be the efficient author of sin, that, forced by the iron rod of Fate, he must produce evil, the assertion is utterly false, and could only have been uttered by one who, having dwelt all his life in the gloomy cave of the Understanding, possessed not even a tolerably correct notion of the true nature of the subject he had in hand, — the character of God. From the above considerations it is apparent that all the requirements of the Reason are fulfilled when it is asserted that all things — the Universe — are dependent upon God; and he is utterly independent.

The paragraphs next succeeding, which have been quoted with entire approbation by Mr. Herbert Spencer, are thoroughly vitiated by their author's indefensible assumption, that cause is "indispensable" to our idea of the Deity. As was remarked above, the notion of cause is incidental.

The Deity may or may not become a cause, as he shall decide. But he has no choice as to whether he shall be a person or not. Hence we may freely admit that "the cause, as such, exists only in relation to its effect: the cause is a cause of the effect; the effect is an effect of the cause." It is also true that "the conception"—idea—"of the Absolute implies a possible existence out of all relation." The position we have taken is in advance of this, for we say, involves an actual existence out of all relation. Introducing, then, not "the idea of succession in time," but the idea of the logical order, we rightly say, "the Absolute exists first by itself, and afterwards becomes a Cause." Nor are we here "checked by the third conception, that of the Infinite." "Causation is a possible mode of existence," and yet "that which exists without causing" is infinite. How is this? It is thus. Infinity is the universality of perfect endowment. Now, taking as the point of departure the first creative nisus or effort of the Deity, this is true. Before that act he was perfect in every possible endowment, and accorded his choice thereto. He was able to create, but did not, for a good and sufficient reason. In and after that act, he was still perfect as before. That act then involved no *essential* change in God. But he was in one mode of being before, and in another mode of being in and after that act. Yet he was equally perfect, and equally blessed, before as after. What then follows? This: that there was some good and sufficient reason why before that act he should be a potential creator, and in that act he should become an actual creator: and this reason preserves the perfection, *i. e.* the infinity of God, equally in both modes. When, then, Mr. Mansel says, "if Causation is a possible mode of existence, that which exists without causing is not infinite, that which becomes a cause has passed beyond its former limits," his utterance is prompted by that pantheistic understanding-conception of God, which thinks him the sum of all that was, and is, and ever shall be, or can be; and that in all this, he is *actual*. On the other hand, as we have seen, all that is required to fulfil the idea of infinity is, that the Being, whom it qualifies, possesses all fulness, has all the forms and springs of being in himself. It is optional with him whether he will create or not; and his remaining out of all relation, or his creating a Universe, and thus establishing relations to and for himself, in no way affect his essential nature, *i. e.* his infinity. He is a person, possessing all possible endowments, and in this does his infinity consist. In this view, "creation at any particular moment of time" is seen to be the only possible hypothesis by which to account for the Universe. Such a *Person*, the necessary Being, must have been in existence before the Universe; and his first act in producing that Universe would mark the first moment of time. No "alternative of Pantheism" is, can be, presented to the advocates of this theory. On the other hand, that scheme is seen to be both impossible and absurd.

One cannot disagree with Mr. Mansel, when in the next paragraph he says, that, "supposing the Absolute to become a cause, it will follow that it operates by means of free will and consciousness." But the difficulties which he then raises lie only in the Understanding, and may be explained thus. Always in God's consciousness *the subject and object are identical.* All that God is, is always present to his Eye. Hence all relations always appear subordinate to, and dependent upon him; and it is a misapprehension of the true idea to suppose, that any relation which falls *in idea* within him, and only becomes actual at his will, is any proper limitation. Both subject and object are thus absolute, being identical; and yet there is no contradiction.

The difficulty is further raised that there cannot be in the absolute Being any interrelations, as of attributes among themselves, or of attributes to the Being. This arises from an erroneous definition of the term absolute. The definition heretofore given in this treatise presents no such difficulty. The possession of these attributes and interrelations is essential to the exclusion by their possessor of another independent Being; and it is a perversion to so use a quality which is essential to a being, that it shall militate against the consistency of his being what he must be. If then "the almost unanimous voice of philosophy, in pronouncing that the absolute is both one and simple," uses the term "simple" in the same sense that it would have when applied to the idea of moral obligation, viz., that it is unanalyzable, then that voice is wrong, just as thoroughly as the voice of antiquity in favor of the Ptolemaic system of Astronomy was wrong; and is to be treated as that was. On such questions *opinions* have no weight. The search is after a knowledge which is sure, and which every man may have within himself. We land, then, in no "inextricable dilemma." The absolute Person we see to be conscious; and to possess complexity in unity, universality in totality. By an immediate intuition we know him as primarily out of all relation, plurality, difference, and likeness; and yet as having, of his own self, established the Universe, which is still entirely dependent upon him; from which he differs, and with which he is not identified.

Again Mr. Mansel says: "A mental attribute to be conceived as infinite, must be in actual exercise on every possible object: otherwise it is potential only, with regard to those on which it is not exercised; and an unrealized potentiality is a limitation." With our interpretation the assertion is true and contains no puzzle. Every mental attribute of the Deity is most assuredly "in actual exercise," upon every one of its "possible objects" *as ideas*. But the objects are not therefore actual. Neither is there any need that they should ever become so. He sees them just as clearly, and knows them just as thoroughly as ideals, as he does as actual objects. All ideal objects are "unrealized potentialities"; and yet they are the opposite of limitations proper. But this sentence, as an expression of the thought which Mr. Mansel seemingly wished to convey, is vitiated by the presence of that understanding-conception that infinity is amount, which must be actual. Once regard infinity as *quality* of the necessarily existent Person, and it directly follows that this or that act, of that Person, in no way disturbs that infinity. The quality conditions the acting being; but the act of that being cannot limit the quality. The quality is, that the act may be; not the reverse. Hence the questions arising from the interrelations of Power and Goodness, Justice and Mercy, are solved at once. Infinity as quality, not amount, pervades them all, and holds them all in perfect harmony, adjusting each to each, in a melody more beautiful than that of the spheres. Even "the existence of Evil" is "compatible with that of" this "perfectly good Being." He does not will that it shall be; neither does he will that it shall not be. If he willed that it should not be, and it was, then he would be "thwarted"; but only on such a hypothesis can the conclusion follow. But he does will that certain creatures shall be, who, though dependent upon him for existence and sustenance, are, like him, final causes, — the final arbiters of their own destinies, who in the choice of ends are unrestrained, and may choose good or ill. He made these creatures, knowing that some of them would choose wrong, and so evil would be: but *he* did not will the evil. He only willed the conditions upon which evil was possible, and placed all proper bars to prevent the evil; and the *a priori* facts of his immutable perfection in endowments, and of his untarnished holiness, are decisive of the consequent fact, that, in willing those conditions, God did the very best possible deed. If it be further asserted that the fact, that the Being who possesses all possible endowments in perfection could not wisely prevent sin, is a limitation; and, further, that it were better to have prevented sin by an unwise act than to have permitted it by a wise act; it can only be replied: This is the same as to say, that it is essential to God's perfection that he be imperfect; or, that it was better for the perfect Being to violate his Self than to permit sin. If any one in his thinking chooses to accept of such alternatives, there remains no ground of argument with him; but only "a certain fearful looking for of judgment and fiery indignation which shall devour the adversary."

Carrying on his presentation of difficulties, Mr. Mansel further remarks: "Let us however suppose for an instant, that these difficulties are surmounted, and the existence of the Absolute securely established on the testimony of reason. Still we have not succeeded in reconciling this idea with that of a Cause: we have done nothing towards explaining how the absolute can give rise to the relative, the infinite to the finite. If the condition of causal activity is a higher state than that of quiescence, the absolute, whether acting voluntarily or involuntarily, has passed from a condition of comparative imperfection to one of comparative perfection; and therefore was not originally perfect. If the state of activity is an inferior state to that of quiescence, the Absolute, in becoming a cause, has lost its original perfection." On this topic we can but repeat the argument heretofore adduced. Let the supposition be entertained that perfection does not belong to a state, but to God's nature, to what God *is*, as ground for what God does, and standing in the logical order before his act; and it will directly appear that a state of quiescence or a state of activity in no way modifies his perfection. What God is, remains permanent and perfect, and his acts are only manifestations of that permanent and perfect. It follows, then, taking the first moment of time as the point of departure, that, before that point, God was in a state of complete blessedness, and that after that point he was also in such a state; and, further, that while these two states are equal, there is not "complete indifference," because there was a reason, clearly seen by the Divine mind, why the passage from quiescence to activity should be when it was, and as it was, and that this reason having been acknowledged in his conduct, gives to the two states equality, and yet differentiates the one from the other.

"Again, how can the Relative be conceived as coming into being?" It cannot be *conceived* at all. The faculty of the mind by which it forms a concept — the discursive Understanding — is impotent to conceive what cannot be conceived — the act of creation. The changes of matter can be concluded into a system, but not the power by which the matter came to be, and the changes were produced. If the how is known at all, it must be seen. The laws of the process must be intuited, as also the process as logically according with those laws. The following is believed to be an intelligible account of the process, and an answer to the above question. The absolute and infinite Person possesses as *a priori* organic elements of his being, all possible endowments in perfect harmony. Hence all laws, and all possible combinations of laws, are at once and always present before the Eye of his Reason, which is thus constituted Universal Genius. These combinations may be conveniently named ideal forms. They arise spontaneously, being in no way dependent upon his will, but are rather *a priori* conditional of any creative activity. So, too, they harmoniously arrange themselves into systems, — archetypes of what may be, some of which may appear nobler, and others inferior. This Person, being such as we have stated, possesses also as endowment all power, and thereby excludes the possibility of there being any "*other*" power. This power is adequate to do all that *power* can do, — to accomplish all that lies within the province of power. So long as the Person sees fit not to exert his power, his ideal forms will be only ideals, and the power will be simply power. But whenever he shall see fit to send forth his power, and organize it according to the ideal forms, the Universe will become. In all this the Person, "of his own will," freely establishes whatever his unerring wisdom shows is most worthy of his dignity; and so the actualities and relations which be thus ordains are no proper limit or restraint, for they in no way lessen his fulness, but are only a manifestation of that fulness, — a declaration of his glory. In a word, Creation is that executive act of God by which he combines with his power that ideal system which he had chosen because best, or *it is the organization of ample power according to perfect law.* If one shall now ask, "How could he send forth the power?" it is to be replied that the question is prompted by the curiosity of the "flesh," man's animal nature; and since no representation — picture — can be made, no answer can be furnished. It is not needed to know *how* God is, or does anything, but only that he does it. All the essential requirements of the problem are met when it is ascertained in the light of the Reason, that all fulness is in God, that from this fulness he established all other beings and their natural relations, and that no relation is *imposed* upon him by another. The view thus advanced avoids the evil of the understanding-conception, that creation is the bringing of something out of nothing. There is an actual self-existent ground, from which the Universe is produced. Neither is the view pantheistic, for it starts with the *a priori* idea of an absolute and infinite Person who is "before all things, and by whom all things consist," — who organizes his own power in accordance with his own ideals, and thus produces the Universe, and all this by free will in self-consciousness.

On page eighty-four, in speaking "of the atheistic alternative, Mr. Mansel makes use of the following language: "A limit is itself a relation; and to conceive a limit as such, is virtually to acknowledge the existence of a correlative on the other side of it." Upon reading this sentence, some sensuous form spontaneously appears in the Sense. Some object is conceived, and something outside it, that bounds it. But let the idea be once formed of a Being who possesses all limitation within himself, and for whom there is no "other side," nor any "correlative," and the difficulty vanishes. We do not seek to account for sensuous objects. It is pure Spirit whom we consider. We do not need to form a concept of "a first moment in time," or "a first unit of space," nor could we if we would. To do so would be for the faculty which forms concepts to transcend the very laws of its organization. What we need is, to see the fact that a Spirit is, who, possessing personality as form, and absoluteness and infinity as qualities, thereby contains all limits and the ground of all being in himself, and antithetical to whom is only negation.

From the ground thus attained there is seen to result, not the dreary Sahara of interminable contradictions, but the fair land of harmonious consistency. A Spirit, sole, personal, self-conscious, the absolute and infinite Person, is the Being we seek and have found; and upon such a Being the soul of man may rest with the unquestioning trust of an infant in its mother's arms. One cannot pass by unnoticed the beautiful spirit of religious reverence which shines through the closing paragraphs of this lecture. It is evident with what dissatisfaction the writer views the sterile puzzles of which he has been treating, and what a relief it is to turn from them to "the God who is 'gracious and merciful, slow to anger, and of great kindness, and repenteth Him of the evil.'" The wonder is, that he did not receive that presentation which his devout spirit has made, as the truth — which it is — and say, "I will accept this as final. My definitions and deductions shall accord with this highest revelation. This shall be my standard of interpretation." Had he done so, far other, and, as it is believed, more satisfactory and truthful would have been the conclusions he would have given us.

In his third Lecture Mr. Mansel is occupied with an examination of the human nature, for the purpose, if possible, of finding "some explanation of the singular phenomenon of human thought," which he has just developed. At the threshold of the investigation the fact of consciousness appears, and he begins the statement of its conditions in the following language: "Now, in the first place, the very conception of Consciousness, in whatever mode it may be manifested, necessarily implies *distinction between one object and another.* To be conscious, we must be conscious of something; and that something can only be known as that which it is, by being distinguished from that which it is not." In this statement Mr. Mansel unconsciously assumes as settled, the very question at issue; for, the position maintained by one class of writers is, that in certain of our mental operations, viz., in intuitions, the mind sees a simple truth, idea, first principle, as it is, in itself, and that there is no distinction in the act of knowledge. It is unquestionably true that, in the examination of objects in the Sense, and the conclusion of judgments in the Understanding, no object can come into consciousness without implying a "distinction between one object and another." But it is also evident that a first truth, to be known as such, must be intuited—seen as it is in itself; and so directly known to have the qualities of necessity and universality which constitute it a first truth. Of this fact Sir William Hamilton seems to have been aware, when he denied the actuality of the Reason,—perceiving, doubtless, that only on the ground of such a denial was his own theory tenable. But if it shall be admitted, as it would seem it must be, that men have necessary and universal convictions, then it must also be admitted that these convictions are not entertained by distinguishing them from other mental operations, but that they are seen of themselves to be true; and thus it appears that there are some modes of consciousness which do not imply the "distinction" claimed. The subsequent sentences seem capable of more than one interpretation. If the author means that "the Infinite" cannot be infinite without he is also finite, so that all distinction ceases, then his meaning is both pantheistic and contradictory; for the word infinite has no meaning, if it is not the opposite of finite, and to identify them is undoubtedly Pantheism. Or if he means "that the Infinite cannot be distinguished" as independent, from the Finite *as independent,* and thus, as possessing some quality with which it was not endowed by the infinite Person, then there can be no doubt of his correctness. But if, as would seem, his idea of infinity is that of amount, is such that it appears inconsistent, contradictory, for the infinite Person to retain his infinity, and still create beings who are really other than himself, and possessing, as quality, finiteness, which he cannot possess as quality, then is his idea of what infinity is wrong. Infinity is quality, and the capacity to thus create is essential to it. All that the Reason requires is, that the finite be created by and wholly dependent upon the infinite Person; then all the relations and conditions are only *improper*, — such as that Person has established, and which, therefore, in no way diminish his glory or detract from his fulness. When, then, Mr. Mansel says, "A consciousness of the Infinite, as such, thus necessarily involves a self-contradiction, for it implies the recognition, by limitation and difference, of that which can only be given as unlimited and indifferent," it is evident that he uses the term infinite to express the understanding-conception of unlimited amount, which is not relevant here, rather than the reason-idea of universality which is not contradictory to a real distinction between the Infinite and finite. There is also involved the unexpressed assumption that we have no knowledge except of the limited and different, or, in other words, that the Understanding is the highest faculty of the mind. It has already been abundantly shown that this is erroneous, — that the Reason knows its objects in themselves, as out of all relation, plurality, difference, or likeness. Dropping now the abstract term "the infinite," and using the concrete and proper form, we may say:

We are conscious of infinity, *i. e.* we are conscious that we see with the eye of Reason infinity as a simple, *a priori* idea; and that it is quality of the Deity.

2. We are conscious of the infinite Person; in that we are conscious, that we see with the eye of Reason the complex *a priori* idea of a perfect Person possessing independence and universality as qualities of his Self. But we are not con-

scious of him in that we exhaustively comprehend him. As is said elsewhere, we know that he is, and to a certain extent, but not wholly what he is.

In further discussing this question Mansel is guilty of another grave psychological error. He says, "Consciousness is essentially a limitation, for it is the determination to one actual out of many possible modifications." There is no truth in this sentence. Consciousness is not a limitation; it is not a determination; it is not a modification. It may be well to state here certain conclusions on this assertion, which will be brought out in the fuller discussion of it, when we come to speak of Mr. Spencer's book. Consciousness is *one*, and retains that oneness throughout all modifications. These occur in the unity as items of experience affect it. Doubtless Dr. Hickok's illustration is the best possible. Consciousness is the *light* in which a spiritual person sees the modifications of himself, *i. e.* the activity of his faculties and capacities. Like Space, only in a different sphere, it is an illimitable indivisible unity, which is, that all limits may be in it — that all objects may come into it. If, then, only one modification — object — comes into it at a time, this is because the faculties which see in its light are thus organized; — the being to whom it belongs is partial; but there is nothing pertaining to consciousness *as such*, which constitutes a limit, — which could bar the infinite Person from seeing all things at once in its light. This Person, then, so far as known, must be known as an actual absolute, infinite Spirit, and hence no "thing"; and further as the originator and sustainer of all "*things*," — which, though dependent on him, in no way take aught from him. He may be known also, as potentially everything, in the sense that all possible combinations, or forms of objects, must ever stand as ideals in his Reason; and he can, at his will, organize his power in accordance therewith. But he must also be known as free to create or not to create; and that the fact that many potential forms remain such, in no way detracts from his infinity.

Another of Mr. Mansel's positions involves conclusions which, we feel assured, he will utterly reject. He says, "If all thought is limitation, — if whatever we conceive is, by the very act of conception, regarded as finite, — the infinite, from a human point of view, is merely a name for the absence of those conditions under which thought is possible." "From a human point of view," and *we*, at least, can take no other, what follows? That the Deity *can have no thoughts*; cannot know what our thoughts are, or that we think. But three suppositions can be made. Either he has no thoughts, is destitute of an intellect; or his intellect is Universal Genius, and he sees all possible objects at once; or there is a faculty different in kind from and higher than the Reason, of which we have, can have, no knowledge. The first, though acknowledged by Hamilton in a passage elsewhere quoted, and logically following from the position taken by Mr. Mansel, is so abhorrent to the soul that it must be unhesitatingly rejected. The second is the position advocated in this treatise. The third is hinted at by Mr. Herbert Spencer. We reject this third, because the Reason affirms it to be impossible; and because, being unnecessary, by the law of parsimony it should not be allowed. To advocate a position of which, in the very terms of it, the intellect can have no possible shadow of knowledge, is, to say the least, no part of the work of a philosopher. "The condition of consciousness is" not "distinction" in the understanding-conception of that term. So consciousness is not a limitation, though all limits when cognized are seen in the light of consciousness. According to the philosophy we advocate, God is a particular being, and is so known; yet he is not known as "one thing out of many," but is known in himself, as being such and such, and yet being *unique*. When Mr. Mansel says, "In assuming the possibility of an infinite object of consciousness, I assume, therefore, that it is at the same time limited and unlimited," he evidently uses those terms with a signification pertinent only to the Understanding. He is thinking of *amount* under the forms of Space and Time; and so his remark has no validity. He who thinks of God rightly, will think of him as the infinite and absolute spiritual Person; and will define infinity and absoluteness in accordance therewith.

If the views now advanced are presentations of truth, a consistent rationalism *must* attribute "consciousness to God." *We* are always conscious of "limitation and change," because partiality and growth are organic with us. But we can perceive no peculiarity in consciousness, which should produce such an effect. On the contrary we see, that if a person has little knowledge, he will be conscious of so much and no more. And if a person has great capabilities, and corresponding information, he is conscious of just so much. Whence, it appears, that the "limitation and change" spring from the nature of the constitution, and not from the consciousness. If, then, there should be one Person who possessed the sum of all excellencies, there could arise no reason from consciousness why he should not be conscious thereof.

Mr. Mansel names as the "second characteristic of Consciousness, that it is only possible in the form of a *relation*. There must be a Subject, or person conscious, and an Object or thing of which he is conscious." This utterance, taken in the sense which Mr. Mansel wishes to convey, involves the denial of consciousness to God. But upon the ground that the subject and object in the Deity are always identical the difficulty vanishes. But how can man be "conscious of the Absolute?" If by this is meant, have an exhaustive comprehension of the absolute Person, the experience is manifestly impossible. But man may have a certain knowledge, *that* such Person is without knowing in all respects *what* he is, just as a child may know that an apple is, without knowing what it is. Again Mr. Mansel uses the terms absolute and infinite to represent a simple unanalyzable Being. In this he is guilty of personifying an abstract term, and then reasoning with regard to the Being as he would with regard to the term. Absoluteness is a simple unanalyzable idea, but it is not God; it is only one quality of God. So with infinity. God is universal complexity; and to reason of him as unanalyzable simplicity is as absurd as to select the color of the apple's skin, and call that the apple, and then reason from it about the apple. So, then, though man cannot comprehend the absolute Person *as such*, he has a positive idea of absoluteness, and a positive knowledge that the Being is who is thus qualified. Upon the subsequent question respecting the partiality of our knowledge of the infinite and absolute Person, a remark made above may be repeated and amplified. We may have a true, clear, thorough knowledge *that* he exists without having an exhaustive knowledge of *what* he is. The former is necessary to us; the latter impossible. So, too, the knowledge by us, of any *a priori* law, will be exhaustive. Yet while we know that it *must* be such, and not otherwise, it neither follows that we know all other *a priori* laws, nor that we know all the exemplifications of this one. And since, as we have heretofore seen, neither absoluteness nor infinity relate to number, and God is not material substance that can be broken into "parts," but an organized Spirit, we see that we may consider the elements of his organization in their logical order; and, remembering that absoluteness and infinity as qualities pervade all, we may examine his nature and attributes without impiety.

Mr. Mansel says further: "But in truth it is obvious, on a moment's reflection, that neither the Absolute nor the Infinite can be represented in the form of a whole composed of parts." This is tantamount to saying, the spiritual cannot be represented under the form of the material — a truth so evident as hardly to need so formal a statement. But what the Divine means is, that that Being cannot be known as having qualities and attributes which may be distinguished in and from himself; which is an error. God is infinite. So is his Knowledge, his Wisdom, his Holiness, his Love, &c. Yet these are distinguished from each other, and from him. All this is consistent, because infinity is *quality*, and permeates them all; and not amount, which jumbles them all into a confused, *indistinguishable* mass.

In speaking of "human consciousness" as "necessarily subject to the law of Time," Mr. Mansel says, "Every object of whose existence we can be in any way conscious is necessarily apprehended by us as succeeding in time to some former object of consciousness, and as itself occupying a certain portion of time." In so far as there is here expressed the law of created beings, under which they must see objects, the remark is true. But when Mr. Mansel proceeds further, and concludes that, because we are under limitation in seeing the object, it is under the same limitation, so far as we apprehend it in being seen, he asserts what is a psychological error. To show this, take the mathematical axiom, "Things which are equal to the same things, are equal to one another." Except under the conditions of Time, we cannot see this, that is, we do, must, occupy a time in observing it. But do we see that the axiom is under any condition of Time? By no means. We see, directly, that it is, *must be*, true, and that in itself it has no relation to Time. It is thus *absolutely* true; and as one of the ideas of the infinite and absolute Person, it possesses these his qualities. We have, then, a faculty, the Reason, which, while it sees its objects in succession, and so under the law of Time, also sees that those objects, whether ideas, or that Being to whom all ideas belong, are, *in themselves*, out of all relation to Time. Thus is the created spiritual person endowed; thus is he like God; thus does he know "the Infinite." Hence, "the command, so often urged upon man by philosophers and theologians, 'In contemplating God, transcend time,'" means, "In all your reflections upon God, behold him in his true aspect, in the reason-idea, as out of all relation." It is true that "to know the infinite" *exhaustively*, "the human mind must itself be infinite." But this knowledge is not required of that mind. Only that knowledge is required which is possible, viz., that the Deity is, and what he is, *in so far as we are in his image.*

Again; personality is not "essentially a limitation and a relation," in the sense that it necessarily detracts aught from any being who possesses it. It rather adds, — is, indeed, a pure addition. We appear to ourselves as limited and related, not because of our personality, but because of our finiteness as *quality* in the personality.

Hence we not only see no reason why the complete and universal Spirit should not have personality, but we see that if he was destitute of it, he must possess a lower form of being, — since this is the highest possible form, — which would be an undoubted limitation; or, in other words, we see that he must be a Person. In what Mr. Mansel subsequently says upon this subject, he presents arguments for the personality of God so strong, that one is bewildered with the question, "How could he escape the conviction which they awaken? How could he reject the cry of his spiritual nature, and accept the barren contradictions of his lower mind?" Let us note a few sentences. "It is by consciousness alone that we know that God exists, or that we are able to offer him any service. It is only by conceiving Him as a Conscious Being, that we can stand in any religious relation to Him at all, — that we can form such a representation of Him as is demanded by our spiritual wants, insufficient though it be to satisfy our intellectual curiosity." "Personality comprises all that we know of that which exists; relation to personality comprises all that we know of that which seems to exist. And when, from the little world of man's consciousness and its objects, we would lift up our eyes to the inexhaustible universe beyond, and ask to whom all this is related, the highest existence is still the highest personality, and the Source of all Being reveals Himself by His name, 'I AM.'" "It is our duty, then, to think of God as personal; and it is our duty to believe that He is infinite." We may at this point quote with profit the words of that Book whose authority Mr. Mansel, without doubt, most heartily acknowledges. "And for this cause God shall send them strong delusion, that they should believe a lie; that they all might be damned who believed not the truth, but had pleasure in unrighteousness." "I have not written unto you because ye know not the truth, but because ye know it, and that no lie is of the truth." Either God is personal or he is not. If he is, then all that we claim is conceded. If he is not personal, and "it is our duty to think" of him as personal, then it is our duty to think and believe a *falsehood.* This no man, at least neither Mr. Mansel nor any other enlightened man, *can* bring his mind to accept as a moral law. The soul instinctively asserts that obligation lies parallel with *truth*, and "that no lie is of the truth." So, then, there can be no duty except where truth is. And the converse may also be accepted, viz: Where an enlightened sense of duty is, there is truth. When, therefore, so learned and truly spiritual a man as Mr. Mansel asserts "that it is our duty to think God personal, and believe him infinite," we unhesitatingly accept it as the utterance of a great fundamental truth in that spiritual realm which is the highest realm of being, and so, as one of the highest truths, and with it we accept all its logical consequences. It is a safe rule anywhere, that if two mental operations seem to clash, and one must be rejected, man should cling to, and trust in the higher — the teaching of the nobler nature. Thus will we do, and from the Divine's own ground will we see the destruction of his philosophy. "It is our duty to think of God as personal," because he is personal; and we know that he is personal because it is our duty to think him so. We need pay no regard to the perplexities of the Understanding. We soar with the eagle above the clouds, and float ever in the light of the Sun. The teachings of the Moral Sense are far more sure, safe, and satisfactory than any discursions of the lower faculty. Therefore it is man's wisdom, in all perplexity to heed the cry of his highest nature, and determine to stand on its teachings, as his highest knowledge, interpret all utterances by this, and reject all which contradict it. At the least, the declaration of this faculty is *as* valid as that of the lower, and is to be more trusted in every disagreement, because higher. Still further, no man would believe that God, in the most solemn, yea, awful moment of his Self-revelation, would declare a lie. The bare thought, fully formed, horrifies the soul as a blasphemy of the damned. Yet, in that supreme act, in the solitude of the Sinaitic wilderness, to one of the greatest, one of the profoundest, most devout of men, He revealed Himself by the pregnant words, "I AM": the most positive, the most unquestionable form in which He could utter the fact of His personality. This, then, and all that is involved in it, we accept as truth; and all perplexities must be interpreted by this surety.

In summing up the results to which an examination of the facts of consciousness conducted him, Mr. Mansel utters the following psychological error: "But a limit is necessarily conceived as a relation between something within and something without itself; and the consciousness of a limit of thought implies, though it does not directly present to us, the existence of something of which we do not and cannot think." Not so; for a limit may be seen to be wholly within the being to whom it belongs, and so *not* to be "a relation between something within and something without itself." This is precisely the case with the Deity. All relations and limits spring from within him, and there is nothing "without" to establish the relation claimed. This absence of all limit from without is rudely expressed in such common phrases as this: "It must be so in the *nature of things*." This "nature of things" is, in philosophical language, the system of *a priori* laws of the Universe, and these are necessary ideas in the Divine Reason. It appears, then, that what must be in the nature of things, finds its limits wholly within, and its relations established by the Deity.

With these remarks the author would close his criticism

upon Mr. Mansel's book. We start from entirely different bases, and these two systems logically follow from their foundations. If Sir William Hamilton is right in his psychology, his follower is unquestionably right in his deductions. But if that psychology is partial, if besides the Understanding there is the Reason, if above the judgment stands the intuition, giving the final standard by which to measure that judgment, then is the philosophical system of the Divine utterly fallacious. The establishment of the validity of the Pure Reason is the annihilation of "the Philosophy of the Unconditioned." On the ground which the author has adopted, it is seen that "God is a spirit," infinite, absolute, self-conscious, personal; and a consistent interpretation of these terms has been given. We have found that certain objects may be seen as out of all relation, plurality, difference, or likeness. Consciousness and personality have also been found to involve no limit, in the proper sense of that term. On the contrary, the one was ascertained to be the light in which any or all objects might be seen under conditions of Time, or at once; and that this seeing was according to the capacity with which the being was endowed, and was not determined by any peculiarity of the consciousness; while the other appeared to be the highest possible form of existence, and that also in which God had revealed himself. From such a ground it is possible to go forward and construct a Rational Theology which shall verify by Reason the teachings of the Bible.

REVIEW OF MR. HERBERT SPENCER'S "FIRST PRINCIPLES."

In the criticisms heretofore made, some points, held in common by the three writers named early in this work, have been, it may be, passed over unnoticed. This was done, because, being held in common, it was believed that an examination of them, as presented by the latest writer, would be most satisfactory. Therefore, what was peculiar in thought or expression to Sir Wm. Hamilton or Mr. Mansel, we have intended to notice when speaking of those writers. But where Mr. Spencer seems to present their very thought as his own, it has appeared better to remark upon it in his latest form of expression. Mr. Spencer also holds views peculiar to himself. These we shall examine in their place. And for convenience' sake, what we have to say will take the form of a running commentary upon those chapters entitled, "Ultimate Religious Ideas," "Ultimate Scientific Ideas," "The Relativity of all Knowledge," and "The Reconciliation." Before entering upon this, however, some general remarks will be pertinent.

1. Like his teachers, Mr. Spencer believes that the Understanding is the highest faculty of the human intellect. This is implied in the following sentence: "Those imbecilities of the understanding that disclose themselves when we try to answer the highest questions of objective science, subjective science proves to be necessitated by the laws of that understanding." — *First Principles*, p. 98.

His illustrations, also, are all, or nearly all, taken from sensuous objects. In speaking of the Universe, evidently the *material* Universe is present to his mind. His questions refer to objects of sense, and he shows plainly enough that any attempt to answer them by the Sense or Understanding is futile. Hence he concludes that they cannot be answered. But those who "know of a surety," that man is more than an animal nature, containing a Sense and an Understanding; that he is also a spiritual person, having an *Eye*, the pure Reason, which can *see* straight to the central Truth, with a clearness and in a light which dims and pales the noonday sun, know also that, and how, these difficulties, insoluble to the lower faculties, are, in this noble alembic, finally dissolved.

2. As Mr. Spencer follows his teachers in the psychology of man's faculties, so does he also in the use of terms. Like them, he employs only such terms as are pertinent to the Sense and Understanding. So also with them he is at fault, in that he raises questions which no Sense or Understanding could suggest even, questions whose very presence are decisive that a Pure Reason is organic in man; and then is guilty of applying to them terms entirely impertinent, — terms belonging only to those lower tribunals before which these questions can never come. For instance, he always employs the word "conceive" to express the effort of the mind in presenting to itself the subjects now under discussion. In some form of noun, verb, or adjective, this word seems to have rained upon his pages; while such terms as "infinite period," "infinitely divisible," "absolutely incompressible," "infinitesimal," and the like, dot them repeatedly. Let us revert, then, a moment to the positions attained in an earlier portion of this work. It was there found that the word conceive was *utterly irrelevant* to any subject except to objects of Sense and the Understanding in its work of classifying them, or generalizing from them, so, also, with regard to the other terms quoted, it was found that they not only presented no object of thought to the mind, but that the words had no relation to each other, and could not properly be used together. For instance, infinite has no more relation to, and can no more qualify period, than the points of the compass are pertinent to, and can

qualify the affections. The phrase, infinite period, is simply absurd, and so also are the others. The words infinite and absolute have nothing to do with amount of any sort. They can be pertinent only to God and his *a priori* ideas. Many, perhaps most of the criticisms in detail we shall have to make, will be based on this single misuse of words; which yet grows naturally out of that denial and perversion of faculties which Mr. Spencer, in common with the other Limitist writers, has attempted. On the other hand, it is to be remembered, that, if we arrive at the truth at all, we must *intuit* it; we must either see it as a simple *a priori* idea, or as a logical deduction from such ideas.

3. A third, and graver error on Mr. Spencer's part is, that he goes on propounding his questions, and asserting that they are insoluble, apparently as unconscious as a sleeper in an enchanted castle that they have all been solved, or at least that the principles on which it would seem that they could be solved have been stated by a man of no mean ability, — Dr. Hickok, — and that until the proposed solutions are thoroughly analyzed and shown to be unsound, his own pages are idle. He implies that there is no cognition higher than a conception, when some very respectable writers have named intuitions as incomparably superior. He speaks of the Understanding as if it were without question the highest faculty of man's intellect, when no less a person than Coleridge said it would satisfy his life's labor to have introduced into English thinking the distinction between the Understanding, as "the faculty judging according to sense," and the Reason, as "the power of universal and necessary convictions," which, being such, must necessarily rank far above the other. And finally he uses the words and phrases above disallowed, and the faculties to which they belong, in an attempt to prove, by the citation of a few items in an experience, what had already been demonstrated by another in a process of as pure reasoning as Calculus. No one, it is believed, can master the volume heretofore alluded to, entitled "Rational Psychology," and so

appreciate the *demonstration* therein contained, of the utter incompetency of the Sense or Understanding to solve such questions as Mr. Spencer has raised by his incident of the partridge, (p. 69,) and the utter irrelevancy to them of the efforts of those faculties, without feeling how tame and unsatisfactory in comparison is the evidence drawn from a few facts in a sensuous experience. One cares not to see a half dozen proofs, more or less that a theory is fallacious who has learned that, and why, the theory *cannot* be true. Let us now take up in order the chapters heretofore mentioned.

"ULTIMATE RELIGIOUS IDEAS."

The summing up of certain reflections with which this chapter opens, concludes thus: "But that when our symbolic conceptions are such that no cumulative or indirect processes of thought can enable us to ascertain that there are corresponding actualities, nor any predictions be made whose fulfilment can prove this, then they are altogether vicious and illusive, and in no way distinguishable from pure fictions,"—p. 29. So far very good; but his use of it is utterly unsound. "And now to consider the bearings of this general truth on our immediate topic — Ultimate Religious Ideas." But this "general truth" has *no* bearings upon "ultimate religious ideas"; how then can you consider them? *No* ideas, and most of all religious ideas, are conceptions, or the results of conceptions — or are the products of "cumulative or indirect processes of thought." They are not results or products *at all.* They are organic, are the spontaneous presentation of what is inborn, and so must be directly seen to be known at all. Man might pile up "cumulative processes of thought" for unnumbered ages, and might form most exact conceptions of objects of Sense,—conceptions are not possible of others,—and he could never creep up to the least and faintest religious idea.

On the next page, speaking of "suppositions respecting the origin of the Universe," Mr. Spencer says, "The deeper question is, whether any one of them is even conceivable in the true sense of that word. Let us successively test them." This is not necessary. It has already been *demonstrated* that a conception, or any effort of the Understanding, cannot touch, or have relation to such topics. But it does not follow, therefore, that no one of them is cognizable at all; which he implies. Take the abstract notion of self-existence, for example. No "vague symbolic conceptions," or any conception at all, of it *can be formed.* A conception is possible only "under relation, difference, and plurality." *This* is a pure, simple idea, and so can only be known in itself by a seeing — an immediate intuition. It is seen by itself, as out of all relation. It is seen as simple, and so is learned by no difference. It is seen as a unit, and so out of all plurality. The discursive faculty cannot pass over it, because there are in it no various points upon which that faculty may fasten. It may, perhaps, better be expressed by the words pure independence. Again, it is *not* properly "existence without a beginning," but rather, existence out of all relation to beginning; and so it is an idea, out of all relation to those faculties which are confined to objects that did begin. Because we can "by no mental effort" "form a conception of existence without a beginning," it does not follow that we cannot *see* that a Being existing out of all relation to beginning *is.* "To this let us add" that the intuition of such a Being is a complete "explanation of the Universe," and does make it "easier to understand" "that it existed an hour ago, a day ago, a year ago"; for we see that this Being primarily is *out of all relation to time,* that there is no such thing as an "infinite period," the phrase being absurd; but that through all the procession of events which we call time he *is*; and that before that procession began — when there was no time, he was. Thus we see that all events are based upon Him who is independent; and that time, in our general use of it, is but the measure of what He produces. We arrive, then, at the conclusion that the Universe is not self-existent, not because self-existence cannot be object to the human mind, and be clearly seen to be an attribute of one Being, but because the Universe is primarily object to faculties in that mind, which cannot entertain such a notion at all; and because this notion is *seen* to be a necessary idea in the province of that higher faculty which entertains as objects both the idea and the Being to whom it primarily belongs.

The theory that the Universe is self-existent is Pantheism, and not the theory that it is self-created, though this latter, in Mr. Spencer's definition of it, seems only a phase of the other. To say that "self-creation is potential existence passing into actual existence by some inherent necessity," is only to remove self-existence one step farther back, as he himself shows. Potential existence is either no existence at all, or it is positive existence. If it is no existence, then we have true self-creation; which is, that out of nothing, and with no cause, actual existence starts itself. This is not only unthinkable, but absurd. But if potential existence is positive, it needs to be accounted for as much as actual. While, then, there can be no doubt as to the validity of the conclusions to which Mr. Spencer arrives, respecting the entire incompetency of the hypotheses of self-existence and self-creation, to account for the Universe, the distinction made above between self-existence as a true and self-creation as a pseudo idea, and the fact that the true idea is a *reality*, should never be lost sight of. By failing to discriminate — as in the Understanding he could not do — between them, and by concluding both as objects alike impossible to the human intellect, and for the same reasons, he has also decided that the "commonly received or theistic hypothesis"— creation by external agency — is equally untenable. In his examination of this, he starts as usual with his ever-present, fallacious assumption, that this is a "conception"; that it can be, *is* founded upon a "cumulative process of thought, or the fulfilment of predictions based on it." These words, phrases, and notions, are all irrelevant. It is not a conception, process, or prediction that we want; it is a *sight.* Hence, no assumptions have to be made or granted. No "proceedings of a human artificer" *can in the least degree* "vaguely symbolize to us" the "method after which the Universe" was "shaped." This differed in *kind* from all possible human methods, and had not one element in common with them.

Mr. Spencer's remarks at this point upon Space do not appear to be well grounded. "An immeasurable void" — Space — is not an entity, is *no* thing, and therefore cannot "exist," neither is any explanation for it needed. His question, "how came it so?" takes, then, this form: How came immeasurable nothing to be nothing? Nothing needs no "explanation." It is only *some* thing which must be accounted for. The theory of creation by external agency being, then, an adequate one to account for the Universe, supplies the following statement. That Being who is primarily out of all relation, produced, from himself, and by his immanent power, into nothing — Space, room, the condition of material existence, — something, matter and the Universe became. "The genesis of the universe" having thus been explained and seen to be "the result of external agency," we are ready to furnish for the question, "how came there to be an external agency?" that true answer, which we have already shadowed forth. That pure spiritual Person who is necessarily existent, or self-existent, *i. e.* who possesses pure independence as an essential attribute, whose being is thus fixed, and is therefore without the province of power, is the external agency which is needed. This Person, differing in kind from the Universe, cannot be found in it, nor concluded from it, but can only be known by being seen, and can only be seen because man possesses the endowment of a spiritual *Eye*, like in kind to His own All-seeing eye, by which spiritual things may be discerned. This Person, being thus seen immediately, is known in a far more satisfactory mode than he could be by any generalizations of the Understanding, could he be represented in these at all. The knowledge of Him is, like His self, *immutable*. We KNOW that we stand on the eternal Rock. Our eye is illuminated with the unwavering Light which radiates from the throne of God. Nor is this any hallucination of the rhapsodist. It is the simple experience which every one enjoys who looks at pure truth in itself. It is the Pure Reason seeing, by an immediate intuition, God as pure spirit, revealed directly to itself. It is, then, because self-existence is a pure, simple idea, organic in man, and seen by him to be an attribute of God, that God is known to be the Creator of the Universe. Having attained to this truth, we readily see that the conclusions which Mr. Spencer states on pages 35, 36, as that "self-existence is rigorously inconceivable"; that the theistic hypothesis equally with the others is "literally unthinkable"; that "our conception of self-existence can be formed only by joining with it the notion of unlimited duration through past time"; so far as they imply our destitution of knowledge on these topics, are the opposite of the facts. We *see*, though we cannot "conceive," self-existence. The theistic hypothesis becomes, therefore, literally thinkable. We see, also, that unlimited duration is an absurdity; that duration must be limited; and that self-existence involves existence out of all relation to duration.

Mr. Spencer then turns to the nature of the Universe, and says: "We find ourselves on the one hand obliged to make certain assumptions, and yet, on the other hand, we find these assumptions cannot be represented in thought." Upon this it may be remarked:

1. What are here called assumptions are properly assertions, which man makes, and cannot help making, except he deny himself; — necessary convictions, first truths, first principles, *a priori* ideas. They are organic, and so are the foundation of all knowledge. They are not results learned from lessons, but are *primary*, and conditional to an ability

to learn. But supposing them to be assumptions, having, at most, no more groundwork than a vague guess, there devolves a labor which Mr. Spencer and his coadjutors have never attempted, and which, we are persuaded, they would find the most difficult of all, viz., to account for the fact of these assumptions. For the question is pertinent and urgent;

2. How came these assumptions to suggest themselves? Where, for instance, did the notion of self come from? Analyze the rocks, study plants and their growth, become familiar with animals and their habits, or exhaust the Sense in an examination of man, and one can find no notion of self. Yet the notion is, and is peculiar to man. How does it arise? Is it "created by the slow action of natural causes?" How comes it to belong, then, to the rudest aboriginal equally with the most civilized and cultivated? Was it "created" from nothing or from something? If from something, how came that something to be? We might ask, Does not the presentation of any phenomenon involve the actuality of a somewhat, in which that phenomenon inheres, and of a receptivity by which it is appreciated? Does not the fact of this assumption, as a mental phenomenon, involve the higher fact of some mental ground, some form, some capacity, which is both organic to the mind, and organized in the mind, in accordance with which the assumption is, and which determines what it must be? Or are we to believe that these assumptions are mere happenings, without law, and for which no reason can be assigned? Again we press the question, How came these assumptions to suggest themselves?

3. "These assumptions cannot be represented in thought." If "thought" is restricted to that mental operation of the Understanding by which it generalizes in accordance with the Sense, the statement is true. But if it is meant, as seems to be implied, that the notions expressed in these assumptions are not, cannot be, clearly and definitely known at all by the mind, then it is directly contrary to the truth. The ideas presented by the phrases are, as was seen above, clear and definite.

Since Mr. Spencer has quoted *in extenso*, and with entire approbation, what Mr. Mansel says respecting "the Cause, the Absolute, and the Infinite," we have placed the full examination of these topics in our remarks upon Mr. Mansel's writings, and shall set down only a few brief notes here.

Upon this topic Mr. Spencer admits that "we are obliged to suppose *some* cause"; or, in other words, that the notion of cause is organic. Then we must "inevitably commit ourselves to the hypothesis of a First Cause." Then, this First Cause "must be infinite." Then, "it must be independent;" "or, to use the established word, it must be absolute." One would almost suppose that a *rational* man penned these decisions, instead of one who denies that he has a *reason*. The illusion is quickly dispelled, however, by the objections he lifts out of the dingy ground-room of the Understanding. It is curious to observe in these pages a fact which we have noticed before, in speaking of Sir William Hamilton's works, viz: how, on the same page, and in the same sentence, the workings of the Understanding and Reason will run along side by side, the former all the while befogging and hindering the latter. Mr. Spencer's conclusions which we have quoted, and his objections which we are to answer, are a striking exemplification of this. Frequently in his remarks he uses the words limited and unlimited, as synonymous with finite and infinite, when they are not so, and cannot be used interchangeably with propriety. The former belong wholly in the Sense and Understanding. The latter belong wholly in the Pure Reason. The former pertain to material objects, to mental images of them, or to number. The latter qualify only spiritual persons, and have no pertinence elsewhere. Limitation is the conception of an object *as bounded*. Illimitation is the conception of an object as without boundaries. Rigidly, it is a simple negation of boundaries, and gives nothing positive in the Concept. Finity or finiteness corresponds in the Reason to limitation in the Sense and Understanding. It does not refer to boundaries at all. It belongs only to created spiritual persons, and expresses the fact that they are partial, and must grow and learn. Only by its place in the antithesis does infinity correspond in the Reason to illimitation in the lower faculties. It is *positive,* and is that quality of the pure spirit which is otherwise known as *universality.* It expresses the idea of *all possible endowments in perfect harmony.* From his misuse of these terms Mr. Spencer is led to speak in an irrelevant manner upon the question, "Is the First Cause finite or infinite?" He uses words and treats the whole matter as if it were a question of material substance, which might be "bounded," with a "region surrounding its boundaries," and the like, which are as out of place as to say white love or yellow kindness. His methods of thought on these topics are also gravely erroneous. He attempts an analysis by the logical Understanding, where a synthesis by the Reason is required, — a synthesis which has already been given by our Creator to man as an original idea. It is not necessary to examine some limited thing, or all limited things, and wander around their boundaries to learn that the First Cause is infinite. We need to make no discursus, but only to look the idea of first cause through and through, and thoroughly analyze it, to find all the truth. By such a process we would find all that Mr. Spencer concedes that "we are obliged to suppose," and further, that such a being *must be* self-existent. And this conviction would be so strong that the mind would rest itself in this decision: "A thousand phantasmagoria of the imagination may be wrong," says the soul, "but this I know must be true, or there is no truth in the Universe."

One sentence in the paragraph now under consideration deserves special notice. It is this. "But if we admit that there can be some thing uncaused, there is no reason to assume a cause for anything." This "assumes" the truth of a major premise all *things* are substantially alike. If the word "thing" is restricted to its exact limits, — objects of sense, — then the sentence pertains wholly to the Sense and

Understanding, and is true. But if, as it would seem, the implication is meant that there are no other entities which can be object to the mind except such "things," then it is a clear *petitio principii.* For the very question at issue is, whether, in fact, there is not one entity — "thing" — which so differs in kind from all others, that it is uncaused, *i. e.* self-existent; and whether the admission that that entity is uncaused does not, because of this seen difference, satisfy the mind, and furnish a reasonable ground on which to account for the subordinate causes which we observe by the Sense.

In speaking of the First Cause as "independent," he says, "but it can have no necessary relation within itself. There can be nothing in it which determines change, and yet nothing which prevents change. For if it contains something which imposes such necessities or restraints, this something must be a cause higher than the First Cause, which is absurd. Thus, the First Cause must be in every sense perfect, complete, total, including within itself all power, and transcending all law." We cannot criticize this better, and mark how curiously truth and error are mixed in it, than by so parodying it that only truth shall be stated. The First Cause possesses within himself all possible relations as belonging to his necessary ideals. Hence, change, in the exact sense of that term, is impossible to him, for there is nothing for him to *change to.* This is not invalidated by his passing from inaction to action; for creation involves no change in God's nature or attributes, and so no real or essential change, which is here meant. But he is the permanent, through whom all changes become. He is not, then, a *simple* unit, but is an organized Being, who is ground for, and comprehends in a unity, all possible laws, forms, and relations, as necessary elements of his necessary existence, — as endowments which necessarily belong to him, and are conditional of his pure independence. Hence, these restraints are not "imposed" upon him, except as his existence is imposed upon him. They belong to his Self, and are conditional of his being. So, then, instead of "transcending all law," he is the embodiment of all law; and his perfection is, that possessing this endowment, he accords his conduct thereto. A being who should "transcend all law" would have no reason why he should act, and no form how he should act, neither would he be an organism, but would be pure lawlessness or pure chaos. Pure chaos cannot organize order; pure lawlessness cannot establish law; and so could not be the First Cause. As Mr. Spencer truly says, "we have no alternative but to regard this First Cause as Infinite and Absolute."

And now having learned, by a true diagnosis of the mental activities, that the positions we have gained are fixed, final, irrevocable; and further, that they are not the "results" of "reasonings," but that first there was a seeing, and then an analysis of what was seen, and that the seeing is *true*, though every other experience be false; we *know* that our position is not "illusive," but that we stand on the rock; and that what we have seen is no "symbolic conception of the illegitimate order," but is pure truth.

For the further consideration of this subject, the reader is referred back to our remarks on that passage in Mr. Mansel's work, which Mr. Spencer has quoted.

A few remarks upon his summing up, p. 43 *et seq.*, will complete the review of this chapter. "Passing over the consideration of credibility, and confining ourselves to that of" consistency, we would find in any rigorous analysis, that Atheism and Pantheism are self-contradictory; but we *have found* that Theism, "when rigorously analyzed," presents an absolutely consistent system, in which all the difficulties of the Understanding are explained to the person by the Reason, and is entirely thinkable. Such a system, based upon the necessary convictions of man, and justly commanding that these shall be the fixed standard, in accordance with which all doubts and queries shall be dissolved and decided, gives a rational satisfaction to man, and discloses to him his eternal Rest.

In proceeding to his final fact, which he derives as the permanent in all religions, Mr. Spencer overlooks another equally permanent, equally common, and incomparably more important fact, viz: that Fetishism, Polytheism, Pantheism, and Monotheism, — all religions alike assert *that a god created the Universe.* In other words, the great common element, in all the popular modes of accounting for the vast system of things in which we live is, *that it is the product of an agency external to itself, and that the external agency is personal.* Take the case of the rude aboriginal, who "assumes a separate personality behind every phenomenon." He does not attempt to account for all objects. His mind is too infantile, and he is too degraded to suspect that those material objects which appear permanent need to be accounted for. It is only the changes which seem to him to need a reason. Behind each change he imagines a sort of personal power, superior to it and man, which produces it, and this satisfies him. He inquires no further; yet he looks in the same direction as the Monotheist. In this crude form of belief, which is named Fetishism, we see that essential idea which can be readily traced through all forms of religion, that some *personal* being, external, and superior to the things that be, produced them. Nor is Atheism a proper exception to this law. For Atheism is not a religion, but the denial of all religion. It is not a doctrine of God, but is a denial that there is any God; and what is most in point, it never was a *popular* belief, but is only a philosophical Sahara over which a few caravans of speculative doubters and negatists wander. Neither can Hindu pantheism be quoted against the position taken: for Brahm is not the Universe; neither are Brahma, Vishnu, and Siva. Brahm does not lose his individuality because the Universe is evolved from him. *Now* he is thought of as one, and the Universe as another, although the Universe is thought to be a part of his essence, and hereafter to be reabsorbed by him. *Now,* this part of his essence which was *produced* through Brahma, Vishnu, and Siva, is *individualized*; and so is one, while he is another. Thus, here also, the idea of a proper external agency is preserved. The facts, then, are decisively in favor of the proposition above laid down. "*Our* investigation" discloses "a fundamental verity in each religion." And the facts and the verity find no consistent ground except in a pure Theism, and there they do find perfect consistency and harmony.

It is required, finally, in closing the discussion of this chapter, to account for the fact that, upon a single idea so many theories of God have fastened themselves; or better, perhaps, that a single idea has developed itself in so many forms. This cannot better be done than in the language of that metaphysician, not second to Plato, the apostle Paul. In his Epistle to the Romans, beginning at the 19th verse of the 1st chapter, he says: "Because that which may be known of God is manifest to them; for God hath shewed it unto them. For the invisible things of him from the creation of the world are clearly seen, being understood by the things which are made, even his eternal power and Godhead, so that they are without excuse. Because that, when they knew God, they glorified him not as God, neither were thankful; but became vain in their imaginations, and their foolish heart was darkened: professing themselves to be wise they became fools, and changed the glory of the incorruptible God into an image made like to corruptible man, and to birds, and four-footed beasts, and creeping things." This passage, which would be worthy the admiring study of ages, did it possess no claim to be the teaching of that Being whom Mr. Spencer asserts it is *impossible for us to know*, gives us in a popular form the truth. Man, having organic in his mind the idea of God, and having in the Universe an ample manifestation to the Sense, of the eternal power and Godhead of the Creator of that Universe, corresponding to that idea, perverted the manifestation to the Sense, and degraded the idea in the Reason, to the service of base passion. By this degradation and perversion the organic idea became so bedizened with the finery of fancy formed in the Understanding, under the direction of the animal nature, as to be lost to the popular mind, — the trappings only being seen. When once the truth was thus lost sight of, and with it all that restraint which a knowledge of the true God would impose, men became vain in their imaginations; their fancy ran riot in all directions. Cutting loose from all law, they plunged into every excess which could be invented; and out of such a stimulated and teeming brain all manner of vagaries were devised. This was the first stage; and of it we find some historic hints in the biblical account of the times, during and previous to the life of Abraham. Where secular history begins the human race had passed into the second stage. Crystallization had begun. Students were commencing the search for truth. Religion was taking upon itself more distinct forms. The organic idea, which could not be wholly obliterated, formed itself distinctly in the consciousness of some gifted individuals, and philosophy began. Philosophy in its purest form, as taught by Socrates and Plato, presented again the lost idea of pure Theism. But the spirituality which enabled them to see the truth, lifted them so far above the common people, that they could affect only a few. And what was most disheartening, that same degradation which originally lost to man the truth, now prevented him from receiving it. Thus it was that by a binding of the Reason to the wheels of Passion, and discursing through the world with the Understanding at the beck of the Sense, the many forms of religion became.

"ULTIMATE SCIENTIFIC IDEAS."

On a former page we have already attempted a positive answer to the question, "What are Space and Time," with which Mr. Spencer opens this chapter. It was there found that, in general terms, they are *a priori* conditions of created being; and, moreover, that they possess characteristics suitable to what they condition, just as the *a priori* conditions of the spiritual person possess characteristics suitable to what they condition. It was further found that this general law is, from the necessity of the case, realized both within the mind and without it; that it is, must be, the form of thought for the perceiving subject, corresponding to the condition of existence for the perceived object. It also appeared that the Universe as object, and the Sense and Understanding as faculties in the subject, thus corresponded; and further, that these faculties could never transcend and comprehend Space and Time, because these were the very conditions of their being; moreover, that by them all spaces and times must be considered with reference to the Universe, and apart from it could not be examined by them at all. Yet it was further found that the Universe might in the presence of the Reason be abstracted; and that, then, pure Space and Time still remained as pure *a priori* conditions, the one as *room*, the other as *opportunity*, for the coming of created being. Space and Time being such conditions, *and nothing more*, are entities only in the same sense that the multiplication table and the moral law are entities. They are *conditions* suited to what they condition. In the light of this result let us examine Mr. Spencer's teachings respecting them.

Strictly speaking, Space and Time do not "exist." If they exist (ex sto), they must stand out somewhere and when. This of course involves the being of a where and a when in which they can stand out; and that where and when must needs be accounted for, and so on *ad infinitum*. Again, Mr. Spencer would seem to speak, in his usual style, as if they, in existing "objectively," had a *formal* objective existence. Yet this, in the very statement of it, appears absurd. The mind apprehends many objects, which do not "exist." They only are. Thus, as has just been said, Space and Time, as conditions of created being, *are*. They are entities but not existences. They are *a priori* entities, and so are *necessarily*. By this they stand in the same category with all pure laws, all first principles.

"Moreover, to deny that Space and Time are things, and so by implication to call them nothings, involves the absurdity that there are two kinds of nothings." This sentence "involves the absurdity" of assuming that "nothing" is an entity. If I say that Space is nothing, I say that it presents no content for a concept, and cannot, because there is no content to be presented. It is then *blank*. Just so of Time. As nothings they are, then, both equally blank, and destitute of meaning. Now if Mr. Spencer wishes to hold that nothing represented by one word, differs from nothing represented by another, we would not lay a straw in his way, but yet would be much surprised if he led a large company.

Again, having decided that they are neither "nonentities nor the attributes of entities, we have no choice but to consider them as entities." But he then goes on to speak of them as "things," evidently using the word in the same sense as if applying it to a material object, as an apple or stone; thereby implying that entity and thing in that sense are synonymous terms. Upon this leap in the dark, this blunder in the use of language, he proceeds to build up a mountain of difficulties. But once take away this foundation, once cease attempting "to represent them in thought as things," and his difficulties vanish. Space is a condition. Perhaps receptivity, indivisibility, and illimitability are attributes. If so, it has attributes, for these certainly belong to it. But whether these shall be called attributes or not, it is certain that Space is, is a pure condition, is thus a positive object to the Reason, is qualified by the characteristics named above; and all this without any contradiction or other insuperable difficulty arising thereby. On the ground now established, we learn that extension and Space are *not* "convertible terms." Extension is an attribute of matter. Space is a condition of phenomena. It is only all *physical* "entities which we actually know as such" that "are limited." From our standpoint, that Space is *no* thing, such remarks as "We find ourselves totally unable to form any mental image of unbounded Space," appear painfully absurd. "We find ourselves" just as "totally unable to form any mental image of unbounded" love. Such phrases as "mental image" have *no relevancy* to either Space or Time. In criticizing Kant's doctrine, which we have found *true* as far as it goes, Mr. Spencer evinces a surprising lack of knowledge of the facts in question. "In the first place," he says, "to assert that Space and Time, as we are conscious of them, are subjective conditions, is by implication to assert that they are not objective realities." But the conclusion does not follow. If the reader will take the trouble to construct the syllogism on which this is based, he will at once perceive the absurdity of the logic. It may be said in general that all conditions of a thinking being are both subjective and objective: they are conditions of his being — subjective; and they are objects of his examination and cognizance — objective. Is not the multiplication table an objective reality, *i. e.,* would it not remain if he be destroyed? And yet is it not also a subjective law; and so was it not originally discovered by introspection and reflection? Again he says, "for that consciousness of Space and Time which we cannot rid ourselves of, is the consciousness of them as existing objectively." Now the fact is, that primarily we do not have *any* consciousness of Space and Time. *Consciousness has to do with phenomena.* When examining the material Universe, the *objects,* and the objects as at a distance from each other and as during, are what we are conscious of. For instance, I view the planets Jupiter and Saturn. They appear as objects in my consciousness. There is a distance between them; but this distance *is* not, except as they *are.* If they are not, the word distance has no meaning with reference to them. Take them away, and I have no consciousness of distance as remaining. These planets continue in existence. They endure. This endurance we call time, but if they should cease, one could not think of endurance in connection with them as remaining. Here we most freely and willingly agree with Mr. Spencer that "the question is, What does consciousness directly testify?" but he will find that consciousness on this side the water testifies very differently from his consciousness: as for instance in the two articles in the "North American Review," heretofore alluded to. Here, "the direct testimony of consciousness is," that spaces and times within the Universe are without the mind; that Space and Time, as *a priori* conditions for the possibility of formal object and during event, are also without the mind; but the "testimony" is none the less clear and "direct" that Space and Time are laws of thought in the mind corresponding to the actualities without the mind. And the question may be asked, it is believed with great force, If this last were not so, how could the mind take any cognizance of the actuality? Again, most truly, Space and Time "cannot be conceived to become non-existent even were the mind to become non-existent." Much more strongly than this should the truth be uttered. They could not become non-existent if the Universe with every sentient being, yea, even — to make an impossible supposition — if the Deity himself, should cease to be. In this they differ no whit from the laws of Mathematics, of Logic, and of Morals. These too would remain as well. Thus is again enforced the truth, which has been stated heretofore, that Space and Time, as *a priori* conditions of the Universe, stand in precisely the same relation to material object and during event that the multiplication table does to intellect, or the moral law to a spiritual person. It will now be doubtless plain that Mr. Spencer's remarks sprang directly from the lower faculties. The Sense in its very organization possesses Space and Time as void forms into which objects may come. So also the Understanding possesses the notional as connecting into a totality. These faculties cannot be in a living man without acting. Activity is their law. Hence images are ever arising and *must* arise in the Sense, and be connected in the Understanding, and all this in the forms and conditions of Space and Time. He who thinks continually in these conditions will always *imagine* that Space and Time are only without him — because he will be thinking only in the iron prison-house of the imagining faculty — and so cannot transcend the conditions it imposes. Now how shall one see these conditions? They do "exist objectively"; or, to phrase it better, they have a true being independent of our minds. In this sense, as we have seen, every *a priori* condition must be objective to the mind. What is objective to the Sense is not Space but a space, *i. e.* a part of Space limited by matter; and, after all, it is the boundaries which are the true object rather than the space, which cannot be "conceived" of if the boundaries be removed. Without further argument, is it not evident that there Space, like all other *a priori* conditions, is object only to the Reason, and that as a condition of material existence?

At the bottom of page 49 we have another of Mr. Spencer's psychological errors: — "For if Space and Time are forms of thought, they can never be thought of; since it is impossible for anything to be at once the *form* of thought and the matter of thought." Although this topic has been amply discussed elsewhere, it may not be uninstructive to recur to it again. Exactly the opposite of Mr. Spencer's remark is the truth. The question at issue here is one of those profound and subtile ones which cannot be approached by argument, but can be decided only by a *seeing*. It is a psychological question pertaining to the profoundest depths of our being. If one says, "I see the forms of thought," and another, "I cannot see them," neither impeaches the other. All that is left is to stimulate the dull faculty of the one until he can see. The following reflections may help us to see. Mr. Spencer's remark implies that we have no higher faculty than the Sense and the Understanding. It implies, also, that we can never have any *self*-knowledge, in the fundamental signification of that phrase. We can observe the conduct of the mind, and study and classify the results; but the laws, the constitution of the activity itself must forever remain closed to us. As was said, when speaking of this subject under a different phase, the eye cannot see and study itself. It is a mechanical organism, capable only of reaction as acted upon, capable only of seeing results, but never able to penetrate to the hidden springs which underlie the event. Just so is it with the Sense and Understanding. They are mere mechanical faculties capable of acting as they are acted upon, but never able to go behind the appearance to its final source. On such a hypothesis as this all science is impossible, but most of all a science of the human mind. If man is enclosed by such walls, no knowledge of his central self can be gained. He may know what he *does*; but what he *is*, is as inscrutable to him as what God is. As such a being, he is only a higher order of brute. He has some dim perceptions, some vague feelings, but he has no *knowledge*; he is *sure* of nothing. He can reach no gronnd which is ultimate, no *Rock* which he knows is *immutable*. Is man such a being? The longings and aspirations of the ages roll back an unceasing No! He is capable of placing himself before himself, of analyzing that self to the very groundwork of his being. All the laws of his constitution, all the forms of his activity, he can clearly and amply place before himself and know them. And how is this? It is because God has endowed him with an EYE like unto His own, which enables man to be self-comprehending, as He is self-comprehending, — the Reason, with which man may read himself as a child reads a book; that man can make "the *form* of thought the *matter* of thought." True, the Understanding is shut out from any consideration of the forms of thought; but man is not simply or mainly an Understanding. He is, in his highest being, a spiritual person, whom God has endowed with the faculty of VISION; and the great organic evil, which the fall wrought into the world, was this very denial of the spiritual light, and this crowding down and out of sight, of the spiritual person beneath the animal nature, this denial of the essential faculties of such person, and this elevation of the lower faculties of the animal nature, the Sense and Understanding, into the highest place, which is involved in all such teachings as we are criticizing.

Mr. Spencer's remarks upon "Matter" are no nearer the truth. In almost his first sentence there is a grievous logical *faux pas.* He says: "Matter is either infinitely divisible or it is not; no third possibility can be named." Yet we will name one, as follows: *The divisibility of matter has no relation to infinity.* And this *third* supposition happens to be the truth. But it will be said that the question should be stated thus: Either there is a limit to the divisibility of matter, or there is no limit. This statement is exhaustive, because limitation belongs to matter. Of these alternatives there can be no hesitation which one to choose. There is a limit to the divisibility of matter. This answer cannot be given by the physical sense; for no one questions but what it is incapable of finding a limit. The mental sense could not give it, because it is a question of actual substance and not of ideal forms. The Reason gives the answer. Matter is limited at both extremes. Its amount is definite, as are its final elements. These "ultimate parts" have "an under and an upper surface, a right and a left side." When, then, one of these parts shall be broken, what results? Not *pieces,* as the materialist, thinking only in the Sense, would have us believe. When a final "part" shall be broken, there will remain *no matter,* — to the sense nothing. To it, the result would be annihilation. But the Reason declares that there would be left *God's power* in its simplicity, — that final Unit out of which all diversity becomes.

The subsequent difficulties raised respecting the solidity of Matter may be explained thus. And for convenience, sake we will limit the term Matter to such substances as are object to the physical sense, like granite, while Force shall be used to comprise those finer substances, like the Ether, which are impalpable to the physical sense. Matter is composed of very minute ultimate particles which do not touch, but which are held together by Force. The space between the atoms, which would otherwise be *in vacuo*, is *full* of Force. We might be more exhaustive in our analysis, and say — which would be true — that a space-filling force composes the Universe; and that Matter is only Force in one of its modifications. But without this the other statement is sufficient. When, then, a portion of matter is compressed, the force which holds the ultimate particles in their places is overcome by an external force, and these particles are brought nearer together. Now, how is it with the moving body and the collision? Bisect a line, and see the truth.

C

A——————B

1

A body with a mass of 4 is moving with a velocity of 4 along the line from A to B. At C it meets another body with a mass of 4 at rest. From thence the two move on towards B with a velocity of 2. What has happened? In the body there was a certain amount of force, which set it in motion and kept it in motion. And just here let us make a point. *No force is ever lost or destroyed. It is only transferred.* When a bullet is fired from a gun, it possesses at one *point* a maximum of force. From that point this force is steadily *transferred* to the air and other substances, until all that it received from the powder is spent. But at any one point in its flight, the sum of the force which has been transferred since the maximum, and of the force yet to be transferred, will always equal the maximum. Now, how is it respecting the question raised by Mr. Spencer? The instant of contact is a point in time, *not a period*, and the transfer of force is instantaneous. C, then, is a *point*, not a period, and the velocity on the one side is 4 and the other side 2, while the momentum or force is exactly equal throughout the line. If it is said that this proves that a body can pass from one velocity to another without passing through the intermediate velocities, we cannot help it. The above are the facts, and they give the truth. The following sentence of Mr. Spencer is, at least, careless. "For when, of two such units, one moving at velocity 4 strikes another at rest, the striking unit must have its velocity 4 instantaneously reduced to velocity 2; must pass from velocity 4 to velocity 2 without any lapse of time, and without passing through intermediate velocities; must be moving with velocities 4 and 2 at the same instant, which is impossible." If there is any sense in the remark, "instantaneously" must mean a *point* of time *without period*. For, if any period is allowed, the sentence has no meaning, since during that period "the striking unit" passes through all "intermediate velocities." But if by instantaneously he means *without period*, then the last clause of the sentence is illogical, since instant there evidently means a period. For if it means point, then it contradicts the first clause. There, it is asserted that 4 was "*reduced*" to 2, *i. e.* that at one point the velocity was 4, and at the next point it was 2, and that there was *no time* between. If 4 was instantaneously reduced to 2, then the velocity 2 was next after the velocity 4, and not coeval with it. Thus it appears that these two clauses which were meant to be synonymous are contradictory.

Bearing in mind what we have heretofore learned respecting atoms, we shall not be troubled by the objections to the Newtonian theory which follow. In reply to the question, "What is the constitution of these units?" the answer, "We have no alternative but to regard each of them as a small piece of matter," would be true if the Sense was the only faculty which could examine them. But even upon this theory Mr. Spencer's remarks "respecting the parts of which each atom consists," are entirely out of place; for the hypothesis that it is an ultimate atom excludes the supposition of "parts," since that phrase has no meaning except it refers to a final, indivisible, material unit. All that the Sense could say, would be, "What this atom is I know not, but that it is, and *is not divisible*, I believe." But when we see by the Reason that the ultimate atom, when dissolved, becomes God's power, all difficulty in the question vanishes. Having thus answered the above objections, it is unnecessary to notice the similar ones raised against Boscovich's theory, which is a modification of that of Newton.

Mr. Spencer next examines certain phenomena of motion. The fact that he seeks for absolute motion by the *physical sense*, a faculty which was only given us to perceive relative — phenomenal — motion, and is, *in its kind*, incapable of finding the absolute motion, (for if it should see it, it could not *know* it,) is sufficient to condemn all that he has said on this subject. For the presentations which he has made of the phenomena given us by the Sense does not exhaust the subject. The perplexities therein developed are all resolvable, as will appear further on. The phenomena adduced on page 55 are, then, merely *appearances* in the physical sense; and the motion is merely relative. In the first instance, the captain walks East with reference to the ship and globe. In the second, he walks East with reference to the ship; the ship sails West with reference to the globe; while the resultant motion is, that he is *stationary* with reference to this larger object. What, then, can the Sense give us? Only resultant motion, at the most. So we see that "our ideas of Motion" are not "illusive," but *deficient.* The motion is just what it appears, measured from a given object. It is *relative*, and this is all the Sense *can* give. Our author acknowledges that "we tacitly assume that there are real motions"; that "we take for granted that there are fixed points in space, with respect to which all motions are absolute; and we find it impossible to rid ourselves of this idea." A question instantly arises, and it seems to be one which he is bound to entertain, viz: How comes this idea to be? We press this question upon Mr. Spencer, being persuaded that he will find it much more perplexing than those he has entertained. Undoubtedly, "absolute motion cannot even be imagined." *No* motion can be imagined, though the moving body may be. But by no means does it follow, "much less known." This involves that the knowing faculty is inferior to, and more circumscribed than, the imagining faculty, when the very opposite is the fact. Neither does it follow from what is said in the paragraph beginning with, "For motion is change of place," that "while we are obliged to think that there is absolute motion, we find absolute motion incomprehensible." The Universe is limited and bounded, and is a sphere. We *may* assume that the centre of the sphere is at rest. Instantly absolute motion becomes comprehensible, for it is motion measured from that point. Surely there can be no harm in the *supposition*. The Reason shows us that the supposition is the truth; and that that centre is the throne of the eternal God. In this view not only is motion, apart from the "limitations of space," totally unthinkable, but it is absolutely impossible. Motion *cannot* be, except as a formal body is. Hence, to speak of motion in "unlimited space" is simply absurd. Formal object *cannot* be, except as *thereby* a limit is established in Space. Hence it is evident that "absolute motion" is not motion with reference to "unlimited Space," which would be the same as motion without a moving; but is motion with reference to that point fixed in Space, around which all things revolve, but which is itself at perfect rest.

"Another insuperable difficulty presents itself, when we contemplate the transfer of Motion." Motion is simply the moving of a body, and *cannot be transferred*. The *force* which causes the motion is what is transferred. All that can be said of motion is, that it is, that it increases, that it diminishes, that it ceases. If the moving body impinges upon another moving body, and causes it to move, it is not motion that is transferred, but the force which causes the motion.

The motion in the impinging body is diminished, and a new motion is begun in the body which was at rest. Again it is asked: "In what respect does a body after impact differ from itself before impact?" And further on: "The motion you say has been communicated. But how? What has been communicated? The striking body has not transferred a *thing* to the body struck; and it is equally out of the question to say that it has transferred an *attribute*." Observe now that a somewhat is unquestionably communicated; and the question is: — What is it? Query. Does Mr. Spencer mean to comprehend the Universe in "thing" and "attribute"? He would seem to. If he does, he gives a decision by assertion without explanation or proof, which involves the very question at issue, which is, Is the somewhat transferred a "thing" or an "attribute"; and a decision directly contrary to the acknowledgment that a somewhat has been communicated? On the above-named hypothesis his statement should be as follows: A somewhat has been communicated. "Thing" and "attribute" comprise all the Universe. Neither a thing, nor an attribute has been communicated, *i. e.* no somewhat has been communicated; which contradicts the evidence and the acknowledgment. If on the other hand Mr. Spencer means that "thing" and "attribute" comprise only a part of the Universe, then the question is not fairly met. It may be more convenient for the moment to conclude the Universe in the two terms thing and attribute; and then, as attribute is essential to the object it qualifies, and so cannot be communicated, it will follow that a thing has been communicated. This thing we call force. It is not in hand now to inquire what force is. It is manifest to the Sense that the body is in a different state after impact, than it was before. Something has been put into the body, which, though not directly appreciable to the Sense, is indirectly appreciable by the results, and which is as real an addition as water is to a bowl, when poured in. Before the impact the body was destitute of that kind of force — motor force would be a convenient term — which tended to move it. After the impact a sufficiency of that force was present to produce the motion. It may be asked, where does this force go to when the motion diminishes till the body stops. It passes into the substances which cause the diminution until there is no surplus in the moving body, and at the point of equilibrium motion ceases. If it be now asked, where does this force ultimately go to, it is to be said that it comes from God, and goes to God, who is the Final. The Sense gives only subordinate answers, but the Reason leads us to the Supreme.

If the view adopted be true, Mr. Spencer's halving and halving again "the rate of movement forever," is irrelevant. It is not a *mental operation* but an *actual fact* which is to be accounted for. Take a striking illustration. A ball lying on smooth ice is struck with a hockey. Away it goes skimming over the glassy surface with a steadily diminishing velocity till it ceases. It starts, it proceeds, it stops. These are the facts; and the mental operation must accord with them. There is put into the ball, at the instant of contact, a certain amount of motor force. From that instant onward, that force flows out of the ball into the resisting substances by which it is surrounded, until none is left. And it is just as pertinent to ask how all the water can flow out of a pail, as how all the motor force can flow out of a moving substance. "The smallest movement is separated" by no more of "an impassable gap from no movement," *than it is from a larger movement above it.* That which will account for a movement four becoming two, will account for a movement two becoming zero. The "puzzle," then, may be explained thus. Time is the procession of events. Let it be represented by a line. Take a point in that line, which will then mark its division but represent *no period.* On one side of that point is rest; on the other motion. That point is the point of contact, and occupies no period. At this point the motion is maximum. The force instantly begins to flow off, and continues in a steady stream until none is left, and the body is again at rest.

Here, also, we take a point. This is the point of zero. It again divides the line. Before the bisection is motion; after the bisection is rest. All this cannot be perceived by the Sense, nor conceived by the Understanding. It is seen by the Reason. Now observe the actual phenomenon. The ball starts, proceeds, stops. From maximum to zero there is a steady diminution, or nearly enough so for the experiment; at least the diminution can be averaged for the illustration. Then comparing motion with time, the same difficulty falls upon the one as the other. If the motion is halved, the time must be; and so, "mentally," it is impossible to imagine how a moment of time can pass. To the halving faculty — the Sense — this is true, and so we are compelled to correct our course of procedure. This it is. The Sense and Understanding being impotent to discover an absolute unit of any kind, the Sense *assumes* for itself what meets all practical wants — a standard unit, by which it measures parts in Space and Time. So motion must be measured by some assumed standard; and as, like time, — duration, — it can be represented by a line, let them have a common standard. Suppose, then, that the ball's flight occupies ten minutes of time. The line from m to z will be divided into ten exactly equal spaces; and it will be no more difficult to account for the flow of force from 10 to 9, than from 1 to 0. Also let it be observed that the force, like time, is a unit, which the Sense, for its convenience, divides into parts; but that neither those parts, nor any parts, have any real existence. As Time is an indivisible whole, measured off for convenience, so any given force is such a whole, and is so measured off. All this appearing and measuring are phenomenal in the Sense. It is the Reason which sees that they can be *only* phenomenal, and that behind the appearance is pure Spirit — God, who is primarily out of all relation.

On page 58, near the close of his illustration of the chair, Mr. Spencer says: "It suffices to remark that since the force as known to us is an affection of consciousness, we cannot conceive the force as existing in the chair under the same form without endowing the chair with consciousness." This very strange assertion can only be true, provided a major premiss, No force can be conceived to exist without involving an affection of consciousness in the object in which it *apparently* inheres, is true. Such a premiss seems worse than absurd; it seems silly. We cannot learn that force exists, without our consciousness is affected thereby; but this is a very different thing from our being unable to conceive of a force as *existing*, without there is a consciousness in the object through which it *appears*. If Mr. Spencer had said that no force can be, without being exerted, and no force can be exerted, without an affection of the consciousness of the exertor, he would have uttered the truth. We would then have the following result. Primarily all force is exerted by the Deity; and he is conscious thereof. He draws the chair down just as really as though the hand were visible. Secondarily spiritual persons are endowed by their Creator with the ability to exert his force for their uses, and so I lift the chair. The great error, which appears on every page of Mr. Spencer's book and invalidates all his conclusions, shows itself fully here. He presents images from the Sense, and then tries to satisfy the Reason — the faculty which calls for an absolute account — by the analyses of that Sense. His attempt to "halve the rate," his remark that "the smallest movement is separated by an impassable gap from no movement," and many such, are only pertinent to the Sense, can never be explained by the Sense, and are found by the Reason to need, and be capable of, no such kind of explanation as the Sense attempts; but that the phenomena are appearances in *wholes*, whose partitions cannot be absolute, and that these wholes are accounted for by the being of an absolute and infinite Person — God, who is utterly impalpable to the Sense, and can be known only by the Reason.

The improper use of the Sense mentioned above, is, if possible, more emphatically exemplified in the remarks upon "the connection between Force and Matter." "Our ultimate test of Matter is the ability to resist." This is true to the Sense, but no farther. "Resist" what? Other matter, of course. Thus is the sensuousness made manifest. In the Sense, then, we have a material object. But Force is not object to the Sense directly, but only indirectly by its effects through Matter. The Sense, in its percept, deems the force other than the matter. Hence it is really no more difficult for the Sense to answer the question, How could the Sun send a force through 95,000,000 of miles of void to the Earth and hold it, than through solid rock that distance? All that the Sense *can do* is to present the phenomena. It is utterly impotent to account for the least of them.

In the following passage, on page 61, Mr. Spencer seems to have been unaccountably led astray. He says: "Let the atoms be twice as far apart, and their attractions and repulsions will both be reduced to one fourth of their present amounts. Let them be brought within half the distance, and their attractions and repulsions will both be quadrupled. Whence it follows that this matter will as readily as not assume any other density; and can offer no resistance to any external agents." Now if this be true, there can be no "external agents" to which to offer any "resistance." It is simply to assert that all force neutralizes itself; and that matter is impossible. But the conclusion does not "follow." It is evidently based on the supposition that the "attractions and repulsions" are *contra*-acting forces which exactly balance each other, and so the molecules are held in their position by *no* force. Instead of this, they are *co*-acting forces, which are wholly expended in holding the molecules in their places. The repulsions, then, are expended in resisting pressure from without which seeks to crowd the particles in upon themselves and thus disturb their equilibrium; while the attractions are expended in holding the particles down to their natural distance from each other when any disturbing force attempts to separate them. Hence, referring to the two cases mentioned, in the first instance the power of resistance is reduced to one fourth, and this corresponds with the fact; and in the second instance the power of resistance is increased fourfold, and this corresponds with the fact.

We thus arrive at the end of Mr. Spencer's remarks concerning the material Universe and of our strictures thereon. Perhaps the reader's mind cannot better be satisfied as to the validity of these strictures than by presenting an outline of the system furnished by the Reason, and upon which they are based.

The Reason gives, by a direct and immediate intuition, and as a necessary *a priori* idea, God. This is a *spontaneous*, synthetical act, precisely the same in kind with that which gives a simple *a priori* principle, as idea. In it the Reason intuits, not a single principle seen to be necessary simply, but the fact that all possible principles *must* be combined in a perfectly harmonious unity, in a single Being, who thereby possesses all possible endowments; and so is utterly independent, and is seen to be the absolute and infinite Person, the perfect Spirit. This act is no conclusion of the One from the many in a synthetical judgment, but is entirely different. It is the neccssary seeing of the many in the One; and so is not a judgment but an intuition, not a guess but a certainty. God, then, is known, when known at all, not "by plurality, difference, and relation," but by an *immediate* insight into his unity, and so is directly known as he is. And the whole Universe is, that creatures might be, to whom this revelation was possible. Among the other necessary endowments which this intuition reveals, is that of immanent power commensurate with his dignity, and adequate to realize in actual creatures the necessary *a priori* ideas, which he also possesses as endowments. Power is, then, a simple idea, incapable of analysis; and which cannot therefore be defined, except by synonymous terms; and to which President Hopkins's remark upon moral obligation is equally pertinent; viz: "that we can only state the occasion on which it arises." From these data the *a priori* idea of the Universe may be developed as follows: —

God, the absolute and infinite Person, possesses, as inherent endowment forever immanent in himself, Universal Genius; which is at once capacity and faculty, in which he sees, and by which he sees, all possible ideas, and these in all possible combinations or ideals. Thus has he all possible knowledge. From the various ideal systems which thus are, he, having perfect wisdom, and according his choice to the behest of his own worth, selects that one which is thus seen to be best; and thereby determines the forms and laws under which the Universe shall become. He also possesses, as inherent endowment, all power; *i. e.* the ability to realize every one of his ideals; but *not* the ability to violate the natural laws of his being, as to make two and two five. The ideal system is only ideal: the power is simply power; and so long as the two remain isolated, no-thing will be. Therefore, in order to the realization of his ideal, it must be combined with the power; *i. e.*, the power must be organized according to the ideal. How, then, can the power, having been sent forth from God, be organized? Thus. If the power goes forth in its simplicity, it will be expended uselessly, because there is no substance upon which it may be exercised. It follows, then, that, if exercised at all, it must be exercised upon *itself*. When, therefore, God would create the Universe, he sent forth two "pencils," or columns of power, of equal and sufficient volume, which, acting upon each other from opposite directions, just held each other in balance, and thus force was. These two "pencils," thus balancing each other, would result in a sphere of "space-filling force." The point of contact would determine the first place in Space, and the first point in Time; from which, if attainable, an absolute measure of each could be made. All we have now attained is the single duality "space-filling force," which is wholly homogeneous, is of sufficient volume to constitute the Universe, and yet by no means *is* the Universe. There is only Chaos, "without form and void, and darkness" is "upon the face of the deep." Now must "the Spirit of God move upon the face of the waters"; then through vast and to us immeasurable periods of time, through cycle and epicycle, the work of organization will go on. Ever moving under forms laid down in the *a priori* ideal, God's power turns upon itself, as out of the crush of elemental chaos the Universe is being evolved. During this process, whatever of the force is to act under the law of heat in the *a priori* ideal, assumes that form and the heat force becomes; whatever is to act under the law of magnetism, assumes that form, and magnetic force becomes; so of light, and the various forms of matter. At length, in the revolution of the cycles, the Universe attains that degree of preparation which fits it for living things to be, and the life force is organized; and by degrees all its various forms are brought forth. After another vast period that point is reached when an animal may be organized, which shall be the dwelling-place for a time of a being whose life is utterly different in kind from any animal life, and man appears. Now in all these vast processes, be it observed that God is personally present, that the first energy was his, and that every subsequent energizing act is his special aud personal act. He organized the duality, force. He then organized this force into heat-force, light-force, magnetic-force, matter-force, life-force, and soul-force. And so it is that his personal supervision and energy is actually present in every atom of the Universe. When we turn from this process of thought to the sensible facts, and speak of granite, sandstone, schist, clay, herbage, animals, yes, of the thousand kinds of substance which appear to the eye, it is to be remembered that all these are but *forms to the Sense* of that "reason-conception," force, — that primal duality, which power acting upon itself becomes. Now as the machine can never carve any other image than those for which it is specially constructed, and must work just as it is made to work, so the

Sense, which is purely mechanical, can never do any other than the work for which it was made, can never transcend the laws of its organization. It can only give forms — results, but is impotent to go behind them. It can only say *that things are*, but never say *what* or *why* they are.

Seen in the light of the theory which has thus been presented, Mr. Spencer's difficulties vanish. Matter is force. Motion is matter affected by another form of force. The "puzzle" of motion and rest is only phenomenal to the Sense; it is an appearance of force acting through another force. It may also be said that the Universe is solid force. There is no void in it. There is no nook, no crevice or cranny, that is not full of force. To seek, then, for some medium through which force may traverse vast distances, is the perfection of superfluity. From centre to circumference it is present, and controls all things, and is all things. So it is no more difficult to see how force reaches forth and holds worlds in their place, than how it draws down the pebble which a boy has thrown into the air. It is no substance which must travel over the distance, it is rather an inflexible rod which swings the worlds round in their orbits. Whether, then, we look at calcined crags or lilies of the valley, whether astronomy, or geology, or chemistry be our study, the objects grouped under those sciences will be found to be equally the results of this one force, acting under different laws, and taking upon itself different forms, and becoming different objects.

That faculty and that line of thought, which have given so readily the solution of the difficulties brought to view by Mr. Spencer's examination of the outer world, will afford us an easier solution, if possible, of the difficulties which he has raised respecting the inner world. That which is not of us, but is far from us, may perchance be imperfectly known; but ourselves, what we are, and the laws of our being, may be certainly and accurately known. And this is the highest knowledge. It may be important, as an element of culture, that we become acquainted with many facts respecting the outer world. It cannot but be of the utmost importance, that we know ourselves; for thus only can we fulfil the behest of that likeness to God, in which we were originally created. We seek for, we may obtain, we *have obtained* knowledge in the inner world, — a knowledge sure, steadfast, immutable.

It seems to be more than a mere verbal criticism, rather a fundamental one, that it is not "our states of consciousness" which "occur in succession"; but that the modifications in our consciousness so occur. Consciousness is *one*, and retains that oneness throughout all modifications. These occur in the unity, as items of experience affect it. Is this series of modifications "of consciousness infinite or finite"? To this question experience *can* give no answer. All experiments are irrelevant; because these can only be after the faculty of consciousness is. They can go no further back than the *forms* of the activity. These they may find, but they cannot account for. A law lies on all those powers by which an experiment may be made, which forever estops them from attaining to the substance of the power which lies back of the form. The eye cannot examine itself. The Sense, as mental capacity for the reception of impressions, cannot analyze its constituents. The Understanding, as connective faculty concluding in judgments, is impotent to discover why it must judge one way and not another. It is only when we ascend to the Reason that we reach the region of true knowledge. Here, overlooking, analyzing all the conduct of the lower powers, and holding the self right in the full blaze of the Eye of self, Man attains a true and fundamental *self-knowledge*. From this Mount of Vision we know that infinity and finiteness have no pertinence to modifications of consciousness, or in fact to any series. We attain to the further knowledge that this series is, *must be*, limited; because the constituted beings, in whom it in each case inheres, are limited, and had a beginning. It matters not now to inquire how a self-conscious person could be created. It is sufficient to know that one has been created. This fact involves the further fact that consciousness, as an actuality, began in the order of nature, after the being to whom it belongs as endowment, or, in other words, an organization must be, before the modifications which inhere in that organization can become. The attainment of this as necessary law is far more satisfactory than any experience could be, were it possible; for we can never know but that an experience may be modified; but a law given in the intuition is immutable. The fact, ascertained many pages back, that the subject and the object are identical under the final examination of the Reason, enables us to attain the present end of the chain. The question is one of fact, and is purely psychological. It cannot be passed upon, or in any way interfered with, by logical processes. It is only by examination, by seeing, that the truth can be known. Faraday ridiculed as preposterous the pretension that a vessel propelled by steam could cross the ocean, and demonstrated, to his entire satisfaction, the impossibility of the event. Yet the Savannah crossed, and laughed at him. Just so here, all arguing is folly. The question is one of fact in experience. And upon it the soul gives undoubted answer, as we have stated. Nor is it so difficult, as some would have us believe, to see how this may be. Consciousness is an indivisible unity, and, as we have before seen, may best be defined as the light in which the person intuits his own acts and activities. This unity is abiding, and is ground for the modifications. It is, then, *now*, and the person now knows what the present modification *is*. The person does not need to look to memory and learn what the former modification was. It immediately knows what the modification *is* now. Thus a simple attainment of the psychological truth through a careful examination dispels as a morning mist the whole cloud of Mr. Spencer's difficulties. Well might President Hopkins say, "The only question is, what is it that consciousness gives? If we say that it does thus give both the subject and the object, that simple affirmation sweeps away in a moment the whole basis of the ideal and skeptical philosophy. It becomes as the spear of Ithuriel, and its simple touch will change what seemed whole continents of solid speculation into mere banks of German fog.'' We have learned, then, that it is not possible, or necessary, either to "perceive" or "conceive" the terminations of consciousness, because this involves the discovery, by *mechanical* faculties, of their own being and state before they became activities on the one hand, which is a contradiction, and on the other an utter transcending of the sphere of their capability, the attempt to do which would be a greater folly than would be that of the hand to see Jupiter. But we have intuited the law, which declares the necessity of a beginning for us and all creatures; and we ever live in the light of the present end. When, then, Mr. Spencer says that "Consciousness implies perpetual change and the perpetual establishment of relations between its successive phases," we know that he has uttered a fundamental psychological error, in fact, that almost the opposite is the truth. Consciousness is the permanent, the abiding, the changeless. It is the light of the personal Eye. Into it all changes come; but they are only *incidental.* In the finite and partial person, they come, because such person *must grow*; and so, because of his partiality and incompleteness, they become necessary incidents; but let there be a Person having all knowledge, who therefore cannot learn, having all perfection, who therefore cannot change, and it is plain that these facts in no way interfere with his consciousness. All variety is immanent in its light, and no change can come into it because *there is no change to come*; but this Person sees *all* his endowments *at once,* in the unity of this his light, just as we see *some* of our endowments in the unity of this our light. The change is not in the consciousness, but in the objects which come into it. This view also disposes of the theory that "any mental affection must be known as like these foregoing ones or unlike those"; that, "if it is not thought of in connection with others — not distinguished or identified by comparison with others, it is not recognized — is not a state of consciousness at all." Such comparison we have found only incidental in consciousness, pertaining to things in the Sense and Understanding, and not essential. Thus does a true psychology dissipate all these difficulties as a true cosmology explained the perplexities "of Motion and Rest."

Take another step and we can answer the question "What is this that thinks?" It is a spiritual person. What, then, is a spiritual person? A substance — a kind of force — the nature of which we need inquire about no further than to know that it is suitable to the use which is made of it, which is organized, according to a set of constituting laws, into such spiritual person. The substance without the laws would be simple substance, and nothing more. The laws without the substance would be only laws, and could give no being having no ground in which to inhere. But the substance as ground and the complete set of laws as inhering in the ground, and being its organization when combined, become a spiritual person who thinks. The *ego*, that is the sense of personality, is only one of the forms of activity of this being, and therefore cannot be said to think. The pages now before us are all vitiated by the theory that "successive impressions and ideas constitute consciousness." Once attain to the true psychology of the person, and learn that consciousness is as stated above, — an abiding light into which modifications come, — and there arises no difficulty in believing in the reality of self, and in entirely justifying that belief by Reason. Yea, more, from such a standpoint it is utter unreason, the height of folly, to doubt for an instant, for immanent and central in the light of Reason lies the solemn fact of man's selfhood. We arrive, then, directly at Mr. Spencer's conclusion, that "Clearly, a true cognition of self implies a state in which the knowing and the known are one — in which subject and object are identified," and we *know* that such a state is an actuality. Mr. Mansel may hold that such an assertion is the annihilation of both, but he is wholly wrong. The Savannah has crossed the Atlantic.

We attain, then, exactly the opposite result from Mr. Spencer. We have seen that "Ultimate Scientific Ideas are all" presentative "of realities" which can "be comprehended." We have, indeed, found it to be true, that, "after no matter how great a progress in the colligation of facts and the establishment of generalizations ever wider and wider, — after the merging of limited and derivative truths in truths that are larger and deeper, has been carried no matter how far, — the fundamental truth remains as much beyond reach as ever." But having learned this, we do not arrive at the conclusion that "the explanation of that which is explicable does but bring out into greater clearness the inexplicableness of that which remains behind." On the other hand we know that such a conclusion is erroneous, and *that the method by which it is reached is a false method, and utterly irrelevant to the object sought.* Could this lesson but be thoroughly learned, Mr. Spencer's work, and our work, would not have been in vain. Only by a method differing from this IN KIND — a method in which there is no "colligation of facts," and no "generalizations" concluded therefrom, but a simple, direct insight into Pure Truth — can "the fundamental truth" be known; and thus it may be known by every human soul. "*God made man in his own image.*" In our scheme there is ample room for the man of Science, with the eye of Sense, to run through the Universe, and gather facts. With telescope and microscope, he may pursue them, and capture innumerable multitudes of them. But having done this, we count it folly to attempt to generalize truth therefrom. But holding up the facts in the clear light of Reason, and searching them through and through, we *see* in them the immutable principle, known by a spontaneous, immediate, intuitive knowledge to be immutable, and thus we "*know the truth.*"

"THE RELATIVITY OF ALL KNOWLEDGE."

In the opening of this chapter, Mr. Spencer states the result, which, in his opinion, philosophy has attained as follows: "All possible conceptions have been one by one tried and found wanting; and so the entire field of speculation has been gradually exhausted without positive result: the only result arrived at being the negative one above stated — that the reality existing behind all appearances is, and must ever be, unknown." He then sets down a considerable list of names of philosophers, who are claimed by Sir William Hamilton as supporters of that position. Such a parade of names may be grateful to the feelings of the Limitists, but it is no support to their cause. The questions at issue are of such a nature that no array of dignities, of learning, of profound *opinions*, can have a feather's weight in the decision. For instance, take Problem XLVII, of the first book of Euclid. What weight have human opinions with reference to its validity? Though a thousand mathematicians should deny its truth, it would be just as convincing as now; and when a thousand mathematicians assert its truth, they add no item to the vividness of the conviction. The school-boy, who never heard of one of them, when he first reads it, knows it must be so, and that this is an inevitable necessity, beyond the possibility of any power or will to change. On principles simple, fixed, and final, just like those of mathematics, seen by the same Eye and known with the same intellectual certainty, and by logical processes just as pure, conclusive, *demonstrative* as those of geometry, *and by such alone*, can the questions now before us be settled. But though names and opinions have no weight in the final decision, though a demonstration is demanded and must be given, still it is interesting to note the absence of two names, representatives of a class, which must ever awaken, among the devout and pure-hearted, attention and love, and whose teachings, however unnoticed by Mr. Spencer, are a leaven working in the minds and hearts of men, which develop with continually increasing distinctness the solemn and sublime truth, that the human mind is capable of absolute knowledge. Plato, with serious, yea, sad countenance, the butt of jeer and scoff from the wits and comedians of his day, went about teaching those who hung upon his lips, that in every human soul were Ideas which God had implanted, and which were final truth. And Jesus Christ, with a countenance more beautifully serious, more sweetly sad, said to those Jews which believed on him, "If ye continue in my word, then are ye my disciples indeed; *and ye shall know the truth*, and the truth shall make you free." It may seem to men who grope about in the dismal cavern of the animal nature — the Sense and Understanding — wise to refuse the light, and reject the truths of the Pure Reason and the God-man, and to call the motley conglomeration of facts which they gather, but cannot explain, philosophy; but no soul which craves "the Higher Life" will, can be satisfied with such attainments. It yearns for, it cries after, yea, with ceaseless iteration it urges its supplication for the highest truth; and it shall attain to it, because God, in giving the tongue to cry, gave also the Eye to see. The Spiritual person in man, made in the very image of God, can never be satisfied till, stripped of the weight of the animal nature, it sees with its own Eye the Pure Reason, God as the Highest Truth. And to bring it by culture, by every possible manifestation of his wondrous nature, up to this high Mount of Vision, is one object of God in his system of the Universe.

The teaching of the Word — that august personage, "who came forth from God, and went to God," has been alluded to above. It deserves more than an allusion, more than any notice which can be given it here. It is astonishing, though perhaps not wholly unaccountable, that the writings of the apostles John and Paul have received so little attention from the metaphysicians of the world, as declarations of metaphysical truths. Even the most devout students of them do not seem to have appreciated their inestimable value in this regard. The reason for this undoubtedly is, that their transcendent importance as declarations of religious truth has shone with such dazzling effulgence upon the eyes of those who have loved them, that the lesser, but harmoniously combining beams of a true spiritual philosophy have been unnoticed in the glory of the nobler light. It will not, therefore, we trust, be deemed irreverent to say that, laying aside all questions of the Divinity of Christ, or of the inspiration of the Bible, and considering the writings of John and Paul merely as human productions, written at some time nobody knows when, and by some men nobody knows who, they are the most wonderful revelations, the profoundest metaphysical treatises the world has ever seen. In them the highest truths, those most difficult of attainment by processes of reflection, are stated in simple, clear language, and *they answer exactly to the teachings of the Reason.* Upon this, President Hopkins says: "The identity which we found in the last lecture between the teaching of the constitution of man and the law of God, was not sought. The result was reached because the analysis would go there. I was myself surprised at the exactness of the coincidence." Nor is this coincidence to be observed simply in the statement of the moral law. In all questions pertaining to man's nature and state, the two will be found in exact accord. No law is affirmed by either, but is accorded to by the other. In fine, whoever wrote the Book must have had an accurate and exhaustive knowledge of Man, about whom he wrote. Without any reference then to their religious bearings, but simply as expositions of metaphysical truths, the writings of the two authors named deserve our most careful attention. What we seek for are laws, final, fixed laws, which are seen by a direct intuition to be such; and these writings are of great value, because they cultivate and assist the Reason in its search for these highest Truths.

One need have no hesitation, then, in rejecting the authority of Mr. Spencer's names, aye, even if they were a thousand more. We seek for, and can obtain, that which he cannot give us — a demonstration; which he cannot give us because he denies the very existence of that faculty by which alone a demonstration is possible. As his empiricism is worthless, so is his rationality. No "deduction" from any "*product* of thought, or process of thought," is in any way applicable to the question in hand. Intuitions are the mental actions needed. Light is neither product nor process. We pass over, then, his whole illustration of the partridge. It proves nothing. He leads us through an interminable series of questions to no goal; and says there is none. He gives the soul a stone, when it cries for bread. One sentence of his is doubtless true. "Manifestly, as the *most* general cognition at which we arrive cannot be reduced to a more general one, it cannot be understood." Of course not. When the Understanding has attained to the last generalization *by these very terms*, it cannot go any farther. But by no means does his conclusion follow, that "Of necessity, therefore, explanation must eventually bring us down to the inexplicable. The deepest truth which we can get at must be unaccountable. Comprehension must become something other than comprehension, before the ultimate fact can be comprehended." How shall we account for the last generalization, and show this conclusion to be false? Thus. Hitherto there have been, properly speaking, no comprehensions, only perceptions in the Sense and connections in the Understanding. "The sense *distinguishes* quality and *conjoins* quantity; the understanding *connects* phenomena; the reason *comprehends* the whole operation of both." The Reason, then, overseeing the operations of the lower faculties, and possessing within itself the *a priori* laws in accordance with which they are, *sees* directly and immediately why they are, and thus comprehends and accounts for them. It sees that there is an end to every process of generalization; and it then sees, what the Understanding could never guess, that *after* — in the order of our procedure — the last generalization there is an eternal truth, in accordance with which process and conclusion were and must be. There remains, then, no inexplicable, for the final truth is seen and known in its very self.

The passages quoted at this point from Hamilton and Mansel have been heretofore examined, and need no further notice. We will pass on then to his subsequent reflections upon them. It is worthy of remark, as a general criticism upon these comments, that there is scarcely one, if there is a single expression in the remainder of this chapter, which does not refer to the animal nature and its functions. The illustrations are from the material world, and the terms and expressions are suited thereto. With reference to objects in the Sense, and connections in the Understanding, the "fundamental condition of thought," which Mr. Spencer supplies, is unquestionably valuable. There is "likeness" as well as "relation, plurality, and difference." But observe that both these laws alike are pertinent only to the Sense and Understanding, that they belong to *things in nature*, and consequently have no pertinence to the questions now before us. We are discussing *ideas*, not *things*; and those are simple, and can only be seen, while these are complex, and may be perceived, distinguished, and conceived. If any one shall doubt that Mr. Spencer is wholly occupied with things in nature, it would seem that after having read p. 80, he could doubt no longer. "Animals," "species or genus," "mammals, birds, reptiles, or fishes," are objects by which he illustrates his subject. And one is forced to exclaim, "How can he speak of such things when they have nothing to do with the matter in hand? What have God and infinity and absoluteness to do with 'mammals, birds, reptiles, or fishes'?

If we can know only these, why speak of those?" It would seem that the instant they are thus set together and contrasted, the soul must cry out with an irrepressible cry, "It is by an utterly different faculty, and in entirely other modes, that I dwell upon God and the questions concerning him. These modes of the animal nature, by which I know 'mammals,' are different in kind from those of the spiritual person, by which I know God and the eternal truth." And when this distinction becomes clearly appreciated and fixed in one's mind, and the query arises, how could a man so confound the two, and make utter confusion of the subject, as the Limitists have done, he can hardly refrain from quoting Romans I. 20 *et seq.* against them.

Let us observe now Mr. Spencer's corollary. "A cognition of the Real as distinguished from the Phenomenal must, if it exists, conform to this law of cognition in general. The First Cause, the Infinite, the Absolute, to be known at all, must be classed. To be positively thought of, it must be thought of as such or such — as of this or that kind." To begin with the law which is here asserted, is *not* a "general" law, and so does not lie upon all cognition. It is only a special law, and lies only upon a particular kind of cognition. This has been already abundantly shown; yet we reproduce one line of proof. No mathematical law comes under his law of cognition; neither can he, nor any other Limitist, make it appear that it does so come. His law is law only for things in nature, and not for principles. Since then all ideas are known in themselves — are *self-evident,* and since God, infinity, and absoluteness are ideas, they are known in themselves, and need not be classed. So his corollary falls to the ground. Can we have any "sensible experience" of God? Most certainly not. Yet we can have just as much a sensible experience of him as of any other person — of parent, wife, or child. Did you ever see a person — a soul? No. Can you see — "have sensible experience of" — a soul? No. What is it, then, that we have such experience of? Plainly the body — that material frame through which the soul manifests itself. The Universe is that material system through which God manifests himself to those spiritual persons whom he has made; and that manifestation is the same in kind as that of a created soul through the body which is given it. It follows then, — and not only from this, but it may be shown by further illustration, — that every other person is just as really inscrutable to us as God is; and further, that, if we can study and comprehend the soul of our wife or child, we can with equal certainty study, and to some extent comprehend, the soul of God. Or, in other words, if man is only an animal nature, having a Sense and Understanding, all personality is an insoluble mystery; all spiritual persons are alike utterly inscrutable. And this is so, because, upon the hypothesis taken, man is destitute of any faculty which can catch a glimpse of such object. A Sense and Understanding can no more see, or in any possible manner take cognizance of, a spiritual person than a man born blind can see the sun. Again, we say he is destitute of the faculty. Will Mr. Spencer deny the fact of the idea of personality? Will he assert that man has no such notion? Let him once admit that he has, and in that admission is involved the admission of the reality of that faculty by which we know God, for the faculty which cognizes personality, and cognizes God, is one and the same.

Although we do not like certain of Mr. Spencer's terms, yet, to please him, we will use them. Some conclusions, then, may be expressed thus: God as the Deity cannot be "classed"; he is unique. This is involved in the very terms by which we designate him. Yet we cognize him, but this is by an immediate intuition, in which we know him as he is in himself. "We shall see him as he is," says the apostle; and some foretastes of that transcendent revelation are vouchsafed us here on earth. But the infinite Person, *as person*, must be "assimilated" with other persons. Yet his infinity and absoluteness, *as such*, cannot be "grouped." And yet again, *as qualities*, they can be "grouped" with other qualities. Unquestionably between the Creator, *as such*, and the created, *as such*, "there must be a distinction transcending any of the distinctions existing between different divisions of the created." God as self-existent differs in kind from man as dependent, and this difference continues irrevocable; while that same God and that same man are *alike* in kind *as persons*. This is true, because all spiritual persons are composite beings; and while the essential elements of a spiritual person are common to created persons and the uncreated Person, there are *other* characteristics, *not essential* to personality, which belong some to the created, and some to the uncreated, and differentiate them. Or, in other words, God as person, and man as person, are alike. Yet they are diverse in kind, and so diverse in kind that it is out of the range of possibility for that diversity to be removed. How can this be explained? Evidently thus. There are *qualities* transfusing the personality which cannot be interchangeable, and which constitute the diversity. Personality is *form* of being. Qualities transfuse the form. Absoluteness and infinity are qualities which belong to one Person, and are such that they thereby exclude the possibility of their belonging to any other person; and so they constitute that one to whom they belong, unique and supreme. Dependence and partiality are also qualities of a spiritual person, but are qualities of the created spiritual person, and are such as must always subordinate that person to the other. In each instance it is, "*in the nature of things*," impossible for either to pass over and become the other. Each is what he is by the terms of his being, and must stay so.

But from all this it by no means follows that the dependent spiritual person can have no knowledge of the independent spiritual Person. On the other hand, it is the high glory of the independent spiritual Person, that he can create another being "in his own image," to whom he can communicate a knowledge of himself. "Like as a father pitieth his children, so Jehovah pitieth them that fear him." Out of the fact of his Father-hood and our childhood, comes that solemn, and, to the loving soul, joyful fact, that he teaches us the highest knowledge just as really as our earthly parents teach us earthly knowledge. This he could not do if we had not the capacity to receive the knowledge; and we could not have had the capacity, except he had been able, in "the nature of things," and willing to bestow it upon us. While, then, God as "the Unconditioned cannot be classed," and so as unconditioned we do not know him "as of such or such kind," after the manner of the Understanding, yet we may, do, "see him as he is," do know that he is, and is unconditioned, through the insight of the Reason, the eye of the spiritual person, and what it is to be unconditioned.

We now reach a passage which has filled us with unqualified amazement. As much as we had familiarized ourselves with the materialistic teachings of the Limitists, we confess that we were utterly unprepared to meet, even in Mr. Spencer's writings, a theory of man so ineffably degrading, and uttered with so calm and naïve an unconsciousness of the degradation it involved, as the following. Although for want of room his illustrations are omitted, it is believed that the following extracts give a fair and ample presentation of his doctrine.

"All vital actions, considered not separately but in their ensemble, have for their final purpose the balancing of certain outer processes by certain inner processes.

"There are unceasing external forces, tending to bring the matter of which organic bodies consist, into that state of stable equilibrium displayed by inorganic bodies; there are internal forces by which this tendency is constantly antagonized; and the perpetual changes which constitute Life may be regarded as incidental to the maintenance of the antagonism. . . . .

"When we contemplate the lower kinds of life, we see that the correspondences thus maintained are direct and simple;

as in a plant, the vitality of which mainly consists in osmotic and chemical actions responding to the coexistence of light, heat, water, and carbonic acid around it. But in animals, and especially in the higher orders of them, the correspondences become extremely complex. Materials for growth and repair not being, like those which plants require, everywhere present, but being widely dispersed and under special forms, have to be formed, to be secured, and to be reduced to a fit state for assimilation. . . . .

"What is that process by which food when swallowed is reduced to a fit form for assimilation, but a set of mechanical and chemical actions responding to the mechanical and chemical actions which distinguish the food? Whence it becomes manifest, that, while Life in its simplest form is the correspondence of certain inner physico-chemical actions with certain outer physico-chemical actions, each advance to a higher form of Life consists in a better preservation of this primary correspondence by the establishment of other correspondences. Divesting this conception of all superfluities, and reducing it to its most abstract shape, we see that Life is definable as the continuous adjustment of internal relations to external relations. And when we so define it, we discover that the physical and the psychial life are equally comprehended by the definition. We perceive that this, which we call intelligence, shows itself when the external relations to which the internal ones are adjusted begin to be numerous, complex, and remote in time and space; that every advance in Intelligence essentially consists in the establishment of more varied, more complete, and more involved adjustments; and that even the highest achievements of science are resolvable into mental relations of coexistence and sequence, so coördinated as exactly to tally with certain relations of coexistence and sequence that occur externally. . . .

"And lastly let it be noted that what we call *truth*, guiding us to successful action and the consequent maintenance of life, is simply the accurate correspondence of subjective to objective relations; while *error*, leading to failure and therefore towards death, is the absence of such accurate correspondence.

"If, then, Life in all its manifestations, inclusive of Intelligence in its highest forms, consists in the continuous adjustment of internal relations to external relations, the necessarily relative character of our knowledge becomes obvious. The simplest cognition being the establishment of some connection between subjective states, answering to some connection between objective agencies; and each successively more complex cognition being the establishment of some more involved connection of such states, answering to some more involved connection of such agencies; it is clear that the process, no matter how far it be carried, can never bring within the reach of Intelligence either the states themselves or the agencies themselves."

Or, to condense Mr. Spencer's whole teaching into a few plain every-day words, Man is an animal, and only an animal, differing nowhat from the dog and chimpanzee, except in the fact that his life "consists in the establishment of more varied, more complete, and more involved adjustments," than the life of said dog and chimpanzee. Mark particularly the sententious diction of this newly arisen sage. Forget not one syllable of the profound and most important knowledge he would impart. "Life in all its manifestations, inclusive of Intelligence in its highest forms, consists in the continuous adjustment of internal relations to external relations." See, there is not a limit, not a qualification to the assertion! Now turn back a page or two, reader, if thou hast this wonderful philosophy by thee, and gazing, as into a cage in a menagerie, see the being its author would teach thee that thou art. From the highest to the lowest forms, life is one. In its lower forms, life is a set of "direct and simple" "correspondences." "But in animals, *and especially in the higher orders of them*," and, of course, most especially in the human animal as the highest order, "the correspondences become extremely complex." As much as to say, reader, you are not exactly a plant, nor are you yet of quite so low a type as the chimpanzee aforesaid; but the difference is no serious matter. You do not differ half as much from the chimpanzee as the chimpanzee does from the forest he roves in. All the difference there is between you and him is, that the machinery by which "the continuous adjustment of internal relations to external relations" is carried on, is more "complex" in you than in the chimpanzee. He roams the forest, inhabits some cave or hollow tree, and lives on the food which nature spontaneously offers to his hairy hand. You cut down the forest, construct a house, and live on the food which some degree of skill has prepared. He constructs no clothing, nor any covering to shield him from the inclemency of the weather, but is satisfied with tawny, shaggy covering, which nature has provided. You on the contrary are destitute of such a covering, and rob the sheep, and kill the silk-worm, to supply the lack. But in all this there is no *difference in kind.* The mechanism by which life is sustained in you is more "complex," it is true, than that by which life is sustained in him; there arise, therefore, larger needs, and the corresponding "intelligence" to supply those needs. But sweet thought, cheering thought, oh how it supports the soul! Your life in its highest form is only this animal life, — is only the constructive force by which that "extremely complex" machinery carries on "the continuous adjustment of internal relations to external relations." All other notions of life are "superfluities."

Reader, in view of the teaching of this new and widely heralded sage, how many "superfluities" must you and I strip off from our "conception" of life! And with what bitter disappointment and deep sadness should we take up our lamentation for man, and say: How art thou fallen, oh man! thou noblest denizen of earth; yea, how art thou cast down to the ground. But a little ago we believed thee a spiritual being; that thou hadst a nature too noble to rot with the beasts among the clods; that thou wast made fit to live with angels and thy Creator, God. But a little ago we believed thee possessed of a psychical life — a soul; that thou wouldst live forever beyond the stars; and that this soul's life was wholly occupied in the consideration of "heavenly and divine things." A little ago we believed in holiness, and that thou, consecrating thyself to pure and loving employments, shouldst become purer and more beautiful, nobler and more lovely, until perfect love should cast out all fear, and thou shouldst then see God face to face, and rejoice in the sunlight of his smiling countenance. But all this is changed now. Our belief has been found to be a cheat, a bitter mockery to the soul. We have sat at the feet of the English sage, and learned how dismally different is our destiny. Painful is it, oh reader, to listen; and the words of our teacher sweep like a sirocco over the heart; yet we cannot choose but hear.

"The pyschical life" — the life of the soul, "the immortal spark of fire," — and the physical life "are *equally* definable as the continuous adjustment of internal relations to external relations." We had supposed that intelligence in its highest forms was wholly occupied with the contemplation of God and his laws, and the great end of being, and all those tremendous questions which we had thought fitted to occupy the activities of a spiritual person. We are undeceived now. We find we have shot towards the pole opposite to the truth. Now "we perceive that this which we call Intelligence shows itself when the external relations to which the internal ones are adjusted begin to be numerous, complex, and remote in time or space; that *every advance in Intelligence essentially consists in the establishment of more varied, more complete, and more involved adjustments; and that even the highest achievements of science* are resolvable into mental relations of coexistence and sequence, so coördinated as *exactly to tally* with certain relations of coexistence and sequence that occur externally." In such relations consists the life of the "caterpillar." In such relations, *only a little "more complex,"* consists the life of "the sparrow." Such relations only does "the fowler" observe; such only does "the chemist" know. This is the path by which we are led to the last, the highest "truth" which man can attain. Thus do we learn "that what we call *truth*, guiding us to successful action, and the consequent maintenance of life, is *simply* the accurate correspondence of subjective to objective relations; while *error*, leading to failure and therefore towards death, is the absence of such accurate correspondence." What a noble life, oh, reader, what an exalted destiny thine is here declared to be! The largest effort of thine intelligence, "the highest achievement of science," yea, the total object of the life of thy soul, — thy "psychial" life, — is to attain such exceeding skill in the construction of a shelter, in the fitting of apparel, in the preparation of food, in a word, in securing "the accurate correspondence of subjective to objective relations," and thus in attaining the "*truth*" which shall guide "us to successful action and the consequent maintenance of life," that we shall secure forever our animal existence on earth. Study patiently thy lesson, oh human animal! Con it o'er and o'er. Who knows but thou mayest yet attain to this acme of the perfection of thy nature, though it be far below what thou hadst once fondly expected, — mayest attain a perfect knowledge of the "*truth*," and a perfect skill in the application of that truth, *i. e.* in "the continuous adjustment of internal relations to external relations"; and so be guided "to successful action, and the consequent maintenance of life," whereby thou shalt elude forever that merciless hunter who pursues thee, — the grim man-stalker, the skeleton Death. But when bending all thy energies, yea, all the powers of thy soul, to this task, thou mayest recur at some unfortunate moment to the dreams and aspirations which have hitherto lain like golden sunlight on thy pathway. Let no vain regret for what seemed thy nobler destiny ever sadden thy day, or deepen the darkness of thy night. True, thou didst deem thyself capable of something higher than "the continuous adjustment of internal relations to external relations"; didst often occupy thyself with contemplating those "things which eye hath not seen, nor ear heard"; didst deem thyself a son of God, and "a joint-heir with Jesus Christ," "of things incorruptible and undefiled, and which fade not away, eternal in the heavens"; didst sometimes seem to see, with faith's triumphant gaze, those glorious scenes which thou wouldst traverse when in the spirit-land thou shouldst lead a pure spiritual life with other spirits, where all earthliness had been stripped off, all tears had been wiped away, and perfect holiness was thine through all eternity. But all these visions were only dreams; they wholly deluded thee. We have learned from the lips of this latest English sage that thy god is thy belly, and that thou must mind earthly things, so as to keep up "the continuous adjustment of internal relations to external relations." Such being thy lot, and to fulfil such a lot being "the highest achievement of science," permit not thyself to be disturbed by those old-fashioned and sometimes troublesome notions that "*truth*" and those "achievements" pertained to a spiritual person in spiritual relations to God as the moral Governor of the Universe; that man was bound to know the truth and obey it; that his "errors" were violations of perfect law, — the truth he knew, — were *crimes* against Him who is "of too pure eyes to behold iniquity, and cannot look upon sin with the least degree of allowance"; that for these crimes there impended a just penalty — an appalling punishment; and that the only real "failure" was the failure to repent of and forsake the crimes, and thus escape the penalty. Far other is the fact, as thou wilt learn from this wise man's book. As he teaches us, the only "error" we can make, is, to miss in maintaining perfectly "the continuous adjustment of internal relations to external relations," — is to eat too much roast beef and plum-pudding at dinner, or to wear too scanty or too thick clothing, or to expose one's self imprudently in a storm, or by some other carelessness which may produce "the absence of such accurate correspondence" as shall secure unending life, and so lead to his only "failure" — the advance "towards death." When, then, oh reader! by some unfortunate mischance, some "error" into which thine ignorance hath led thee, thou hast rendered thy "failure" inevitable, and art surely descending "towards death," hesitate not to sing with heedless hilarity the old Epicurean song, "Let us eat and drink, for to-morrow we die."

> Sing and be gay
> The livelong day,
> Thinking no whit of to-morrow.
> Enjoy while you may
> All pleasure and play,
> For after death is no sorrow.

Thou hast committed thine only "error" in not maintaining "the accurate correspondence"; thou hast fallen upon thine only "failure," the inevitable advance "towards death." Than death no greater evil can befall thee, and that is already sure. Then let "dance and song," and "women and wine," bestow some snatches of pleasure upon thy fleeting days.

Delightful philosophy, is it not, reader? Poor unfortunate man, and especially poor, befooled, cheated, hopeless Christian man, who has these many years cherished those vain, deceitful dreams of which we spoke a little ago! To be brought down from such lofty aspirations; to be made to know that he is only an animal; that "Life in all its manifestations, inclusive of Intelligence in its highest forms, consists in the continuous adjustment of internal relations to external relations." Do you not join with me in pitying him?

And such is the philosophy which is heralded to us from over the sea as the newly found and wonderful truth, which is to satisfy the hungering soul of man and still its persistent cry for bread. And this is the teacher, mocking that painful cry with such chaff, whom newspaper after newspaper, and periodical after periodical on this side the water, even to those we love best and cherish most, have pronounced one of the profoundest essayists of the day. Perhaps he can give us some sage remarks upon "laughter," as it is observed in the human animal, and on that point compare therewith other animals. But, speaking in all sincerity after the manner of the Book of Common Prayer, we can but say, "From all such philosophers and philosophies, good Lord deliver us."

Few, perhaps none of our readers, will desire to see a denial in terms of such a theory. When a man, aspiring to be a philosopher, advances the doctrine that not only is "Life in its simplest form" — the animal life — "the correspondence of certain inner physico-chemical actions with certain outer physico-chemical actions," but that "*each advance to a higher form of Life* consists in a better preservation of this primary correspondence"; and when, proceeding further, and to be explicit, he asserts that not only "the physical," *but also* "*the psychical life* are *equally*" but "the continuous adjustment of internal relations to external relations"; and when, still further to insult man, and to utter his insult in the most positive, extreme, and unmistakable terms, he asserts "that even the highest achievements of science are resolvable into mental relations of coexistence and sequence, so coördinated as exactly to tally with certain relations of coexistence and sequence that occur externally," — that is, that the highest science is the attainment of a perfect cuisine; in a word, when a human being in this nineteenth century offers to his fellows as the loftiest attainment of philosophy the tenet that the highest form of life cognizable by man is an animal life, and that man can have no other knowledge of himself than as an animal, of a little higher grade, it is true, than other animals, but not different in kind, then the healthy soul, when such a doctrine is presented to it, will reject it as instantaneously as a healthy stomach rejects a roll of tobacco.

With what a sense of relief does one turn from a system of philosophy which, when stripped of its garb of well-chosen words and large-sounding, plausible phrases, appears in such vile shape and hideous proportions, to the teachings of that pure and noble instructor of our youth, that man who, by his gentle, benignant mien, so beautifully illustrates the spirit and life of the Apostle John, — Rev. Mark Hopkins, D. D., President of Williams College. No one who has read his "Lectures on Moral Science," and no lover of truth should fail to do so, will desire an apology for inserting the following extract, wherein is presented a theory upon which the soul of man can rest, as at home the soldier rests, who has just been released from the Libby or Salisbury charnel-house.

"And here, again, we have three great forces with their products. These are the vegetable, the animal, and the rational life.

"Of these, vegetable life is the lowest. Its products are as strictly conditional for animal life as chemical affinity is for vegetable, for the animal is nourished by nothing that has not been previously elaborated by the vegetable. 'The profit of the earth is for all; the king himself is served by the field.'

"Again, we have the animal and sensitive life, capable of enjoyment and suffering, and having the instincts necessary to its preservation. *This,* as man is now constituted, *is conditional for his rational life.* The rational has its roots in that, and manifests itself only through the organization which that builds up.

"*We have, then, finally and highest of all, this rational and moral life, by which man is made in the image of God.* In man, as thus constituted, we first find a being who is capable of choosing his own end, or, rather, of choosing or rejecting the end indicated by his whole nature. This is moral freedom, *and in this is the precise point of transition from all that is below to that which is highest.* For everything below man the end is necessitated. Whatever choice there may be in the agency of animals of means for the attainment of their end, — and they have one somewhat wide, — they have none in respect to the end itself. This, for our purpose, and for all purposes, is the characteristic distinction, so long sought, between man and the brute. Man determines his own end; the end of the brute is necessitated. Up to man everything is driven to its end by a force working from without or from behind; but for him the pillar of cloud and of fire puts itself in front, and he follows it or not, as he chooses.

"In the above cases it will be seen that the process is one of the addition of new forces, with a constant limitation of the field within which the forces act. . . . . . It is to be noticed, however, that while the field of each added and superior force is narrowed, yet nothing is dropped. Each lower force shoots through, and combines itself with all that is higher. Because he is rational, man is not the less subject to gravitation and cohesion and chemical affinity. He has also the organic life that belongs to the animal. In him none of these are dropped; *but the rational life is united with and superinduced upon all these*, so that man is not only a microcosm, but is the natural head and ruler of the world. He partakes of all that is below him, *and becomes man by the addition of something higher*. . . . . Here, then, is our model and law. Have we a lower sensitive and animal nature? Let that nature be cherished and expanded by all its innocent and legitimate enjoyments, for it is an end. But — and here we find the limit — let it be cherished *only as subservient to the higher intellectual life*, for it is also a means." The italics are ours.

Satisfactory, true, and self-sustained as is this theory, — and it is one which like a granite Gothic spire lifts itself high and calm into the atmosphere, standing firm and immovable in its own clear and self-evident truth, unshaken by a thousand assaulting materialistic storms, — we would buttress it with the utterances of other of the earth's noble ones; and this we do not because it is in any degree needful, but because our mind loves to linger round the theme, and to gather the concurrent thought of various rarely endowed minds upon this subject. Exactly in point is the following — one of many passages which might be selected from the works of that profoundest of English metaphysicians and theologians, S. T. Coleridge: —

"And here let me observe that the difficulty and delicacy of this investigation are greatly increased by our not considering the understanding (even our own) in itself, and as it would be were it not accompanied with and modified by the coöperation of the will, the moral feeling, and that faculty, perhaps best distinguished by the name of Reason, of determining that which is universal and necessary, of fixing laws and principles whether speculative or practical, and of contemplating a final purpose or end. This intelligent will — having a self-conscious purpose, under the guidance and light of the reason, by which its acts are made to bear as a whole upon some end in and for itself, and to which the understanding is subservient as an organ or the faculty of selecting and appropriating the means — seems best to account for that progressiveness of the human race, *which so evidently marks an insurmountable distinction and impassable barrier between man and the inferior animals, but which would be inexplicable, were there no other difference than in the degree of their intellectual faculties.*" — *Works*, Vol. I. p. 371. The italics are ours.

The attention of the reader may with profit be also directed to the words of another metaphysician, who has been much longer known, and has enjoyed a wider fame than either of those just mentioned; and whose teachings, however little weight they may seem to have with Mr. Spencer, have been these many years, and still are received and studied with profound respect and loving carefulness by multitudes of persons. We refer to the apostle Paul, "There is, therefore, now no condemnation to those who are in Christ Jesus, who walk not after the flesh, but after the spirit." That is, who do not walk after the law of the animal nature, but who do walk after the law of the spiritual person, for it is of this great psychological distinction that the apostle so fully and continually speaks. "For they that are after the flesh do mind the things of the flesh; but they that are after the spirit, the things of the spirit. For the minding of the flesh is death, but the minding of the spirit is life and peace; because the minding of the flesh is enmity against God, for it is not subject to the law of God, neither indeed can be." *Romans* VIII. 1, 5, 6, 7. This I say, then, "Walk in the spirit, and fulfil not the lust of the flesh. For the flesh lusteth against the spirit, and the spirit against the flesh: and these are contrary the one to the other." — *Galatians* V. 16, 17.

Upon these passages it should be remarked, by way of explanation, that our translators in writing the word spirit with a capital, and thus intimating that it is the Holy Spirit of God which is meant, have led their readers astray. The apostle's repeated use of that term, in contrasting the flesh with the spirit, appears decisive of the fact that he is contrasting, in all such passages, the animal nature with the spiritual person. But if any one is startled by this position and thinks to reject it, let him bear in mind that the law of the spiritual person in man and of the Holy Spirit of God is *identical.*

The reader will hardly desire from us what his own mind will have already accomplished — the construction in our own terms, and the contrasting of the system above embodied with that presented by Mr. Spencer. The human being, Man, is a twofold being, "flesh" and "spirit," an animal nature and a spiritual person. In the animal nature are the Sense and the Understanding. In the spiritual person are the Reason, the spiritual Sensibilities, and the Will. The animal nature is common to man and the brutes. The spiritual person is common to man and God. It is manifest, then, that there is "an insurmountable distinction and impassable barrier" not only "between man and the inferior animals," but between man as spiritual person, and man as animal nature, and that this is a greater distinction than any other in the Universe, except that which exists between the Creator and the created. What relation, then, do these so widely diverse natures bear to each other? Evidently that which President

Hopkins has assigned. "Because he is rational, man is not the less subject to gravitation and cohesion and chemical affinity. He has also the organic life that belongs to the plant, and the sensitive and instinctive life that belongs to the animal." Thus far his life "is the correspondence of certain inner physico-chemical actions with certain outer physico-chemical actions,"—undoubtedly "consists in the continuous adjustment of internal relations to external relations"; and being the highest order of animal, his life "consists in the establishment of more varied, more complete, and more involved adjustments" than that of any other animal. What, then, is this life for? "This, as man is now constituted, is *conditional for his rational life.*" "The rational life is united with and *superinduced upon all these.*" As God made man, and in the natural order, the "flesh," the animal life, is wholly subordinate to the "spirit," the spiritual life. And the spirit, or spiritual person of which Paul writes so much, — does this also, this "Intelligence in its highest form," consist "in the continuous adjustment of internal relations to external relations"? Are the words of the apostle a cheat, a lie, when he says, "For if ye live after the flesh, ye shall die; but if ye through the spirit" — *i. e.* by living with the help of the Holy Spirit, in accordance with the law of the spiritual person — "do mortify the deeds of the body, ye shall live?" And are Mr. Spencer's words, in which he teaches exactly the opposite doctrine, true? wherein he says: "And lastly let it be noted that what we call truth," &c., (see *ante*, p. 168,) wherein he teaches that "if ye live after the flesh," if you are guided by "*truth*," if you are able perfectly to maintain "the accurate correspondence of subjective to objective relations," "ye shall not surely die," you will attain to what is *successful action*, the preservation of "life," of "the continuous adjustment of internal relations to external relations," of the animal life, and thus your bodies will live forever — the highest good for man; but if you "mortify the deeds of the body," if you pay little heed to "the continuous adjustment of internal relations to external relations," you will meet with "*error*, leading to failure and therefore towards death," — the death of the body, the highest evil which can befall man, — and so "ye shall" not "live." Proceeding in the direction already taken, we find that in his normal condition the spiritual person would not be chiefly, much less exclusively, occupied with attending to "the continuous adjustment of internal relations to external relations," but would only regard these in so far as is necessary to preserve the body as the ground through which, in accordance with the present dispensation of God's providence, that person may exert himself and employ his energies upon those objects which belong to his peculiar sphere, even the laws and duties of spiritual beings. The person would indeed employ his superior faculties to assist the lower nature in the preservation of its animal life, but this only as a means. God has ordained that through this means that person shall develop and manifest himself; yet the life, continuance in being, of the soul, is in no way dependent on this means. Strip away the whole animal nature, take from man his body, his Sense and Understanding, leave him — as he would then be — with no possible medium of communication with the Universe, and he, the I am, the spiritual person, would remain intact, as active as ever. He would have lost none of his capacity to see laws and appreciate their force; he would feel the *bindingness* of obligation just as before; and finally, he would be just as able as in the earlier state to make a choice of an ultimate end, though he would be unable to make a single motion towards putting that choice into effect. The spiritual person, then, being such that he has in himself no element of decomposition, has no need, for the preservation of his own existence, to be continually occupied with efforts to maintain "the accurate correspondence of subjective to objective relations." Yet activity is his law, and, moreover, an activity having objects which accord with this his indestructible nature. With what then will such a being naturally occupy himself? There is for him no danger of decay. He possesses within himself the laws and ideals of his action. As such, and created, he is near of kin to that august Being in whose image he was created. His laws are the created person's laws. The end of the Creator should be that also of the created. But God is infinite, while the soul starts a babe, an undeveloped germ, and must begin to learn at the alphabet of knowledge. What nobler, what more sublime and satisfactory occupation could this being, endowed with the faculties of a God, find, than to employ all his power in the contemplation of the eternal laws of the Universe, *i. e.* to the acquisition of an intimate acquaintance with himself and God; and to bend all his energies to the realization by his own efforts of that part in the Universe which God had assigned him, *i. e.*, to accord his will entirely with God's will. This course of life, a spiritual person standing in his normal relation to an animal nature, would pursue as spontaneously as if it were the law of his being. But this which we have portrayed is not the course which human beings do pursue. By no means. One great evil, at least, that "the Fall" brought upon the race of man, is, that human beings are born into the world with the spiritual person all submerged by the animal nature; or, to use Paul's figure, the spirit is enslaved by the flesh; and such is the extent of this that many, perhaps most, men are born and grow up and die, and never know that they have any souls; and finally there arise, as there have arisen through all the ages, just such philosophers as Sir William Hamilton and Mr. Spencer, who in substance deny that men are spiritual persons at all, who say that the highest knowledge is a generalization in the Understanding, a form of a knowledge common to man and the brutes, and that "the highest achievements of science are resolvable into mental relations of coexistence and sequence, so coördinated as exactly to tally with certain relations of coexistence and sequence that occur externally." It is this evil, organic in man, that Paul portrays so vividly; and it is against men who teach such doctrines that he thunders his maledictions.

We have spoken above of the spiritual person as diverse from, superior to, and superinduced upon, the animal nature. This is his *position* in the logical order. We have also spoken of him as submerged under the animal nature, as enslaved to the flesh. By such figures do we strive to express the awfully degraded *condition* in which every human being is born into the world. And mark, this is simply a natural degradation. Let us then, as philosophers, carry our examination one step farther and ask: In this state of things what would be the fitting occupation of the spiritual person. Is it that "continuous adjustment"? He turns from it with loathing. Already he has served the "flesh" a long and grievous bondage. Manifestly, then, he should struggle with all his might to regain his normal condition to become naturally good as well as morally good, — he should fill his soul with thoughts of God, and then he should make every rational exertion to induce others to follow in his footsteps.

We attain, then, a far different result from Mr. Spencer. "The highest achievements of science" for us, our "truth," guiding us "to successful action," is that pure *a priori* truth, the eternal law of God which is written in us, and given to us for our guidance to what is truly "successful action," — the accordance of our wills with the will of God.

What we now reach, and what yet remains to be considered of this chapter, is that passage in which Mr. Spencer enounces, as he believes, a new principle of philosophy, a principle which will symmetrize and complete the Hamiltonian system, and thus establish it as the true and final science for mankind. Since we do not view this principle in the same light with Mr. Spencer, and especially since it is our intention to turn it upon what he has heretofore written, and demolish that with it, there might arise a feeling in many minds that the whole passage should be quoted, that there might be no doubt as to his meaning. This we should willingly do, did our space permit. Yet it seems not in the least necessary. That part of the passage which contains the gist of the subject, followed by a candid epitome of his arguments and illustrations, would appear to be ample for a fair and sufficiently full presentation of his theory, and for a basis upon which we might safely build our criticism. These then will be given.

"There still remains the final question — What must we say concerning that which transcends knowledge? Are we to rest wholly in the consciousness of phenomena? Is the result of inquiry to exclude utterly from our minds everything but the relative; or must we also believe in something beyond the relative?

"The answer of pure logic is held to be, that by the limits of our intelligence we are rigorously confined within the relative; and that anything transcending the relative can be thought of only as a pure negation, or as a non-existence. 'The *absolute* is conceived merely by a negation of conceivability,' writes Sir William Hamilton. 'The *Absolute* and the *Infinite*,' says Mr. Mansel, 'are thus, like the *Inconceivable* and the *Imperceptible*, names indicating, not an object of thought or of consciousness at all, but the mere absence of the conditions under which consciousness is possible.' From each of which extracts may be deduced the conclusion, that, since reason cannot warrant us in affirming the positive existence of what is cognizable only as a negation, we cannot rationally affirm the positive existence of anything beyond phenomena.

"Unavoidable as this conclusion seems, it involves, I think, a grave error. If the premiss be granted, the inference must doubtless be admitted; but the premiss, in the form presented by Sir William Hamilton and Mr. Mansel, is not strictly true. Though, in the foregoing pages, the arguments used by these writers to show that the Absolute is unknowable, have been approvingly quoted; and though these arguments have been enforced by others equally thoroughgoing, yet there remains to be stated a qualification, which saves us from that scepticism otherwise necessitated. It is not to be denied that so long as we confine ourselves to the purely logical aspect of the question, the propositions quoted above must be accepted in their entirety; but when we contemplate its more general, or psychological aspect, we find that these propositions are imperfect statements of the truth; omitting, or rather excluding, as they do, an all-important fact. To speak specifically:— Besides that *definite* consciousness of which Logic formulates the laws, there is also an *indefinite* consciousness which cannot be formulated. Besides complete thoughts, and besides the thoughts which, though incomplete, admit of completion, there are thoughts which it is impossible to complete, and yet which are still real, in the sense that they are normal affections of the intellect.

"Observe in the first place, that every one of the arguments by which the relativity of our knowledge is demonstrated, distinctly postulates the positive existence of something beyond the relative. To say that we cannot know the Absolute, is, by implication, to affirm that there *is* an Absolute. In the very denial of our power to learn *what* the Absolute is, there lies hidden the assumption *that* it is; and the making of this assumption proves that the Absolute has been present to the mind, not as a nothing but as a something. Similarly with every step in the reasoning by which this doctrine is upheld. The Noumenon, everywhere named as the antithesis of the Phenomenon, is throughout necessarily thought of as an actuality. It is rigorously impossible to conceive that our knowledge is a knowledge of Appearances only, without at the same time conceiving a Reality of which they are appearances; for appearance without reality is unthinkable." After carrying on this train of argument a little further, he reaches this just and decisive result. "Clearly, then, the very demonstration that a *definite* consciousness of the Absolute is impossible to us, unavoidably presupposes an indefinite consciousness of it." Carrying the argument further, he says: "Perhaps the best way of showing that, by the necessary conditions of thought, we are obliged to form a positive though vague consciousness of this which transcends distinct consciousness, is to analyze our conception of the antithesis between Relative and Absolute." He follows the presentation of certain "antinomies of thought" with an extract from Sir William Hamilton's words, in which the logician enounces his doctrine that in "correlatives" "the positive alone is real, the negative is only an abstraction of the other"; or, in other words, the one gives a substance of some kind in the mind, the other gives simply nothingness, void, absolute negation. Criticizing this, Mr. Spencer is unquestionably right in saying: "Now the assertion that of such contradictories 'the negative is *only* an abstraction of the other' — 'is *nothing else* than its negation' — is not true. In such correlatives as Equal and Unequal, it is obvious enough that the negative concept contains something besides the negation of the positive one; for the things of which equality is denied are not abolished from consciousness by the denial. And the fact overlooked by Sir William Hamilton is, that the like holds, even with those correlatives of which the negative is inconceivable, in the strict sense of the word." Proceeding with his argument, he establishes, by ample illustration, the fact that a "something constitutes our consciousness of the Non-relative or Absolute." He afterwards shows plainly by quotations, "that both Sir William Hamilton and Mr. Mansel do," in certain places, "distinctly imply that our consciousness of the Absolute, indefinite though it is, is positive not negative." Further on he argues thus: "Though Philosophy condemns successively each attempted conception of the Absolute; though it proves to us that the Absolute is not this, nor that, nor that; though in obedience to it we negative, one after another, each idea as it arises; yet as we cannot expel the entire contents of consciousness, there ever remains behind an element which passes into new shapes. The continual negation of each particular form and limit simply results in the more or less complete abstraction of all forms and limits, and so ends in an indefinite consciousness of the unformed and unlimited." Thus he brings us to "the ultimate difficulty — How can there possibly be constituted a consciousness of the unformed and unlimited, when, by its very nature, consciousness is possible only under forms and limits?" This he accounts for by hypostatizing a "raw material" in consciousness which is, must be, present. He presents his conclusion as follows: "By its very nature, therefore, this ultimate mental element is at once necessarily indefinite and necessarily indestructible. Our consciousness of the unconditioned being literally the unconditioned consciousness, or raw material of thought, to which in thinking we give definite forms, it follows that an ever-present sense of real existence is the very basis of our intelligence." . . . .

"To sum up this somewhat too elaborate argument: —We have seen how, in the very assertion that all our knowledge, properly so called, is Relative, there is involved the assertion that there exists a Non-relative. We have seen how, in each step of the argument by which this doctrine is established, the same assumption is made. We have seen how, from the very necessity of thinking in relations, it follows that the Relative itself is inconceivable, except as related to a real Non-relative. We have seen that, unless a real Non-relative or Absolute be postulated, the Relative itself becomes absolute, and so brings the argument to a contradiction. And on contemplating the process of thought, we have equally seen how impossible it is to get rid of the consciousness of an actuality lying behind appearances; and how, from this impossibility, results our indestructible belief in that actuality."

The approval which has been accorded to certain of the arguments adduced by Mr. Spencer in favor of his especial point, that the Absolute is a positive somewhat in consciousness, and to that point as established, must not be supposed to apply also to that hypothesis of "indefinite consciousness" by which he attempts to reconcile this position with his former teachings. On the contrary, it will be our purpose hereafter to show that this hypothesis is a complete fallacy.

As against the positions taken by Sir William Hamilton and Mr. Mansel, Mr. Spencer's argument may unquestionably be deemed decisive. Admitting the logical accuracy of their reasoning, he very justly turns from the logical to the psychological aspect of the subject, takes exception to their premiss, shows conclusively that it is fallacious, and gives an approximate, though unfortunately a very partial and defective presentation of the truth. Indeed, the main issue which must now be made with him is whether the position he has here taken, and which he puts forth as that peculiar element in his philosophical system, that new truth, which shall harmonize Hamiltonian Limitism with the facts of human nature, is not, when carried to its logical results, in diametrical and irreconcilable antagonism to that whole system, and all that he has before written, and so does not annihilate them. It will be our present endeavor to show that such is the result.

Perhaps we cannot better examine Mr. Spencer's theory than, first, to take up what we believe to be the element of truth in it, and carry out this to its logical results; and afterwards to present what seem to be the elements of error, and show them to be such.

1. "We are obliged to form a positive though vague consciousness of" "the Absolute." Without criticizing his use here of consciousness as if it were a faculty of knowledge, and remembering that we cannot have a consciousness of anything without having a knowledge commensurate with that consciousness, we will see that Mr. Spencer's assertion is tantamount to saying, We have a positive knowledge that the Absolute is. It does not seem that he himself can disallow this. Grant this, and our whole system follows, as does also the fallacy of his own. Our argument will proceed thus. Logic is the science of the pure laws of thought, and is mathematically accurate, and is absolute. Being such, it is law for all intellect, for God as well as man. But three positions can be taken. Either it is true for the Deity, or

else it is false for him, or else it has no reference to him. In the last instance God is Chaos; in the second he and man are in organic contradiction, and he created man so; the first is the one now advocated. The second and third hypotheses refute themselves in the statement of them. Nothing remains but the position taken that the laws of Logic lie equally on God and man. One of those laws is, that, if any assertion is true, all that is logically involved in it is true; in other words, all truth is in absolute and perfect harmony. This is fundamental to the possibility of Logic. Now apply this law to the psychological premiss of Mr. Spencer, that we have a positive knowledge that the Absolute is. A better form of expression would be, The absolute Being is. It follows then that he is in a *mode*, has a *formal* being. But three hypotheses are possible. He is in no mode; he is in one mode; he is in all modes. If he is in no mode, there is no form, no order, no law for his being; which is to say, he is Chaos. Chaos is not God, for Chaos cannot organize an orderly being, and men are orderly beings, and were created. If he is in all modes, he is in a state of utter contradiction. God "is all in every part." He is then all infinite, and all finite. Infinity and finiteness are contradictory and mutually exclusive qualities. God is wholly possessed of contradictory and mutually exclusive qualities, which is more than unthinkable — it is absurd. He is, must be, then, in one mode. Let us pause here for a moment and observe that we have clearly established, from Mr. Spencer's own premiss, the fact that God *is limited*. He must be in one mode to the exclusion of all other modes. He is limited then by the necessity to be what he is; and if he could become what he is not, he would not have been absolute. Since he is absolute, he is, to the exclusion of the possibility of any other independent Being. Other beings are, and must therefore be, dependent on and subordinate to him. Since he is superior to all other beings, he must be in the highest possible mode of being. Personality is the highest possible mode of being. This will appear from the following considerations. A person, possesses the reason and law of his action, and the capacity to act, within himself, and is thus a *final cause*. No higher form of being than this can be needed, and so by the law of parsimony a hypothesis of any other must be excluded. God is then a person.

We have now brought the argument to that point where its connection with the system advocated in this treatise is manifest. If the links are well wrought, and the chain com plete, not only is this system firmly grounded upon Mr. Spencer's premiss, but, as was intimated on an early page, he has in this his special point given partial utterance to what, once established, involves the fallacy not only of all he has written before, but as well of the whole Limitist Philosophy. It remains now to remark upon the errors in his form of expressing the truth.

2. Mr. Spencer's error is twofold. He treats of consciousness as a faculty of knowledge. He speaks of a "vague," an "indefinite consciousness." Let us examine these in their order.

a. He treats of consciousness as a faculty of knowledge. In this he uses the term in the inexact, careless, popular manner, rather than with due precision. As has been observed on a former page, consciousness is the light in which the person sees his faculties act. Thus some feeling is affected. This feeling is cognized by the intellectual faculty, and of this the person is conscious. Hence it is an elliptical expression to say "I am conscious of the feeling." The full form being "I am conscious that I know the feeling." Thus is it with all man's activities. Applying this to the case in hand, it appears, not that we are conscious of the Absolute, but that we are conscious that the proper intellectual faculty, the Pure Reason, presents what absoluteness is, and that the absolute Person is, and through this presentation — intuition — the spiritual person knows these facts. We repeat, then, our position: consciousness is the indivisible unity, the light in which the person sees all his faculties and capacities act; and so is to be considered as different in kind from them all as the peculiar and unique endowment of a spiritual person.

b. Mr. Spencer speaks of a "vague," an "indefinite consciousness." The expression "vague consciousness" being a popular and very common one, deserves a careful examination, and this we hope to give it, keeping in mind meantime the position already attained.

The phrase is used in some such connection as this, "I have a vague or undefined consciousness of impending evil." Let us analyze this experience. In doing so it will be observed that the consciousness, or rather the seeing by the person in the light of consciousness, is positive, clear, and definite, and is the apprehension of a feeling. Again, the feeling is positive and distinct; it is a feeling of dread, of threatening danger. What, then, is vague — is undefined? This. That cause which produces the feeling lies without the reach of the cognitive faculties, and of course cannot be known; because what produces the feeling is unknown, the intellectual apprehension experiences a sense of vagueness; and this it instinctively carries over and applies to the feeling. Yet really the sense of vagueness arises from an ignorance of the cause of the feeling. Strictly speaking, then, it is not consciousness that is vague; and so Mr. Spencer's "*indefinite* consciousness, which cannot be formulated," has no foundation in fact. But this may be shown by another line of thought. Consciousness is commensurate with knowledge, *i. e.*, man can have no knowledge except he is conscious of that knowledge; neither can he have any consciousness except he knows that the consciousness is, and what the consciousness is, *i. e.*, what he is conscious of. Now all knowledge is definite; it is only ignorance that is indefinite. When we say that our knowledge of an object is indefinite, we mean that we partly know its characteristics, and are partly ignorant of them. Thus then also the result above stated follows; and what Mr. Spencer calls "*indefinite* consciousness" is a "*definite* consciousness" that we partly know, and are partly ignorant of the object under consideration.

In the last paragraph but one, of the chapter now under consideration, Mr. Spencer makes a most extraordinary assertion respecting consciousness, which, when examined in the light of the positions we have advocated, affords another decisive evidence of the fallacy of his theory. We quote it again, that the reader may not miss of giving it full attention. "By its very nature, therefore, this ultimate mental element is at once necessarily indefinite and necessarily indestructible. Our consciousness of the unconditioned being literally *the unconditioned consciousness*, or *raw material of thought*, to which in thinking we give definite forms, it follows that an ever-present sense of real existence is the very basis of our intelligence." Upon reading this passage, the question spontaneously arises, What does the writer mean? and it is a question which is not so easily answered. More than one interpretation may be assigned, as will appear upon examination. A problem is given. To find what the "raw material of thought" is. Since man has thoughts, there must be in him the "raw material of thought" — the crude thought-ore which he smelts down in the blast-furnace of the Understanding, giving forth in its stead the refined metal — exact thought. We must then proceed to attain our answer by analyzing man's natural organization.

Since man is a complex, constituted being, there is necessarily a logical order to the parts which are combined in the complexity. He may be considered as a substance in which a constitution inheres, *i. e.*, which is organized according to a *set* of fixed laws, and that set of laws may be stated in their logical order. It is sufficient, however, for our purpose to consider him as an organized substance, the organization being such that he is a person — a selfhood, *self-active* and capable of self-examination. The raw material of *all* the activities of such a person is this organized substance. Take away the substance, and there remains only the set of laws as *abstract* ideas. Again, take away the set of laws, and the substance is simple, unorganized substance. In the combining of the two the person becomes. These, then, are all there is of the person, and therefore in these must the raw material be. From this position it follows directly that any capacity or faculty, or, in general, every activity of the person, is the substance acting in accordance with the law which determines that form of the activity. To explain the term, form of activity. There is a *set* of laws. Each law, by itself, is a simple law, and is incapable of organizing a substance into a being. But when these laws are considered, as they naturally stand in the Divine Reason, in relation to each other, it is seen that this, their standing together, constitutes ideals, or forms of being and activity. To illustrate from an earthly object. The law of gravitation alone could not organize a Universe; neither could the law of cohesion, nor of centripetal, nor centrifugal force, nor any other one law. All these laws must be acting together, — or rather all these laws must stand together in perfect harmony, according to their own nature, thus constituting an ideal form, in accordance with which God may create this Universe. For an illustration of our topic in its highest form, the reader is referred to those pages of Dr. Hickok's "Rational Psychology," where he analyzes personality into its elements of Spontaneity, Autonomy, and Liberty. From that examination it is sufficiently evident that either of these alone cannot organize a person, but that all three must be present in order to constitute such a being. There are, then, various forms of activity in the person, as Reason, Sensibility, and Will, in each of which the organized substance acts in a mode or form, and this form is determined by the set of organizing laws. Consciousness also is such a form. The "raw material of thought," then, must be this substance considered under the peculiar form of activity which we call consciousness, but *before the substance thus formulated has been awakened into activity by those circumstances which are naturally suited to it, for bringing it into action.* Now, by the very terms of the statement it is evident that the substance thus organized in this form, or, to use the common term, consciousness considered apart from and prior to its activity, can never be known *by experience*, i. e., *we can never be conscious of an unconscious state.* "Unconditioned consciousness" is consciousness considered as quiescent because in it have been awakened no "definite forms" — no "thinking." "In the nature of things," then, it is impossible to be conscious of an "unconditioned consciousness." Yet Mr. Spencer says that "our consciousness of the unconditioned," which he has already asserted and proved, is a "positive," and therefore an active state; is identical with, is "literally the unconditioned consciousness," or consciousness in its quiescent state, considered before it had been awakened into activity, which is far more absurd than what was just above shown to be a contradiction.

To escape such a result, a less objectionable interpretation may be given to the dictum in hand. It may be said that it looks upon consciousness only as an activity, and in the logical order after its action has begun. We are, then, conscious, and in this is positive action, but no definite object is present which gives a form in consciousness, and so consciousness *returns upon itself.* We are conscious that we are conscious, which is an awkward way of saying that we are self-conscious, or, more concisely yet, that we are conscious; for accurately this is all, and this is the same as to say that the subject and object are identical in this act. The conclusion from this hypothesis is one which we judge Mr. Spencer will be very loath to accept, and yet it seems logically to follow. Indeed, in a sentence we are about to quote, he seems to make a most marked distinction between self-consciousness and this "consciousness of the unconditioned," which he calls its "obverse."

But whatever Mr. Spencer's notion of the "raw material of thought" is, what more especially claims our attention and is most strange, is his application of that notion. To present this more clearly, we will quote further from the passage already under examination. "As we can in successive mental acts get rid of all particular conditions, and replace them by others, but cannot get rid of that undifferentiated substance of consciousness, which is conditioned anew in every thought, there ever remains with us a sense of that which exists persistently and independently of conditions. At the same time that by the laws of thought we are rigorously prevented from forming a conception of absolute existence, we are by the laws of thought equally prevented from ridding ourselves of the consciousness of absolute existence: this consciousness being, as we here see, the obverse of our self-consciousness." Now, by comparing this extract with the other, which it immediately follows, it seems plain that Mr. Spencer uses as synonymous the phrases "consciousness of the unconditioned," "unconditioned consciousness," "raw material of thought," "undifferentiated substance of consciousness," and "consciousness of absolute existence." Let us note, now, certain conclusions, which seem to follow from this use of language. We are conscious "of absolute existence." No person can be conscious except he is conscious of some state or condition of his being. Absolute existence is, therefore, a state or condition of our being. Also this "consciousness of absolute existence" — as it seems *our* absolute existence — is the "raw material of thought." But, again, as was shown above, this "raw material," this "undifferentiated substance of consciousness," if it is anything, is consciousness considered as capacity, and in the logical order before it becomes, or is, active; and it further appeared that of this quiescent state we could have no knowledge by experience. But since the above phrases are synonymous, it follows that "consciousness of absolute existence" is the "undifferentiated substance of consciousness," is a consciousness of which we can have no knowledge by experience, is a consciousness of which we can have no consciousness. Is this philosophy?

It would be but fair to suppose that there is some fact which Mr. Spencer has endeavored to express in the language we are criticizing. There is such a fact, a statement of which will complete this criticism. Unquestionably, in self-examination, a man may abstract all "successive mental acts," may consider himself as he *is*, in the logical order before he *has experiences.* In this he will find "that an ever-present sense of real existence is the very basis of our intelligence"; or, in other words, that it is an organic law of our being that there cannot be an experience without a being to entertain the experience; and hence that it is impossible for a man to think or act, except on the assumption that he is. But all this has nothing to do with a "consciousness of the unconditioned," or of "absolute existence"; for our existence is not absolute, and it is *our* existence of which we are conscious. The reality and abidingness of *our* existence is ground for *our* experience, nothing more. Even if it were possible for us to have a consciousness of our state before any experience, or to actually now abstract all experience, and be conscious of our consciousness unmodified by any object, *i. e.* to be conscious of unconsciousness, this would not be a "consciousness of absolute existence." We could find no more in it, and deduce no more from it, than that our existence was involved in our experience. Such a consciousness would indeed appear "unconditioned" by the coming into it of any activity, which would give a form in it; but this would give us no notion of true unconditionedness — true "absolute existence." This consciousness, though undisturbed by any experience, would yet be conditioned, would have been created, and be dependent upon God for continuance in existence, and for a chance to come into circumstances, where it could be modified by experiences, and so could grow. While, then, Mr. Spencer's theory gives us the fact of the notion of the necessity of our existence to our experience, it in no way accounts for the fact of our consciousness of the unconditioned, be that what it may.

But to return from this considerable digression to the result which was attained a few pages back, viz: that what Mr. Spencer calls "*indefinite* consciousness" is a "*definite* consciousness" that we partly know, and are partly ignorant of the object under consideration. Let this conclusion be applied to the topic which immediately concerns us, — the character of God.

But three suppositions are possible. Either we know nothing of God, not even that he is; or we have a partial knowledge of him, we know that he is, and all which we can logically deduce from this; or we know him exhaustively. The latter, no one pretends, and therefore it needs no notice. The first, even if our own arguments are not deemed satisfactory, has been thoroughly refuted by Mr. Spencer, and so is to be set aside. Only the second remains. Respecting this, his position is that we know that God is and no more. Admit this for a moment. We are conscious then of a positive, certain, inalienable knowledge that God is; but that with reference to any and all questions which may arise concerning him we are in total ignorance. Here, again, it is apparent that it is not our consciousness or knowledge that is vague; it is our ignorance.

We might suggest the question — of what use can it be to man to know that God is, and be utterly and necessarily, yea, organically ignorant of what he is? Let the reader answer the question to his own mind. It is required to show how the theory advocated in this book will appear in the light of the second hypothesis above stated.

Man knows that God is, and what God is so far as he can logically deduce it from this premiss; but, in so far as God is such, that he cannot be thus known, except wherein he makes a direct revelation to us, he must be forever inscrutable. To illustrate. If the fact that God is, be admitted, it logically follows that he must be self-existent. Self-existence is a positive idea in the Reason, and so here is a second element of knowledge respecting the Deity. Thus we may go on through all that it is possible to deduce, and the system thus wrought will be The Science of Natural Theology, a science as pure and sure as pure equations. Its results will be what God must be. Looking into the Universe we will find what must be corresponding with what is, and our knowledge will be complete. Again, in many regards God may be utterly inscrutable to us, since he may possess characteristics which we cannot attain by logical deductions. For instance, let it be granted that the doctrine of the Trinity is true — that there are three persons in one Godhead. This would be a fact which man could never attain, could never make the faintest guess at. He might, unaided, attain to the belief that God would forgive; he might, with the profound and sad-eyed man of Greece, become convinced that some god must come from heaven to lead men to the truth; but the notion of the Trinity could never come to him, except God himself with carefulness revealed it. Respecting those matters of which we cannot know except by revelation, this only can be demanded; and this by inherent endowment man has a right to demand; viz: that what is revealed shall not contradict the law already "written in the heart." Yet, once more, there are certain characteristics of God that must forever be utterly inscrutable to every created being, and this, because such is their nature and relation to the Deity, that one cannot be endowed with a faculty capable of attaining the knowledge in question. Such for instance are the questions, How is God self-existent, how could he be eternal, how exercise his power, and the like? These are questions respecting which no possible reason can arise why we should know them, except the gratification of curiosity, which in reality is no reason at all, and therefore the inability in question is no detriment to man.

By the discussion which may now be brought to a close, two positions seem to be established. 1. That we have, as Mr. Spencer affirms, a positive consciousness that the absolute Being is, and that this and all which we can logically deduce from this are objects of knowledge to us; in other words, that the system advocated in this volume directly follows from that premiss. 2. That any doctrine of "indefinite consciousness" is erroneous, that the vagueness is not in our consciousness, but in our knowledge; and further, that the hypothesis of a consciousness of the "raw material of thought" is absurd.

"THE RECONCILIATION."

It would naturally seem, that, after what is believed to be the thorough refutation of the limitist scheme, which has been given in the preceding comments on Mr. Spencer's three philosophical chapters, the one named in our heading would need scarce more than a notice. But so far is this from being the case, that some of the worst features in the results of his system stand out in clearest relief here. Before proceeding to consider these, let us note a most important admission. He speaks of his conclusion as bringing "the results of speculation into harmony with those of common sense," and then makes the, for him, extraordinary statement, "Common Sense asserts the existence of reality." In these two remarks it would appear to be implied that Common Sense is a final standard with which any position must be reconciled. The question instantly arises, What is Common Sense? The writer has never seen a definition, and would submit for the reader's consideration the following.

Common Sense *is the practical Pure Reason;* it is that faculty by which the spiritual person sees in the light of consciousness the *a priori* law as inherent in the fact presented by the Sense.

For the sake of completeness its complement may be defined thus:

Judgment is the practical Understanding; it is that faculty

by which the spiritual person selects such means as he thinks so conformed to that law thus intuited, as to be best suited to accomplish the object in view.

A man has good Common Sense, who quickly sees the informing law in the fact; and good judgment, who skilfully selects and adapts his means to the circumstances of the case, and the end sought. Of course it will not be understood that it is herein implied that every person who exercises this faculty has a defined and systematic knowledge of it.

The reader will readily see the results which directly follow from Mr. Spencer's premiss. It is true that "Common Sense asserts the existence of a reality," and this assertion is true; but with equal truth does it assert the law of logic; that, if a premiss is true, *all that is logically involved in it is true.* It appears, then, that Mr. Spencer has unwittingly acknowledged the fundamental principle of what may be called the Coleridgian system, the psychological fact of the Pure Reason, and thus again has furnished a basis for the demolition of his own.

It was said above that some of the evil results of Mr. Spencer's system assumed in this chapter their worst phases. This remark is illustrated in the following extract: "We are obliged to regard every phenomenon as a manifestation of some Power by which we are acted upon; phenomena being, so far as we can ascertain, unlimited in their diffusion, we are obliged to regard this Power as omnipresent; and criticism teaches us that this Power is wholly incomprehensible. In this consciousness of an Incomprehensible Omnipresent Power we have just that consciousness on which Religion dwells. And so we arrive at the point where Religion and Science coalesce." The evils referred to may be developed as follows: "We are obliged to regard every phenomenon as a manifestation of some Power by which we are acted upon." This may be expressed in another form thus: Every phenomenon is a manifestation of some Power by which we are acted upon. Some doubt may arise respecting the precise meaning of this sentence, unless the exact signification of the term phenomenon be ascertained. It might be confined to material appearances, appreciable by one of the five senses. But the context seems to leave no doubt but that Mr. Spencer uses it in the wider sense of every somewhat in the Universe, since he speaks of "phenomena" as "unlimited." Putting the definition for the term, the sentence stands: Every somewhat in the Universe is "a manifestation of some Power by which we are acted upon." It follows, then, that there is no somewhat in the Universe, except we are acted upon by it. Our being arises to be accounted for. Either we began to be, and were created, or the ground of our being is in ourselves, our being is pure independence, and nothing further is to be asked. This latter will be rejected. Then we were created. But we were not created by Mr. Spencer's "some Power," because it only *acts upon us*. In his creation, man was not acted upon, because there was no man to be acted upon; but in that act a being was originated *who might be acted upon*. Then, however, we came into being, another than "some Power" was the cause of us. But the act of creating man was a somewhat. Every somewhat *in* the Universe is "a manifestation of some Power." This is not such a manifestation. Therefore the creation of man took place outside the Universe. Or does Mr. Spencer prefer to say that the creation of man is "a manifestation of some Power acting upon" him!

The position above taken seems the more favorable one for Mr. Spencer. If, to avoid the difficulties which spring from it, he limits the term phenomenon, as for instance to material appearances, then his assertion that phenomena are unlimited is a contradiction, and he has no ground on which to establish the omnipresence of his Power.

But another line of criticism may be pursued. Strictly speaking, all events are phenomena. Let there be named an event which is universally known and acknowledged, and which, in the nature of the case, cannot be "a manifestation of some Power by which we are acted upon," and in that statement also will the errors of the passage under consideration be established. The experiencing by the human soul of a sense of guilt, of a consciousness of ill-desert, is such an event. No "Power" can make a sinless soul feel guilty; no "Power" *can relieve a sinful soul from feeling guilty.* The feeling of guilt does not arise from the defiance of Power, *it arises from the violation of Law.* And not only may this experience be named, but every other experience of the moral nature of man. In this connection let it be observed that Mr. Spencer always elsewhere uses the term phenomenon to represent material phenomena in the material universe. Throughout all his pages the reader is challenged to find a single instance in which he attempts to account for any other phenomena than these and their concomitants, the affections of the intellect in the animal nature. Indeed, so thoroughly is his philosophy vitiated by this omission, that one could never learn from anything he has said in these pages, that man had a moral nature at all, that there were any phenomena of sin and repentance which needed to be accounted for. In this, Sir William Hamilton and Mr. Mansel are just as bad as he. Yet in this the Limitists have done well; it is impossible, on the basis of their system, to render such an account. To test the matter, the following problem is presented.

To account, on the basis of the Limitist Philosophy, for the fact that the nations of men have universally made public acknowledgment of their guilt, in having violated the law of a superior being; and that they have offered propitiatory sacrifices therefor, except in the case of those persons and nations who have received the Bible, or have learned through the Koran one of its leading features, that there is but one God, and who in either case believe that the needful sacrifice has already been made.

Another pernicious result of the system under examination is, that it affords no better ground for the doctrine of Deity's omnipresence than *experience.* Mr. Spencer's words are: "phenomena being, *so far as we can ascertain*, unlimited in their diffusion, we are obliged to regard this Power as omnipresent." Now, if he, or one of his friends, should happen to get wings some day, and should just take a turn through space, and should happen also to find a limit to phenomena, and, skirting in astonishment along that boundary, should happen to light upon an open place and a bridge, which invited them to pass across to another sphere or system of phenomena, made by another "Power," — said bridge being constructed "'alf and 'alf" by the two aforesaid Powers, — then there would be nothing to do but for the said explorer to fly back again to England, as fast as ever he could, and relate to all the other Limitists his new experience; and they, having no ground on which to argue against or above experience, must needs receive the declaration of their colaborator, with its inevitable conclusion, that the Power by which we are here acted upon is limited, and so is not omnipresent. But when, instead of such a fallacious philosophy, men shall receive the doctrine, based not upon human experience, but upon God's inborn ideas that phenomena are limited and God is omnipresent, and that upon these facts experience can afford no decision, we shall begin to eliminate the real difficulties of philosophy, and to approach the attainment of the unison between human philosophy and the Divine Philosophy.

Attached to the above is the conclusion reached by Mr. Spencer in an earlier part of his work, that "criticism teaches us that this Power is wholly incomprehensible." We might, it is believed, ask with pertinence, What better, then, is man than the brute? But the subject is recurred to at this time, only to quote against this position a sentence from a somewhat older book than "First Principles," a book which, did it deserve no other regard than as a human production, would seem, from its perfect agreement with the facts of human nature, to be the true basis for all philosophy. The sentence is this: "Beloved, let us love one another, for love is of

God; and every one that loveth, is born of God, *and* KNOWETH GOD."

But the gross materialism of Mr. Spencer's philosophy presents its worst phase in his completed doctrine of God. Mark. A "phenomenon" is "a manifestation of some Power." "In this consciousness of an Incomprehensible Omnipresent Power we have just that consciousness on which Religion dwells. And so we arrive at the point where Religion and Science coalesce." An "Incomprehensible Omnipresent Power" is all the Deity Mr. Spencer allows to mankind. This Power is omnipresent, so that we can never escape it; and incomprehensible, so that we can never know the law of its action, or even if it have a law. At any moment it may fall on us and crush us. At any moment this globe may become one vast Vesuvius, and all its cities Herculaneums and Pompeiis. Of such a Deity the children of men may either live in continual dread, or in continual disregard; they may either spend their lives clad in sackcloth, or purple and fine linen; bread and water may be their fare, or their table may be spread like that of Dives; by merciless mortification of the flesh, by scourges and iron chains, they may seek to propitiate, if possible, this incomprehensible, omnipresent Power; or, reckless of consequences, they may laugh and dance and be gay, saying, we know nothing of this Power, he may crush us any moment, let us take the good of life while we can. The symbols of such a Deity are the "rough and ragged rocks," the hills, the snow-crowned mountains Titan-piled; the avalanche starting with ominous thunder, to rush with crash and roar and terrible destruction upon the hapless village beneath it; the flood gathering its waters from vast ranges of hills into a single valley, spreading into great lakes, drowning cattle, carrying off houses and their agonized inhabitants, sweeping away dams, rending bridges from their foundations, in fine, ruthlessly destroying the little gatherings of man, and leaving the country, over which its devastating waters flowed, a mournful desolation; and finally, perhaps the completest symbol of all may be found in that collection of the united streams and lakes of tens upon tens of thousands of miles of the earth's surface, into the aorta of the world, over the rough, rocky bed of which the crowded waters rush and roar, with rage and foam, until they come suddenly to the swift tremendous plunge of Niagara.

It should be further noticed, that this philosophy is in direct antagonism with that of the Bible, — that, if Spencerianism is true, the Bible is a falsehood and a cheat. Instead of Mr. Spencer's "Power," the Bible presents us a doctrine of God as follows: "And God said unto Moses, I AM THAT I AM. And he said, Thus shalt thou say unto the children of Israel, I AM hath sent me unto you." — *Exodus* IV. 14. This declaration, the most highly metaphysical of any but one man ever heard, all the Limitists, even devout Mr. Mansel, either in distinct terms, or by implication, deny. That other declaration is this: "Beloved, let us love one another: for love is of God; and every one that loveth is born of God, and knoweth God. He that loveth not, knoweth not God; *for God is love.*" — 1 *John* IV. 7, 8. Direct as is the antagonism between the two philosophies now presented, the later one appears in an especially bad light from the fact, that, being very recent and supported by a mere handful of men, its advocates have utterly neglected to take any notice of the other and elder one, although the adherents of this may be numbered by millions, and among them have been and are many of the ablest of earth's thinkers. True, the great majority of Bible readers do not study it as a philosophical treatise, but rather as a book of religious and spiritual instruction; yet, since it is the most profoundly philosophical book which has ever been in the hands of man, and professedly teaches us not only the philosophy of man, but also the philosophy of God, it certainly would seem that the advocates of the new and innovating system should have taken up that one which it sought to supplant, and have made an attempt, commensurate with the magnitude of the work before them, to show its position to be fallacious and unworthy of regard. Instead of this they have nowhere recognized the existence even of this philosophy except in the single instance of a quotation by Mr. Mansel, in which he seems tacitly to acknowledge the antagonism we have noted. In Mr. Spencer's volume this neglect is especially noteworthy. Judging from internal evidence, one would much sooner conclude that it was written by a Hindu pundit, in a temple of Buddha, than by an Englishman, in a land of Bibles and Christian churches. Now, although the Bible may stand in his estimation no higher than the Bahgavat-Gita, yet the mere fact that it *is*, and that it presents a most profound philosophy, which is so largely received in his own and neighboring nations, made it imperative upon him not only to take some notice of it, but to meet and answer it, as we have indicated above.

Another fault in Mr. Spencer's philosophy, one which he will be less willing to admit, perhaps, than the above, and, at the same time, one which will be more likely forcibly to move a certain class of mind, is, that it is in direct antagonism to human nature. Not only is the Bible a falsehood and a cheat, if Mr. Spencer's philosophical system is trne, but human nature is equally a falsehood and a cheat. To specify. Human nature universally considers God, or its gods, as persons; or, in other words, all human beings, or at least with very rare exceptions, spontaneously ascribe personality to Deity. This position is in no wise negatived by the fact of the Buddhist priesthood of India, or of a class of philosophical atheists in any other country. Man is endowed with the power of self-education; and if an individual sees, in the religion in which he is brought up, some inconsistency, which he, thinking it, as it may be, integral, for philosophical reasons rejects, and all religion with it, he may educate himself into speculative atheism. But no child is an atheist. Not even Shelley became such, until he had dashed against some of the distorted and monstrous *human* theologies of his day. But counting all the Buddhists, and all the German atheists, and all the English atheists, and all the American atheists, and all other atheists wherever they may be found, they will not number one tenth of the human race. On what ground can the unanimity of the other nine tenths be accounted for? There appears none possible, but that the notion that God is a person, *is organic in human nature.* Another equally universal and spontaneous utterance of mankind is, that there is a likeness, in some way, between God and man. There are the grossest, and in many instances most degrading modes of representing this; but under them all, and through them all, the indelible notion appears. The unanimity and pertinacity of this notion, appearing in every part of the globe, and under every variety of circumstance, and reappearing after every revolution, which, tearing down old customs and worships, established new ones, can without doubt only be accounted for on the precise ground of the other, — that the notion *is organic in man.* A third utterance of the human race, standing in the same category with these two, is, that the Deity can be propitiated by sacrifice. This also has had revolting, yea most hideous and unrighteous forms of expression, even to human sacrifices. But the notion has remained indestructible through all ages, and must therefore be accounted for, as have been the others. Over against the I AM, which human nature presents and the Bible supports; over against Him in whose image man and the Bible say man was created; and over against Him who, those two still agreeing witnesses also affirm, is moved by his great heart of Love to have mercy on those creatures who come to him with repentance, Mr. Spencer gives us, as the result of *Science*, an incomprehensible omnipresent *Power*; only a Power, nothing more; and that "utterly inscrutable." For our part, whatever others may do, we will believe in human nature and the Bible. On the truthfulness of these two witnesses, as on the Central Rock in the Universe, we plant ourselves. Here do we find our Gibraltar.

Mr. Spencer further says that on the consciousness of this

Power "Religion dwells." Now, so far is this assertion from according with the fact, that on his hypothesis it is impossible to account for the presence of religion as a constitutive element of the human race. Religion was primarily worship, the reverential acknowledgment, by the sinless creature, of the authority of the Creator, combined with the adoration of His absolute Holiness; but since sin has marred the race, it has been coupled with the offering in some forms of a propitiatory sacrifice. But if the Deity is only Power; or equally, if this is all the notion we can form of him, we are utterly at a loss to find aught in him to worship, much less can we account for the fact of the religious nature in us, and most of all are we confounded by the persistent assertion, by this religious nature, of the personality and mercy of God, for Power can be neither personal nor merciful.

Mr. Spencer proceeds to strengthen as well as he can his position by stating that "from age to age Science has continually defeated it (Religion) wherever they have come into collision, and has obliged it to relinquish one or more of its positions." In this assertion, also, he manifests either a want of acquaintance with the facts or a failure to comprehend their significance. Religion may properly be divided into two classes.

1. Those religions which have appeared to grow up spontaneously among men, having all the errors and deformities which a fleshly imagination would produce.

2. The religion of Jesus Christ.

1. From the three great ideas mentioned above, no Science has ever driven even the religions of this class. It has, indeed, corrected many *forms of expression*, and has sometimes driven *individuals*, who failed to distinguish between the form, and the idea which the form overlies, into a rejection of the truth itself.

2. Respecting the religion of Jesus Christ, Mr. Spencer's remark has no shadow of foundation. Since the beginning of its promulgation by Jehovah, and especially since the com-

pletion of that promulgation by our Saviour and his apostles, not one whit of its practical law or its philosophy has been abated; nay, more, to-day, in these American States, there may be found a more widespread, thoroughly believed, firmly held, and intelligent conviction of God's personality, and personal supervision of the affairs of men, of his Fatherhood, and of that fatherhood exercised in bringing "order out of confusion," in so conducting the most terrible of conflicts, that it shall manifestly redound, not only to the glory of himself, but to the very best good of man, so manifestly to so great a good, that all the loss of life, and all the suffering, is felt to be not worthy to be compared to the good achieved, and that too *most strongly by the sufferers*, than was ever before manifested by any nation under heaven. The truth is, that, in spite of all its efforts to the contrary, criticism has ever been utterly impotent to eliminate from human thinking the elements we have presented. Its utmost triumph has been to force a change in the form of expression; and in the Bible it meets with forms of expression which it ever has been, is now, and ever shall be, as helpless to change as a paralytic would be to overturn the Himalaya.

The discussion of the topic immediately in hand may perhaps be now properly closed with the simple allusion to a single fact. Just as far as a race of human beings descends in the gradations of degradation, just so far does it come to look upon Deity simply as power. African Fetishism is the doctrine that Deity is an incomprehensible power, rendered into the form of a popular religion; only the religion stands one step higher than the philosophy, in that it assumes a sort of personality for the Power.

On page 102 the following extract will be found: "And now observe that all along, the agent which has effected the purification has been Science. We habitually overlook the fact that this has been one of its functions. Religion ignores its immense debt to Science; and Science is scarcely at all conscious how much Religion owes it. Yet it is demonstrable that every step by which Religion has progressed from its first low conception to the comparatively high one it has now reached, Science has helped it, or rather forced it to take; and that even now, Science is urging further steps in the same direction." In this passage half truths are so sweepingly asserted as universal that it becomes simply untrue. The evil may be stated under two heads.

1. It is too philosophical. Mr. Spencer undertakes to be altogether too profound. Since he has observed that certain changes for the better have been made in some human religions, by the study of the natural sciences, he jumps to the conclusion that religion has been under a state of steady growth; and of course readily assumes — for there is not a shadow of other basis for his assertion — that the "first" "conception" of religion was very "low." This assumption we utterly deny, and demand of Mr. Spencer his proof. For ourselves we are willing to come down from the impregnable fortresses of the Bible upon the common ground of the Grecian Mythology, and on this do battle against him. In this we are taught that the Golden Age came *first*, in which was a life of spotless purity; after which were the silver and brazen ages, and the Iron Age in which was crime, and the "low conception" of religion came *last*. How marked is the general agreement of this with the Bible account!

2. But more and worse may be charged on this passage than that it is too philosophical. Mr. Spencer constructs his philosophy first and cuts his facts to match it. This is a common mistake among men, and which they are unconscious of. Now the fact is, Science was *not* "the agent which effected the purification." Religion owes a very small debt to Science. Science can never be more than a supplement, "a handmaid" to Religion. Religion's first position was not a low one, but nearly the highest. Afterwards it sunk very low; but men sunk it there. Science never "helped it" or "forced it" one atom upwards. Science alone only degrades Religion and gives new wings and hands to crime. This will be

especially manifest to those who remember what Mr. Spencer's doctrine of Science is. He says: "That even the *highest* achievements of Science are resolvable into mental relations of coexistence and sequence, so coördinated as exactly to tally with certain relations of coexistence and sequence that occur externally." Of course the highest *object* of Science will be "*truth*"; and this, our teacher tells us, "is simply the accurate correspondence of subjective to objective relations." To interpret. A science of medicine, a science of ablutions, a science of clothing, a science of ventilation, a science of temperature, and to some largely, to many chiefly, a science of *cookery* do, combined, constitute Science, and the preservation of the body is its highest attainment. Is this Science "the agent which has effected the purification of Religion?" What then is the truth?

"Lo this have I found, that God hath made man upright; but they have sought out many inventions." — *Eccl.* VII. 29. The first religion was a communion with God. The Creator taught man, as a father would his children. But when man sinned, he began to seek out many inventions, and sank to that awful state of degradation hinted at in the fragmentary sketches of the popular manners and customs of the times of Abraham, — *Gen.* XII. XXV.; which Paul epitomizes with such fiery vigor in the first chapter of Romans, and which may be found fully paralleled in our own day. At the proper time, God took mankind in hand, and began to develop his great plan for giving purity to religion. So he raised up Moses, and gave to Israel the Levitical law. Or if Mr. Spencer shall deny the biblical account of the origin of the five books of Moses, he at least cannot deny that they have a being; and, placing them on the same ground of examination and criticism as Herodotus, that they were written more than a thousand years before the Christian era. Now mark. Whoever wrote them, they remained as they were first framed, and no one of the prophets, who came after, added one new idea. They only emphasized and amplified "The Law."

So far then as this part of Religion was concerned, Science never helped a particle. Yea, more, the words to Moses in the wilderness were never paralleled in the utterances of man before the Christian era.

" In the fulness of time God sent his own Son." However defective was the former dispensation, he, who appeared to most of the men of his day as only a carpenter's son, declared to mankind the final and perfect truth. As the system taught by Moses was not the result of any philosophical developments, but was incomparably superior to the religion of the most civilized people of the world, at whose court Moses was brought up, and was manifestly constructed *de novo*, and from some kind of revelation, so this, which the carpenter's son taught, was incomparably superior to any utterance which the human soul had up to that time, or has since, made. It comes forth at once complete and pure. It utters the highest principles in the simplest language. Indeed, nothing new was left to say when John finished his writing; and the canon might well be closed. And since that day, has Religion advanced? Not a syllable. The purest water is drank at the old fountain. But it will be said that the cause of Religion among men has advanced. Very true, but Science did not advance it. You can yet count the years on your fingers since men of Science generally ceased to be strenuously hostile to Religion. Religion, in every instance, has advanced just where it has gone back, and drank at the old fountains. Who, then, has purified Religion? God is "the agent which has effected the purification." God is he to whom Religion owes "its immense debt," not Science. He it is who has brought her up to her present high position.

When, now, we see how completely Mr. Spencer — to use a commonplace but very forcible phrase — has "ruled God out of the ring," how impertinent seems his rebuke, administered a few pages further on, in the passage beginning, "Volumes might be written upon the impiety of the pious," to those who believe that God means what he says, and that men may know him. These men at least stand on a far higher plane than he who teaches that an "incomprehensible omnipresent Power" is all there is for us to worship, and his words will sound to them like the crackling of thorns under a pot.

There does not appear in this chapter any further topic that has not already been touched upon. With these remarks, then, the examination of this chapter, and of Mr. Spencer's First Principles, may be closed.

CONCLUSION.

If it has ever been the reader's lot to examine Paley's "Evidences of Christianity," or the "Sermons of President Dwight on the Existence of God"; and if he has risen from their perusal with a feeling of utter unsatisfaction, enduring the same craving for a sure truth harassing as before, he will have partly shared the experience which drove the author forward, until he arrived at the foundation principles of this treatise. Those works, and all of that class are, for the object they have in view, worthless; not because the various statements they make are untrue, nor because elegant language and beauty of style are wanting; but because they are radically defective in that, their *method* is irrelevant to the subject in hand; because in all the arguments that have been or can be brought forward there is nothing decisive and final; because the skeptic can thrust the sharp sword of his criticism through every one of them; because, in fine, the very root of the matter, their method itself is false, and men have attempted to establish by a series of arguments what must be ground for the possibility of an argument, and can only be established by the opposite, the *a priori* method. Though the Limitist Philosophy has no positive value, it has this negative one, that it has established, by the most thorough-going criticism, the worthlessness of the *a posteriori* processes of thought on the matter in hand. Yea, more, the existence of *any* spiritual person cannot be proved in that way. You can prove that the boy's body climbs the tree; but never that he has a soul. This is always taken for granted. Lest the author should appear singular in this view, he would call the attention of the reader to a passage in Coleridge's writings in which he at once sets forth the beauty of the style and incompetency of the logic of Dr. Paley's book. "I have, I am aware, in this present work, furnished occasion for a charge of having expressed myself with slight and irreverence of celebrated names, especially of the late Dr. Paley. O, if I were fond and ambitious of literary honor, of public applause, how well content should I be to excite but one third of the admiration which, in my inmost being, I feel for the head and heart of Paley! And how gladly would I surrender all hope of contemporary praise, could I even approach to the incomparable grace, propriety, and persuasive facility of his writings! But on this very account, I feel myself bound in conscience *to throw the whole force of my intellect in the way of this triumphal car*, on which the tutelary genius of modern idolatry is borne, even at the risk of being crushed under the wheels."

Instead of the method now condemned, there is one taught us in the Book, and the only one taught us there, which is open to every human being, for which every human being has the faculty, and respecting which all that is needed is, that the person exercise what he already has. The boy could not learn his arithmetic, except he set himself resolutely to his task; and no man can learn of God, except he also fulfils the conditions, except he consecrate himself wholly to the acquisition of this knowledge, except his soul is poured out in love to God; "for every one that *loveth, is born of God, and knoweth God.*" We come then to the knowledge of God by a direct and immediate act of the soul. The Reason, the Sensibility, and the Will, give forth their combined and highest action in the attainment of this knowledge. As an intellectual achievement, this is the highest possible to the Reason. She attains then, to the Ultima Thule of all effort, and of this she is fully conscious. Nor is there awakened any feverish complaining that there are no more worlds to conquer. In the contemplation of the ineffable Goodness she finds her everlasting occupation, and her eternal rest. Plainly, then, both Reason and Revelation teach but a single, and that the *a priori* method, by which to establish for man the fact of the being of God. Let us buttress this conclusion with other lines of thought.

Reader, now that it is suggested to you, does it not seem in the highest degree improbable, that the most important truths which can pertain to man, truths which do not concern primarily the affairs of this life, but of his most exalted life, the life of the spiritual person as the companion of its Creator, should be based upon an inferior, less satisfactory, and less adequate foundation of knowledge, than those of our childhood's studies, of the arithmetic and the algebra? The boy who cons the first pages of his arithmetical text-book, soon learns what he knows to be *self-evident* truths. He who should offer to *prove* the truth of the multiplication-table, would only expose himself to ridicule. When the boy has attained to youth, and advanced in his studies, the pages of the algebra and geometry are laid before him, and he finds new and higher orders of self-evident truths. Would any evidence, any argument, strengthen his conviction of the validity of the axioms? Yea, rather, if one should begin to offer arguments, would he not instinctively and rightfully feel that the confession was thereby tacitly made, that self-evidence was not satisfactory; and would he not, finding his spontaneous impulse, and his education, so contradictory, be *liable* to fall into complete skepticism? If now there be this spontaneous, yea, abiding, yea, unalterable, yea, universal conviction respecting matters of subordinate importance, can it be possible, — I repeat the question, for it seems to carry with it irresistibly its own and the decisive answer, — can it be possible that the decisions of questions of the highest moment, that the knowledge of the principles of our moral being and of the moral government to which we are amenable, and most of all of the Governor who is at once Creator, Lawgiver, and Judge, is not based on at least equally spontaneous, yea, abiding, yea, unalterable, yea, universal convictions? And when the teacher seemingly, and may it not with truth be said *actually*, distrusting the reliability of such a conviction, goes about to bolster up his belief, and the belief of his pupil, in the existence of God, and thereto rakes together, with painstaking labor, many sticks and straws of evidence, instead of looking up to the truth which shines directly down upon him with steady ineffable effulgence, is it at all strange that the sharper-eyed pupil, keenly appreciating the contradiction between his spontaneous conviction and his teaching, should become uncertain which to follow, a doubter, and finally a confirmed skeptic? If, then, it is incredible that the fundamental principles of man's moral nature — that to which all the other elements of his being are subordinate, and for which they were created — are established on inferior grounds, and those less satisfactory than the grounds of other principles; and if, on the other hand, the conviction is irresistible, that they are established on the highest grounds, and since the truths of mathematics are also based on the highest ground, self-evidence, and since there can be none higher than the highest, it follows that the moral principles of the Universe, so far as they can be known by man, have *precisely the same foundation of truthfulness as the principles of mathematics — they are* SELF-EVIDENT.

But some good reader will check at the result now attained because it involves the position that the human Reason is the final standard of truth for man. Good reader, this position is involved, and is true; and for the sake of Christ's religion it must be taken. The only possible ground for a thoroughly satisfactory and thoroughly unanswerable Christian Philosophy, is the principle that *The human Reason is the final standard of truth for man.*

It has been customary for the devout Bible-reader to esteem that book as his final standard; and to such an extent in many instances has his reverential regard for it been carried, that the expression will hardly be too strong for truth, that it has become an object of worship; and upon the mind of such a one the above assertion will produce a shock. While the author would treat with respect every religious feeling, he would still remind such a person that the Bible is the moral school-book of the spiritual person in man, which God himself prepared for man's use, and must in every case be inferior and subordinate to the being whom it was meant to educate; and furthermore, that, by the very fact of making man, God established in him the standard, and the right to require that this fact be recognized. Mark, God made the standard and thus established the right. This principle may be supported by the following considerations:

1. The church universally has acted upon it; and none have employed it more vigorously than those who have in terms most bitterly opposed it. One of the class just referred to affirms that the Bible is the standard of truth. "Admit," says a friend standing by, "that it would be if it were what it purports to be; but what evidence is there that this is the case." Thereupon the champion presents evidence from the fathers, and evidence from the book itself; and finally closes by saying, that such an array of evidence is ample to satisfy any *reasonable* man of its truth and validity. His argument is undoubtedly satisfactory; but if he has not appealed to a reasonable man, *i. e.* to the Reason, *i. e.*, if he has not acknowledged a standard for *the* standard, and thus has not tacitly, unconsciously and yet decisively employed the Reason as the highest standard of truth, then his conduct has for us no adequate expression.

2. Nicodemus and Christ, in express terms, recognized the validity of this standard. Said the ruler to Christ, "We know that thou art a teacher come from God: for no man can do these miracles that thou doest, except God be with him." — *John* III. 2. In these words, he both recognized the validity of the standard, and the fact that its requirements had been met. But decisively emphatic are the words of our Saviour: "If I had not done among them the works which none other man did, they had not had sin: but now have they both seen and hated both me and my Father." — *John* XV. 24. As if he had said, "While I appeared among

them simply as a man, I had no right to claim from them a belief in my mission; but when I had given them adequate and ample evidence of my heavenly character, when, in a word, I had by my works satisfied all the rational demands for evidence which they could make, then no excuse remained for their rejection of me."

The doctrine of this treatise, that man may know the truth, and know God, is one which will never be too largely reflected upon by the human mind, or too fully illustrated in human thought. In no better strain can we bring our work to a close than by offering some reflections on those words of Jesus Christ which have formed the title of our book.

"Then said Jesus to those Jews which believed on him, 'If ye continue in my word, *then* are ye my disciples indeed; and ye shall know the truth, and the truth shall make you free.'" — *John* VIII. 31, 32. Throughout all the acts of Christ, as recorded in John, and especially during the last days of his life, there may be traced the marks of a superhuman effort to express to the Jews, in the most skilful manner, the nature and purport of his mission. He appeared to them a man; and yet it would seem as if the Godhead in him struggled with language to overcome its infirmities, and express with perfectest skill his extraordinary character and work. But "he came unto his own, and his own received him not." Being then such, even the Divine Man, Jesus Christ possessed in his own right *an absolute and exhaustive metaphysic*. We study out some laws in some of their applications; he knew all laws in all their applications. In these his last days he was engaged in making the most profound and highly philosophical revelations to his followers that one being ever made to another. Or does the reader prefer to call them religious? Very well: for here Religion and Philosophy are identical. Being engaged in such a labor, it is certain that no merely human teacher ever used words with the careful balancing, the skilful selection, the certain exactitude, that Jesus did. Hence in the most emphatic sense may it be said, that, whether he used figurative or literal language, he meant just what he said. The terms used in the text quoted are literal terms, and undoubtedly the passage is to be taken in its most literal signification. In these words then, in this passage of the highest philosophical import, is to be found the basis of the whole *a priori* philosophy. They were spoken of the most important truths, those which pertain to the soul's everlasting welfare; but as the greater includes the less, so do they include all lesser science. In positive and unmistakable terms has Christ declared the fact of knowledge. God knows all truth. In so far as we also know the truth, in so far are we like him. And mark, this is knowledge, a purely intellectual act. Love is indeed a *condition* of the act, but it is not the very act itself.

On this subject it is believed that the Christian church has failed to assert the most accurate doctrine. Too generally has this knowledge been termed a spiritual knowledge, meaning thereby, a sort of an impression of happiness made upon the spiritual sensibility; and this state of bliss has been represented as in the highest degree desirable. Beyond all question it is true, that, when the spiritual person, with the eye of Reason, sees, and thus knows the truth, seeing it and knowing it because his whole being, will, and intellect is consecrated to, wrapt in the effort, and he is searching for it as for hid treasures, there will roll over his soul some ripples of that ineffable Delight which is a boundless ocean in Deity. But this state of the Sensibility follows after, and is dependent upon, the act of love, and the act of knowledge. There should be, there was made in Christ's mind, a distinction in the various psychical modifications of him who had sold all that he had to buy the one pearl. The words of Christ are to be taken, then, as the words of the perfect philosopher, and the perfect religionist. Bearing, as he did, the destiny of a world on his heart, and burdened beyond all utterance by the mighty load, his soul was full of the theme for which he was suffering, he could speak to man only of his highest needs and his highest capabilities. The truth which man may know, then, is not only eternal,—all truth is eternal,—but it is that eternal truth most important to him, the *a priori* laws of the spiritual person and of all his relations. The what he is, the why he is, and the what he ought to become, are the objects of his examination. When, then, a spiritual person has performed his highest act, the act of unconditional and entire consecration to the search after the truth, *i. e.* to God; and when, having done this, he ever after puts away all lusts of the flesh, he shall in this condition become absorbed, wrapt away in the contemplation of the truth; then his spiritual eye will be open, and will dart with its far-glancing, searching gaze throughout the mysteries of the Universe, and he will know the truth. Before, when he was absorbed in the pursuit of the things of Sense, he could see almost no *a priori* principles at all, and what he did see, only in their practical bearing upon those material and transitory things which perish with their using; but now balancing himself on tireless pinion in the upper ether, anon he stoops to notice the largest and highest and most important of those objects which formerly with so much painful and painstaking labor he climbed the rugged heights of sense to examine, and having touched upon them cursorily, to supply the need of the hour, he again spreads his powerful God-given wings of faith and love, and soars upward, upward, upward, towards the eternal Sun, the infinite Person, the final Truth, God. Then does he come to comprehend, "to KNOW, with all saints, what is the height and depth and length and breadth of the love of God." Then do the pure *a priori* laws, especially those of the relations of spiritual persons, *i. e.* of the moral government of God, come full into the field of his vision. Then in the clear blaze, in the noonday effulgence of the ineffable, eternal Sun, does he see the Law which binds God as it binds man,—that Law so terrible in its demands upon him who had violated it, that the infinite Person himself could find no other way of escape for sinning man but in sending "his only-begotten Son into the world." And he who is lifted up to this knowledge needs no other revelation. All other knowledge is a child's lesson-book to him. All lower study is tasteless; all lower life is neglected, forgotten. He studies forever the pure equations of truth; he lives in the bosom of God. Such an one may all his life-long have been utterly ignorant of books. A poor negro on some rice plantation, he may have learned of God only by the hearing of the ear, but by one act, in a moment, in the twinkling of an eye, he has passed all the gradations of earthly knowledge, and taken his seat on the topmost form in heaven. He received little instruction from men; but forevermore God is his teacher.

This of which we have been speaking is, be it remembered, no rhapsody of the imagination. It is a simple literal fact respecting man's intellect. It is the same in kind, though of far nobler import, as if upon this act of consecration there should be revealed to every consecrated one, in a sudden overwhelming burst of light, the whole *a priori* system of the physical Universe. This is not so revealed because it is not essential, and so would only gratify curiosity. The other and the higher is revealed, because it is essential to man's spiritual life.

In the culminating act, then, of a spiritual person, in the unreserved, the absolute consecration of the whole being to the search after truth, do we find that common goal to which an *a priori* philosophy inevitably leads us, and which the purest, Christ's, religion teaches us. Thus does it appear that in their highest idea Philosophy and Religion are identical. The Rock upon which both alike are grounded is eternal. The principles of both have the highest possible evidence, for they are self-evident; and, having them given by the intuition of the Reason, a man can cipher out the whole natural scheme of the Universe as he would cipher out a problem in equations. He has not done it because he is wicked; and God has given him the Bible, as the mathematical astronomy of the moral heavens, as a school-book to lead him back to the goal of his lost purity.

How beautiful, then, art thou, O Religion, supernal daughter of the Deity! how noble in thy magnificent preëminence! how dazzling in thy transcendent loveliness! Thou sittest afar on a throne of pearl; thy diadem the Morning Stars, thy robe the glory of God. Founded is thy throne on Eternity; and from eternity to eternity all thy laws are enduring truth. Sitting thus, O Queen, more firmly throned than the snow-capped mountains, calmer than the ocean's depths, in the surety of thy self-conscious integrity and truth, thou mayest, with mien of noblest dignity, in unwavering confidence, throw down the gauntlet of thy challenge to the assembled doubters of the Universe.

It may be that to some minds, unaccustomed to venturing out fearlessly on the ocean of thought, with an unwavering trust in the pole-star truth in the human soul, certain of the positions attained and maintained in this volume will seem to involve the destruction of all essential distinction between the Creator and the created. If the universe is a definite and limited object, some created being may, at some period, come to know every atom of it. Moreover, if there is a definite number of the qualities and attributes — the endowments of Deity, some one may learn the number, and what they are, and come at length to have a knowledge equal to God's knowledge. Even if this possibility should be admitted, — which it is not, for a reason to appear further on, — yet it would in no way involve that the creature had, in any the least degree, reduced the difference in *kind* which subsists between him and the Creator. A consideration of the following distinctive marks will, it would seem, be decisive upon this point.

God is self-existent. His creatures are dependent upon him. Self-existence is an essential, inherent, untransferable attribute of Deity; and so is not a possible attainment for any creature. Every creature is necessarily dependent upon the Creator every moment, for his continuance in being.

Let him attain ever so high a state of knowledge; let him, if the supposition were rational, acquire a knowledge equal to that of Deity; let him be endowed with all the power he could use, and he would not have made, nor could he make an effort even, in the direction of removing his dependence upon his Creator. In the very height of his glory, in the acme of his attainment, it would need only that God rest an instant, cease to sustain him, and he would not be, he would have gone out, as the light goes out on a burner when one turns the faucet.

Again, the mode by which their knowledge is attained is different in kind; and the creature never can acquire the Creator's mode. The Deity possesses his knowledge as a necessary endowment, given to him at once, by a spontaneous intuition. Hence he could never learn, for there was no knowledge which he did not already possess. Thus he is out of all relation to Time. The creature, on the other hand, can never acquire any knowledge except through processes; and, what is more, can never review the knowledge already acquired, except by a process which occupies a time. This relation of the creature to Time is organic; and this distinction between the creature and Creator is thus also irremovable.

Another organic distinction is that observed in the mode of seeing ideals. The Divine Reason not only gives ideas, *a priori* laws, but it gives all possible images, which those laws, standing in their natural relations to each other, can become. Thus all ideals are realized to him, whether the creative energy goes forth, and power is organized in accordance therewith, or not. Here again the creature is of the opposite kind. The creature can never have an idea until he has been educated by contact with a material universe; and then can never construct an ideal, except he have first seen the elements of that ideal realized in material forms. To illustrate: The infant has no ideas; and there is no radical difference between the beginning of a human being and any other created spiritual person. He has a rudimentary Reason, but it must grow before it can make its presentations, and the means of its education must be a material system. Let a spiritual person be created, and set in the Universe, utterly isolated, with no medium of communication, and it would stay forever just what it was at the beginning, a dry seed. The necessity of alliance with a material Universe is equally apparent in the mature spiritual person. Such a one cannot construct a single ideal, except he have seen all the elements already in material forms. He who will attempt to construct an ideal of any *thing*, which never has been, as a griffin, and not put into it any form of animals which have been on earth, will immediately appreciate the unquestionableness of this position. Therefore it is that no one can, "by searching, find out God." The creature can only learn what the Creator declares to him.

Still another element of distinction, equally marked and decisive as those just named, may be mentioned. The Deity possesses as inherent and immanent endowment Power, or the ability of himself to realize his ideals in objects. Thus is he the Creator. If this were not so, there could have been no Universe, for there was no substance and no one to furnish a substance but he. The creature, on the other hand, cannot receive as a gift, neither attain by culture the power to create. Hence he can only realize his ideals in materials furnished to his hand. Pigments and brushes and chisels and marble must be before painters and sculptors can become.

Each and every one of the distinctions above made is *organic*. They cannot be eliminated. In fact their removal is not a possible object of effort. The creature may *wish* them removed; but no line of thought can be studied out by which a movement can be made towards the attainment of that wish. It would seem, then, that, such being the facts, the fullest scope might fearlessly be allowed to the legitimate use of every power of the creature. Such, it is believed, is God's design.

THE END.

CPSIA information can be obtained
at www.ICGtesting.com
Printed in the USA
LVHW101934050422
715402LV00003B/47

9 783752 588859